STUNG

STUNG

JERRY B. JENKINS
TIM LaHAYE

with CHRIS FABRY

TYNDALE HOUSE PUBLISHERS, INC.
WHEATON, ILLINOIS

Visit areUthirsty.com

Visit Tyndale's exciting Web site at www.tyndale.com

Discover the latest Left Behind news at www.leftbehind.com

Stung is a special edition compilation of the following Left Behind®: The Kids titles:

#17: Terror in the Stadium copyright © 2001 by Jerry B. Jenkins and Tim LaHaye. All rights reserved.

#18: Darkening Skies copyright © 2001 by Jerry B. Jenkins and Tim LaHaye. All rights reserved.

#19: Attack of Apollyon copyright © 2002 by Jerry B. Jenkins and Tim LaHaye. All rights reserved.

Cover photo copyright © 2003 by Jonathan Blair/Corbis Images. All rights reserved.

Published in association with the literary agency of Alive Communications, Inc., 7680 Goddard Street, Suite 200, Colorado Springs, CO 80920.

Designed by Jenny Swanson

Library of Congress Cataloging-in-Publication Data

Jenkins, Jerry B.
  Stung / Jerry B. Jenkins, Tim LaHaye.
     p. cm. — ([Left behind—the kids]) #5 (Vol. 17–19)
  Summary: A compilation of three stories from the Left behind: the kids series in which four teens, left behind after the Rapture, battle the forces of evil.
  ISBN 0-8423-8355-7 (hc)
  [1. End of the world—Fiction. 2. Christian life—Fiction.] I. LaHaye, Tim F. II. Title.
  PZ7.J4138St 2004
  [Fic]—dc22   2003021833

Printed in the United States of America

08   07   06   05   04
9   8   7   6   5   4   3   2   1

1

JUDD raised his hands and knelt with the others. Melinda pointed her gun around and tried to support Felicia, who was pale and almost unconscious, her head hanging.

"On your faces!" Melinda shouted.

Charlie, Vicki's weird friend, wandered in, holding a candle. His eyes grew large when he recognized the two Morale Monitors. "I didn't know the water was bad, I promise!"

"On the floor!" Melinda yelled.

What had Conrad and Lionel told Judd about the girls? He knew they were fiercely loyal to the Global Community and their leader, Commander Blancka. Vicki said she thought the GC had turned on them and wanted them dead. Judd watched for his chance to surprise them.

"You don't have to do this," Vicki said. "We're not going to hurt you."

"Shut up!" Melinda shouted. She stared at Vicki.

"You guys all look weird. What happened to your hair?"
Melinda let go of Felicia, and the girl fell to the floor.
Mr. Stein was still kneeling with his hands folded in
prayer.

Melinda fired into the ceiling, and plaster fell. "I said,
on the ground!"

Nine of us, two of them, Judd thought. *If we rush
Melinda, we can overpower her, but someone might get killed.*

Judd caught Lionel's eye. Lionel clenched his teeth
and shook his head. Vicki crawled toward Felicia and put
a hand on her neck.

"Touch her and you die!" Melinda said, pointing the
gun at Vicki.

Judd lurched forward, but Melinda quickly put the
gun in his face. "You want it first, Thompson?"

Mark grabbed Judd's ankles.

"Stop," Vicki said. "I feel a pulse." She put an ear
over Felicia's face. "Hardly breathing. Help me get her
to a bed."

Mr. Stein moved to help.

"Leave her alone!" Melinda shouted. She fired
another bullet into the ceiling, sending the kids scrambling.

"She's dying," Vicki said. "There may not be much
time."

Melinda brushed dirty hair from her face. "Why
would you help her?"

Vicki lifted Felicia's shoulders. "Put her in my room.
It's closest."

Melinda didn't move.

"Judd, get hot water from the stove and some rags," Vicki said. "Conrad, drinking water. A lot of it."

"Not him," Melinda said, pointing to Conrad. She nodded to Shelly. "You."

"I'll get blankets, too," Shelly said.

Judd shoved a pot of water over the fire on the ancient stove. The schoolhouse still had no electricity.

"The rest of you stay here," he heard Melinda say from the other room. She called out, "And if you guys try to run, I'll shoot them."

Judd gathered rags and opened a drawer, where he found a heavy rolling pin. He banged it against his palm.

Vicki feared Felicia was near death. Mr. Stein helped prop up her head.

"If she drank from the well," he said, "there is nothing we can do. The Scriptures say thousands will die from Wormwood."

Melinda barked orders in the other room. Shelly brought water and blankets. Vicki tried to get Felicia to drink, but she didn't respond. "If we can get her to drink, it might wash out some of the poison."

Judd brought the warm water and rags to Vicki's room, and Vicki cleaned Felicia's face. She grabbed the rolling pin from him. "You want to get us killed, Judd?"

"We have to do something," he said.

Vicki tossed it under the bed. Melinda came running.

"If we can't get Felicia to drink clean water," Vicki said, "well . . . it doesn't look good."

Melinda ordered the others into the next room. Judd glanced at Vicki on his way out.

"Why are you doing this?" Melinda asked Vicki.

"She's sick. Why are *you* doing this?"

Melinda laughed. "I'm taking every one of you back. You're enemies of the Global Community."

"So are you," Vicki said.

"What? I've been loyal to the GC since the day I signed on as a Morale Monitor."

"Then you don't know?" Vicki said.

"Know what?"

"The GC is after you. I'm surprised they haven't killed you already."

Melinda stared. "You're lying. Why would they be after us?"

Felicia coughed and gagged, turning in the bed. She grabbed her stomach and screamed, "Make it stop! Make it stop!"

Vicki tried to hold her down, but Felicia clawed at Vicki's face. "Help me!" Vicki yelled.

"Felicia, it's me," Melinda said as she helped Vicki. "Try to drink some good water."

"I don't want a drink!" Felicia screamed. She writhed and fell back, unconscious again.

Vicki felt for a pulse. Felicia's heart was racing.

"I have to get her to a hospital," Melinda said.

"Impossible," Vicki said. "She'll be dead before you get to the main road. And if the GC finds you, you'll be dead too."

Melinda stared out the window.

"Did you drink from the well?" Vicki said.

Melinda shook her head. "I had the cup to my mouth when she fell and started shaking."

"Wormwood," Vicki muttered.

"Worm what?"

"The comet's name," Vicki said. "The Bible predicted it would fall and poison the water. It also said people would die."

Melinda rolled her eyes. "That's right. You're part of the cult."

Vicki ignored her. "It happened, didn't it?"

Melinda stared at Felicia.

"Did she drink a lot?" Vicki said.

Melinda nodded.

Vicki handed Melinda a drink of fresh water. "You have to be thirsty."

Melinda eyed it warily. "How do I know it's not poisoned?"

Vicki grabbed it, took a drink, and handed it back.

Melinda sipped the water, then drank deeply. Vicki said, "How did you find us?"

"You came back for the dog. The GC planted a chip in his neck that sends out a signal. Felicia and I grabbed the locator and followed."

"You were in GC headquarters?" Vicki said.

"We wanted to find you guys bad."

"What took so long then?"

"We lost the signal, but we spotted Lionel at a pay phone. We tried to follow him, but he was too fast. Took us a couple of days to find this place."

5

"The GC didn't see you?" Vicki said.

Melinda squinted. "How did you know the GC are after us?"

"Commander Blancka's been killed by the GC," Vicki said. "People who had anything to do with the Morale Monitors are being wiped out."

Vicki dripped water into Felicia's mouth. "My guess is that the GC wanted to erase any evidence that we ever existed. Didn't want to look bad."

Melinda looked away. "They did come after us. We saw them whack Blancka and figured we'd be next. I thought if we could catch Stein or any of you, we'd prove our loyalty."

"And save your own skin."

"Exactly," Melinda said. She stuck her head in the next room and pointed to Shelly. "I saw rope outside. Bring it in here. And don't get any ideas about running if you care about your friends."

Felicia spat water. Her eyes were red and hideous. Her skin, pale when she had arrived, now looked green.

What a terrible way to die, Vicki thought.

"I can't breathe," Felicia gasped.

"Drink more water," Vicki pleaded. "It's the only thing—"

Felicia grabbed Vicki's arm. "I can feel it going through me," she wheezed. "It's like acid eating me up."

Vicki screamed for Judd. Melinda let him through.

"You know CPR, right?" Vicki said.

Judd felt Felicia's wrist.

"She has a pulse," Vicki said. "It's her breathing."

"Do something!" Melinda said.

Judd put his mouth over Felicia's and blew hard. The girl's cheeks puffed out.

"No good," Judd said. "Airway's blocked. Or maybe her throat's tightened up."

"What can we do?" Vicki said.

"I'm not sure," Judd said. He pulled out his pocket-knife. "Hand me that ballpoint pen."

Judd took the pen apart, then leaned over Felicia, his hands shaking.

Mr. Stein pushed past Melinda, knelt, and tilted Felicia's head. "Put the pen in the boiling water, Judd; then sterilize the knife over the fire. Hurry!"

Melinda looked over Mr. Stein's shoulder. "Is she going to be okay?"

"It may only prolong her agony," Mr. Stein said, "but we have to try." He shouted for Judd to return. "There's no time. She's turning blue!"

Judd rushed back with the pen and knife. Mr. Stein made a small cut at the base of Felicia's throat. Vicki wiped away the blood as Mr. Stein inserted the pen.

"You're going to kill her!" Melinda screamed.

As Mr. Stein blew through the pen, Judd said, "She'll die if we don't get her some air."

Vicki put a hand on Melinda's shoulder. She jerked away, scowling, then went to check on the others. Color returned to Felicia's face as Vicki watched her lungs fill.

Vicki knelt by her ear. "Felicia, I don't know if you can hear me, but I have to tell you something. God loves you. He died for you so you could live with him. If you can hear me, pray this with me—"

"Get away!" Melinda shouted as she ran back in, pushing Mr. Stein away as well.

Felicia opened her eyes and stared at Melinda. The pen-tube in her neck looked eerie. She tried to take a breath, but her lungs didn't fill. Then came a horrible gurgling sound.

Mr. Stein felt the girl's wrist. He stood and left the room. Judd followed.

"What?" Melinda said. "What happened?"

Vicki looked away and covered her mouth. Mr. Stein returned with a sheet. He pulled the pen from Felicia's neck and draped the sheet over her body.

Vicki couldn't hold back the tears.

"You can't," Lionel said, grabbing Judd's arm. "The gun might go off and kill somebody."

"I've had about fifteen chances to knock her down," Judd said. "I know I can do it."

"But you can't be sure."

"Then let's both get her."

Lionel shook his head. "You heard Vicki talking to her. She's getting through. Don't blow it now by going all macho."

"And if she comes in here and blows you and Conrad away, you'll wish I had."

Vicki wiped her eyes.

"What did you say to her?" Melinda said.

"I wanted her to know God loves her."

Melinda's eyes glazed. "You still think there's a God after all that's happened?"

"After all that's happened, I can't believe you don't."

Melinda pulled Vicki to her feet. "Get in there with the rest of them."

From the corner of her eye, Vicki saw Judd fly through the doorway. "No!" she screamed, as the gun went off.

2

LIONEL found Judd and Melinda struggling on the floor. The gun had been knocked to the far wall. Vicki lay motionless atop Felicia's body. Lionel held Melinda while Judd grabbed the gun. Melinda kicked free and retreated to the corner, panting.

"Vick!" Judd screamed, rushing to her. "Are you hit?"

Lionel and Judd gently rolled Vicki onto her back. Her mouth was bloody. Judd patted her cheek until she came to.

Vicki felt her lip and winced. "I heard the gun. What happened?"

"We've got Melinda under control," Judd said. "She's not going to hurt anybody."

Vicki gasped. "You rushed her!"

"I had to do something," Judd said.

"Things *were* under control. Melinda wasn't going to shoot anybody. You could have gotten me killed!"

Lionel waved Conrad into the room, then looked at Judd and Vicki. "We have to talk."

Conrad kept an eye on Melinda while Judd, Vicki, and Lionel met upstairs.

"We've got decisions to make," Lionel said, "and having you two at each other's throat is not gonna help. You guys promised to work together, but that's not happening."

"We can work together," Judd said.

Vicki held a rag to her bloody lip and rolled her eyes.

"First, what do we do with Melinda?" Lionel said.

"And with people like Charlie?" Judd said.

"He's not a threat," Vicki said. "He just doesn't understand things yet."

"He didn't listen," Judd said. "He drank a little water when we told him not to, and he's the one Melinda and Felicia—"

"Melinda said she followed Lionel," Vicki said. "Besides, he's not going to run off and bring the GC back with him. He seems really interested in God. Give him a couple weeks."

"Melinda's another story," Judd said.

"What are you going to do, shoot her?" Vicki said.

"We ought to hold her. Lock her up."

"That's cruel," Vicki said. "This isn't a prison. Besides, she's hurting. She just lost her best friend."

"She threatened to shoot us! And she wanted to take us all back to the GC. What do you want to do, let her go?"

Vicki took the rag away. Her lip had stopped bleeding but was still swollen. "We have to get her to trust us."

"Trust *us?*" Judd said.

Lionel looked closer at Vicki's lip. "Wish we had ice."

"We will once we get the generator started," Vicki said. She looked out the window. "It's a risk keeping Melinda or letting her go. I think we have to let her make the choice."

Judd shook his head. "That makes no sense. She's made her choice. She's GC."

"You don't know what she told me," Vicki said. "She knows the Global Community is after her."

"And she suddenly comes over to our side, just like that?"

"Not right away," Vicki said, "but a little compassion, a little friendship and concern could go a long way. Outside, she's dead."

Judd put his elbows on his knees and sighed. "We need to bury Felicia."

"After the funeral, I say we put it to Melinda," Vicki said.

"And if she decides to go back to the GC?" Judd said.

"Then we'll have to find a new place," Vicki said.

"And that wrecks Z's idea of using this place for storage."

Vicki paused. "Let me talk to her."

Vicki asked Conrad to join her in the hall. She took the gun and emptied the bullets into her pocket. "Does she have any more ammo on her?"

Conrad handed her a handful of bullets. "This is all both of them were carrying."

"I need to speak with Melinda alone," Vicki said. "Did she say anything to you?"

Conrad shook his head. "She just stared out the window."

Vicki called for Phoenix, and together they went back into the room to see Melinda.

Melinda closed her eyes.

"You have three options," Vicki said. "Take your chances with the GC. Run as far from them as you can. Or stay with us."

"I'd rather die," Melinda said.

Vicki nodded. "And you probably will. They killed Commander Blancka."

"When I tell them you guys are here—"

"You won't have a chance," Vicki said. She drew close to Melinda and knelt. "They'll shoot you on sight."

"Then I'll hide."

"Sooner or later they'll catch you," Vicki said.

Phoenix ambled over to Melinda and swished his tail back and forth. Soon he put his head on Melinda's lap. She didn't even seem to notice.

Vicki turned the gun over in her hands. "If you stayed, we'd offer you protection and food. They wouldn't find you."

"In return for . . ."

"Everybody pitches in," Vicki said. "Plus, you'd attend our studies."

"I'm not going to believe like you guys," Melinda said. "Ever."

"Maybe not," Vicki said. "But you have to admit, it's a better deal than Commander Blancka got."

14

Phoenix nuzzled Melinda's hand. The girl drew back. Phoenix licked the girl's arm, and she put her hand back on Phoenix's head.

Vicki handed the gun to Melinda and stood. "This is yours." She paused in the doorway. "The guys will dig Felicia's grave at sunup. We'll have the funeral in the afternoon. We'd like you to be there."

Melinda took the gun. "What if I take off tonight?"

That would change everything. Their lives would be thrown into turmoil. Vicki's plans for the old school-house would be wrecked.

"Your choice," Vicki said. "If you have to, you have to."

Vicki closed the door, then opened it a crack. "If you go, take blankets with you. It's going to be nippy tonight."

Vicki put food and blankets by Melinda's door and went to bed, listening for any sign of Melinda leaving. At midnight she opened her door and saw the food still in the hallway, but the blankets were gone.

"Please, God," Vicki said, "convince her to stay."

Vicki wrestled with leaving. Could God have brought them here only to have them abandon the place? Was the dream of training kids just that—a dream?

The next morning Vicki found Judd and Mr. Stein in the kitchen.

"I see our guest is still here," Judd said.

"How do you know?" Vicki said.

"Looked in her window," Judd said. He returned Vicki's icy stare. "We have a right to know if she's gone or not, don't we?"

"Don't blow this for me, Judd."

Mr. Stein said, "That girl has been through so much. I only hope we can get through to her before something happens to her."

Mr. Stein used Judd's laptop to log on to Tsion Ben-Judah's Web site. Judd and Vicki ate in silence.

"The rabbi writes about the Meeting of the Witnesses," Mr. Stein said.

"Still scheduled for next week?" Vicki said.

"Yes. And thousands of house churches have begun— run by Jews who have become believers in Jesus as Messiah."

"House churches," Vicki said. "I like that. This is going to be a house church for the Young Tribulation Force."

"It's going to be more than that," Judd said. "Z is going to run supplies through here and help feed people who won't obey Carpathia."

"What else does it say?" Vicki said.

"The house churches base their teachings on Tsion Ben-Judah's daily messages over the Internet," Mr. Stein said. "Though the Global Community urges everyone to join the Enigma Babylon One World Faith, tens of thousands of such churches meet every day.

"Tsion urges congregations to send their leaders to the great meeting, in spite of warnings from the GC. Nicolae Carpathia has tried again and again to cancel it."

Mr. Stein scrolled through the message excitedly.

"Oh, listen to this! Dr. Ben-Judah writes, 'We will be in Jerusalem as scheduled, with or without your approval, permission, or promised protection. The glory of the Lord will be our rear guard.'"

"He called Carpathia's bluff," Judd said.

"We must get the generator started," Mr. Stein said. "I want to be able to keep your computer going twenty-four hours a day while the meetings are taking place."

Conrad burst into the kitchen, out of breath. "Judd, come with me."

Judd followed Conrad around to the front and down the hill. Shelly stood holding a dirty shovel beside a deep hole. Mark pecked at a rock in the bottom. Conrad pointed. "We were digging the grave and we hit that. Then we found another rock the same size, and another, and now there's a whole section of them, along with big beams of wood."

"Looks like a tomb," Judd said. "Have you seen what's inside?"

"It's like they're cemented together," Mark said.

"Cover it over and we'll dig the grave farther up the hill," Judd said.

"What?" Mark said. "We're almost—"

"Melinda is still inside," Judd said.

"What's that got to do with—"

"This may turn out to be nothing," Judd interrupted. "Then again, it might be something we don't want her to see. We'll dig again after the funeral."

Vicki was glad when Melinda joined them at the kitchen table later that morning. Melinda eyed Mr. Stein and pushed back a plate of food. "If you guys hadn't gotten away, the commander would still be alive. Felicia too."

"They were going to execute me," Mr. Stein said. "We had to do something."

Lionel made a wooden stretcher and placed Felicia's body on it. Melinda walked beside Vicki as they followed the procession up the hill to the burial site.

Conrad and Judd gently placed the wrapped body in the hole. Vicki put a hand on Melinda's shoulder as the group awkwardly looked at one another.

Finally, Lionel spoke. "I didn't know Felicia well, but I do know how dedicated she was as a Morale Monitor. She would have made a great member of the Young Trib Force."

Mr. Stein shifted from one foot to another. "I lost my only daughter in the earthquake." He turned to Melinda. "I am deeply saddened for your loss."

"It should've been me," Melinda said. "If I'd have taken the first drink, you'd be burying me."

"You're here for a reason," Vicki said.

Melinda backed away. "I know why you're being so nice. You want me to keep quiet about this place. But that would betray what Felicia and I were trying to do in the first place."

Judd's cell phone rang.

"I won't stay here," Melinda continued. "And you can't make me."

Judd handed the phone to Mr. Stein as Melinda raced toward the schoolhouse. "Taylor Graham," Judd said. "He got the number from Boyd at the gas station. Said it was urgent."

As Conrad and Lionel shoveled dirt into the grave, Judd approached Vicki. "Sorry about Melinda. Guess we're going to have to move."

"I thought I was getting through to her," Vicki said.

"Maybe you were," Judd said. "People have to make their own choices."

Mr. Stein snapped the phone shut, his face ashen. "It is a miracle," he said. "A true miracle of God. I am going to Israel. I am going to the Meeting of the Witnesses."

3

JUDD couldn't believe it. Mr. Stein going to Israel?

"Taylor has access to a plane," Mr. Stein said. "He said there is an airfield near us."

"You know where he got that plane," Judd said. "It's GC property."

"I thought Taylor didn't want anything to do with us," Vicki said.

"He knows I have money," Mr. Stein said. "He said he wants to keep his promise. I think he needs cash."

"Wait," Judd said. "If he's going after Carpathia, why is he going to Israel? Nick's not there."

Mr. Stein shrugged. "Perhaps he will continue to New Babylon."

Judd sighed. "Something's not right. It may be a GC trap."

"You know Taylor would never let the GC take him alive," Vicki said. "I'm happy for Mr. Stein."

"Does sound weird," Lionel said. "And the GC will be looking for that plane."

"I'm leaving that to Taylor," Mr. Stein said. "I need to contact a guide to help me in Israel. I've never been there."

Judd's mind swirled. "I've been twice. I could help you."

"I had dibs on the next trip," Lionel said. "Besides, we're needed here. If we have to move everybody to—"

"We're not moving," Vicki said. "Even if Melinda leaves, this is where we're supposed to be."

"Vick—," Judd said.

"Trust me on this," Vicki interrupted. "God gave us this school for a reason. We're not running."

"Vick, Melinda could lead them right to you," Judd said.

"We stand or fall here," Vicki said. "Take Lionel and go—if it's okay with you, Mr. Stein."

"Yes, I would love the company," Mr. Stein said.

"Then it's settled," Vicki said.

Vicki found Melinda gathering supplies at the schoolhouse.

"Before you go, I want you to have something," Vicki said. She handed some bullets and Felicia's gun to her.

"Why are you giving me these?" Melinda said.

"In case you meet up with the GC. I don't think you'll use them against us."

Melinda rolled the bullets in her hand and sat.

"How'd you guys change your looks? I almost didn't recognize you."

Vicki explained, without telling about Z. "We have new IDs and everything. Hopefully it'll protect us from the GC."

Melinda sighed heavily. "The Global Community promised a better life. Conrad and Lionel don't know."

"Know what?"

"Where I came from. What I've seen."

"Tell me," Vicki said. She sat and stared at Melinda.

Finally, the girl spoke. "I grew up in the East. My dad sold insurance and we moved around a lot. Pittsburgh. Buffalo. Richmond. It was almost like being in the military. You make some friends, and it's time to move again."

"That's tough," Vicki said.

"Yeah, but not as tough as it got after the disappearances. That whole thing tanked my dad's business. Things got rough at home. He drank a lot and screamed at me. I'd take off for a few days, then come back."

"What about your mom?"

Melinda shook her head.

"How'd you meet Felicia?" Vicki said.

"School. Her family life wasn't any better. We'd sit at lunch and plan our escape. She had an uncle who invited us. Even mailed us some money. One Monday morning we got on a bus and headed north. Thought our problems were solved." Melinda closed her eyes. "That was the worst week of my life, until now."

"What happened?" Vicki said.

"I can't tell you everything," Melinda said. "It's too awful. The guy was a creep. He sold drugs. He basically locked us up."

"That's terrible," Vicki said.

"Only thing we could do was watch TV. That's when we saw Nicolae Carpathia. Everything he did—peace treaties, an end to war—that's what we were looking for. Sounded like heaven on earth. Felicia and I decided to get out of there and sign up."

"You escaped?" Vicki said.

"We tricked a guy into letting us out. Told him we'd show him where Felicia's uncle hid his stash."

"Cool," Vicki said.

"We found a GC post and heard about the Morale Monitors. Felicia and I signed up, and they sent us into training."

"That's where you met Conrad and Lionel," Vicki said.

Melinda nodded. "Our first job was Chicago."

"You thought the Morale Monitors would be the answer."

Melinda slumped in her chair. "I don't know what went wrong. I blamed it on Lionel and Conrad at first. I couldn't believe they'd work against us. Then Commander Blancka . . . it doesn't make sense."

Vicki didn't want to come on too strong, but she knew Melinda needed to hear the truth. "Can I give you my theory?" she said.

Melinda rubbed her forehead. "I think I know what's coming, but go ahead."

"I met this journalist," Vicki said, "a guy who's a lot

smarter than me, and he investigated Carpathia and the whole Global Community plan. Melinda, their goal is not world peace. Carpathia and his people want control."

"I don't mind people being in control if they want peace for everybody."

"They don't," Vicki said. "They want to run the world, and if anyone gets in their way or messes up . . . well, look at what happened to Commander Blancka."

"Pretty hard to believe," Melinda said.

"Everything I'm telling you was predicted in the Bible. The disappearances, the earthquake, the peace treaty with Israel, the comets—everything. I can show you."

"Religion's not my thing," Melinda said.

"Mine either," Vicki said, "but this is not religion. This is the truth. Stay. I'll explain it all. What do you have to lose?"

"You really think the GC will do the same to me as they did to the commander?"

"If I were you, I wouldn't want to chance it," Vicki said.

Melinda rolled the gun over and looked at Vicki. "All right. But the minute I find out you're hiding something or lying to me, I'm out of here."

"Deal," Vicki said.

Judd talked with Taylor Graham by phone and explained that he and Lionel would accompany Mr. Stein.

"I only agreed to take one," Taylor said.

Judd handed the phone to Mr. Stein.

"How many seats are there on that plane?" Stein said. "Six? Good, then we will have three extras for anyone else that might—"

Mr. Stein held the phone away from his ear. Taylor Graham yelled something.

"It's my money," Mr. Stein said. "If they don't come, I stay."

After a few moments, Mr. Stein handed the phone back to Judd.

"All right, listen," Taylor Graham said. "There's a landing strip in a ritzy development about ten miles from you."

"The earthquake didn't destroy—?"

"These people have more money than Carpathia himself," Taylor said. "The strip's been repaired. The problem is tight security. There's a guard 24-7 and a fence all the way around. I need you to turn on the landing lights. I'll wait two minutes at the end of the runway. If you're not there, I'm gone."

"Why don't we just come to you?" Judd said.

Taylor laughed. "It'd take too much time."

"Isn't there anywhere else you could land?" Judd said.

"I've scoped it out," Taylor said. "This is the way it goes down. If you can't make this happen, forget it."

"We'll be there," Judd said.

Taylor gave Judd the exact location and the time he would arrive.

"We'll need to leave soon if we're going to make it," Judd said when he hung up.

Suddenly there was an explosion, and a grinding

sound came from the other end of the house. Judd and Mr. Stein rushed through billowy black smoke and found Lionel high-fiving Conrad.

Conrad stood by the generator, covered with grease. "We did it!"

Judd inspected the machine. "As long as you can find gas, this should give you power."

"We found three underground gas tanks," Conrad said. "Must be Z's work."

"Get cleaned up," Judd said to Lionel. "We're heading out." Judd took Vicki aside. "Is Melinda gone?"

"She's staying for now."

"Good," Judd said. "I'll leave my laptop so you guys can watch the coverage of the meetings. Don't let her know about Taylor or where we're going."

Vicki nodded. "I know. Give us an update when you can."

"You can take two of the cycles and ditch them," Conrad said. "They're just sitting here."

Judd sensed something was wrong with Conrad. "Did you want to go with us?"

Conrad shook his head. "It's my brother. Talk some sense into Taylor if you can. He's going to get himself killed."

Judd patted Conrad on the shoulder as Darrion slipped an envelope into Judd's hand. "Give Taylor this. Maybe it will help."

Mr. Stein showed Vicki where he had hidden the rest of his money. "Use as much of it as you need."

Judd and Lionel pushed the cycles to the road and

started them. Traveling after dark was difficult. Judd wasn't familiar with the roads. Finally, he spotted the well-lit water tower Taylor had described.

"It's only a couple of miles from here," Judd said to Mr. Stein sitting behind him.

When they came within a few hundred yards of the gated community, Judd and Lionel turned off their cycles and hid them in some tall grass. They walked the rest of the way.

Mr. Stein huffed and puffed as he carried the heavy duffel bag filled with cash. "How much longer?"

"We've got about an hour to figure out how to get inside," Judd said.

"Are there security guards all around?" Lionel said.

"Only one," Judd said, "but I'm sure they have cameras and sensors around the fence. We have to time this just right."

Mr. Stein wiped his brow. "I don't know if I can handle this much excitement."

Judd spotted a delivery truck. "Wait here."

Judd ran through a field and darted to the other side of the road as the delivery truck stopped by the guard-house. Judd saw a camera above him and stayed in the shadows.

"Okay, we got one package for Kendall, number 418, and another one for Miller," the man in the truck said.

"Miller again?" the guard said. "Busy place."

The guard signed for the packages and the driver left. Judd checked his watch. Only forty-five minutes before Taylor touched down.

"What did you see?" Lionel asked when Judd returned.

"It's tight. They don't even let delivery guys inside. But I have an idea."

Judd took some cash and told Mr. Stein and Lionel to stay on the south side of the fence. "When you hear Taylor's plane, climb over and meet me at the end of the airstrip."

Judd grabbed a motorcycle and raced to a nearby gas station. "Anybody know where I can get a pizza around here?"

A girl behind the counter gave him a name and phone number. "It won't do you any good," she said. "They don't deliver to a pay phone."

"If you order, would they deliver?" Judd said.

"They might," she said coyly.

Judd pulled out a fifty-dollar bill. "Would this convince you?"

The girl looked over her glasses and snatched the bill. "You must want a pizza pretty bad."

A noisy car chugged into the station thirty-five minutes later. Judd handed the man a fifty, and he stared at it. "I can't make change for this."

"Keep it," Judd said.

"You mean it?" the man said.

Judd jumped on his motorcycle and roared off, holding the pizza tightly. Taylor was only ten minutes from touchdown.

Judd pulled into the guard station and smiled. "Got a delivery here."

The guard eyed Judd warily. "Where's your sign?"

"They're trying to save money," Judd said as he looked around the guard's station and whistled. "I've never delivered here before. Is this the place where the planes land?"

"Yeah. Who's the pizza for?"

"You control the runway lights in here?"

The guard leaned close. "Who's the pizza for?"

"Sorry," Judd said. "It's for Miller. Which house is it?"

The guard looked at his logbook.

"Is there a problem?" Judd said.

The guard picked up a phone. "They're supposed to tell security when they order. . . . Yes, Mrs. Miller, this is the front gate."

Judd saw a panel of switches for the runway lights on the office wall. He put the pizza down and climbed onto his motorcycle.

"Ma'am, we have a pizza here. Did you order—"

Judd sped under the barrier and past the well-manicured shrubbery.

"Hey, come back here!" the guard yelled.

Judd rounded the corner and shot through a yard. He hid the bike behind a tree and sprinted into the shadows. Moments later a jeep roared by. Judd ran to the guardhouse. A jet passed overhead.

An alarm rang, and Judd saw Lionel and Mr. Stein on a small monitor. They crawled over the fence near the runway.

"Right on time," Judd muttered. He flipped switches and bolted outside. Judd ran behind houses. Dogs barked. When the plane touched down, he raced toward it. Lionel and Mr. Stein stayed low at the end of the runway. Taylor rolled to a stop and opened the door. Mr. Stein and Lionel scampered aboard and waved for Judd. The engines screamed as Judd jumped into the plane.

"Everybody buckle in!" Taylor shouted. "We've got company."

Through the cockpit window Judd saw the jeep coming at them. Taylor swerved left, then right and off the runway to miss the oncoming car. When the jeep passed, Taylor gunned the engine. Within a few seconds they were airborne and heading toward the Middle East.

4

JUDD couldn't sleep. When the plane left Chicago, Mr. Stein sighed with relief. His eyes shimmered with excitement.

Judd asked Mr. Stein where they would stay in Jerusalem, but he wouldn't discuss it.

"I can make us a reservation," Judd said.

Mr. Stein held up a hand. "God will provide."

Taylor tuned in a Global Community frequency and listened. He had a stolen GC codebook and followed the security forces' movements.

"Did you kill anyone getting this plane?" Judd said.

"Why are you so worried about the GC?" Taylor said. "They're your enemy."

"There's a chance anybody can turn around," Judd said. "A lot of GC people were forced into service. Our job is just to give the message."

"Well, my job is to stop the GC wherever I can and, ultimately, to kill Nicolae Carpathia."

"I wouldn't advertise that if I were you," Lionel said.

"Before I get to him," Taylor continued, "I'll probably have to take out other GC posts."

Judd shook his head.

"I know you all want to tell people about Jesus and do good stuff so God will like you and all that. I've told you before, if that rings your bell, go ahead. But I've seen what the GC does to good people. They're destroying everything I know and love. They talk peace, but they're armed to the teeth. They talk freedom, but they send people to prison. Oh, sorry. They call them reeducation camps."

"You can't do it alone," Judd said.

"Maybe not," Taylor said. "But I'm giving them a run for their money." Taylor eyed Mr. Stein. "Speaking of which, where's the cash you promised?"

Mr. Stein opened the duffel bag and produced an envelope filled with large bills. Taylor grinned. "This should keep me going for a while."

Judd remembered the letter in his pocket. He handed it to Taylor. "Darrion asked me to give you this."

Taylor took it and said, "How's Conrad?"

"He's worried about you," Lionel said.

The radio squawked, and a man gave a report about a plane using a private airfield in Illinois. "A local guard on the ground reports seeing a GC insignia on the side of the plane," the man said. "This may be the stolen jet we're looking for."

"We're way ahead of them," Taylor said, opening the letter and checking his watch. "We should be in Tel Aviv in good time."

"Why Tel Aviv?" Judd said.

"This plane needs a new paint job. I've lined up somebody to do it." Taylor read Darrion's note privately.

Lionel signaled for Judd. "Do you realize the danger we're in? This is a stolen airplane, the pilot's killed several GC personnel, crashed a GC helicopter, and he isn't finished yet."

"I've been thinking the same thing," Judd said.

Taylor stuffed the letter in his shirt and waved Judd forward. "All right, you guys are taking a chance riding with me. You deserve to know what's happened.

"Some people did get killed at the base, but the GC press reported that it was a terrorist attack. It was just me. I wired explosives in the other planes and choppers. They were supposed to explode just after I took off. A couple of guys saw me and scrambled before I could get away. Those were the only two who got killed, I swear.

"I'm not a killing machine, and I don't want innocent people to get hurt. But this is a war. I'm going to stop the Global Community, or at least slow them down as much as I can."

"You could do a lot more damage to them on our side," Judd said.

"You guys are weak," Taylor said. "These people don't understand anything but strength. Plus, you don't have a plan."

"Our goal is to change people one at a time," Lionel said. "From reading the Bible, we know we can't overthrow the system, but having people on the inside will help."

"You do it your way. I'll do it mine."

"Why did you let us come with you?" Judd said.

"I need the money. Now I have it. This will be my last run with you guys."

"What about the return flight?" Mr. Stein said.

"Never discussed that," Taylor said.

"What?!" Judd yelled.

"Calm down. It's nothing personal. I've got a job to do and I can't wait in Israel."

"I'm through talking to him," Judd said. He stomped back to his seat and strapped himself in.

Lionel leaned close to Taylor and said something. The two talked for a few minutes. Then Taylor motioned for them all to sit. "Some turbulence up ahead. Buckle in and get some rest."

Vicki kept track of Melinda and tried to make her as comfortable as possible. When Melinda asked about Judd, Vicki hesitated. "I'm not going to lie to you, but I don't feel I can tell you the truth."

"You don't trust me," Melinda said.

Vicki smiled. "You threatened us. Give it some time."

Melinda nodded. "Okay. But if you lie to me and I find out, I'm gone."

Conrad came through the door, out of breath and covered with dirt. He glanced at Melinda, then turned to Vicki. "Can I see you a minute? Alone?"

Vicki excused herself and went outside with Conrad. He led her toward the river to the original site of Felicia's grave.

"I got up early to figure this out," Conrad said. He told Vicki about the stone he had found and Judd's instructions to dig it up after the burial. "With all the excitement about the trip, we didn't have time."

Vicki climbed into the freshly dug hole. On one side, she saw stones intricately woven together. Conrad had chipped away at the underground wall until one of the stones came loose. Vicki helped work the stone back and forth until it was almost out. Conrad used the end of his shovel, and the stone dropped inside. It fell a few feet with a *thunk*.

"It's hollow in there," Conrad said. He stuck his head through the opening and peered inside.

"Don't do that," Vicki said. "You don't know what's in there."

"Maybe it's some kind of vault," Conrad said.

"Why would they put it out here?" Vicki said.

"I'll try to get another stone out," Conrad said. "Get a flashlight."

When Vicki returned, Conrad had opened a hole big enough to crawl through. Vicki shone the light into the darkness. There were cobwebs and some debris on the dirt floor, but the room looked clear.

Conrad crawled through and dropped to the ground. His voice echoed. "It's at least six feet high. Come on down."

Vicki looked at the schoolhouse. No one stirred. Conrad helped her down.

"This is no vault," Conrad said. "The thing keeps on going in both directions."

Vicki followed as they walked away from the house. The walls of the passage looked ancient, but they were in good shape.

"Whoever built this sure knew what they were doing," Conrad said.

"What if it caves in?" Vicki said.

Conrad banged the top of the passage with his hand and winced. "It's solid."

The passage dipped downhill as they walked farther. The earthen floor became muddy.

"Stop!" Vicki said. She put a finger to her lips. "Hear that? It's water."

Conrad kept going. Finally, they came to the end. The flashlight shone on a thick, wooden door with a huge padlock. The lock was rusty. Conrad banged it with the flashlight but it didn't open.

"What do you think's on the other side?" Conrad said.

"We'll have to go outside to find out," Vicki said.

The two traced their way back to the hole. Conrad picked up an old piece of cloth from the ground and stuffed it in his pocket. Vicki started to climb out, but Conrad tugged at her sleeve. "Let's see where it goes the other way."

The passage led uphill. At times it was so steep Vicki and Conrad had to crawl. They found another door in better shape. However, instead of a padlock, there was only a round door knocker.

"I've seen these in those old horror movies," Vicki said.

"Yeah, the castles with all the fog."

Conrad pulled on the knocker, but the door didn't budge. The sound echoed throughout the passage. He knocked a few more times.

"Guess there's nobody home," Conrad said. "Let's get outta here."

They climbed back through the passage and out of the hole. They brushed themselves off. Conrad pointed toward the river. "I'm going to see where it ends."

Someone ran from the house. Shelly rounded the corner and spotted Vicki and Conrad. "Come quick!" she shouted. "The house is haunted."

"What's going on?" Vicki said.

"It's weird," Shelly said. "We heard something banging. When we went downstairs, it stopped."

Approaching Tel Aviv, Judd woke Lionel. "What did you and Taylor talk about?" Judd said.

Lionel rubbed his eyes and kept his voice low. "Darrion told me what she wrote in the letter. I figured it had to affect him."

"Did it?"

"He didn't break down crying, but I could tell she hit a nerve," Lionel said. "He said he'd do anything he could to help her."

"What did she say in the letter?"

"She thanked him for everything he did for her family. Talked about what happened to her dad just before he died. Then she said if her dad and mom were alive they'd want him to believe in God too."

"Pretty powerful," Judd said.

Lionel patted Judd on the shoulder. "Keep praying."

As the plane touched down on the outskirts of Tel Aviv, that was exactly what Judd was doing.

———————————

Vicki and Conrad followed Shelly back to the schoolhouse. Charlie, who had survived swallowing some of the bitter water, was spooked.

"I heard the noise. It's a ghost. I know it," Charlie said. "It must be a big one, and it must really be mad at somebody 'cause it kept banging."

"It's not a ghost," Vicki said, putting a hand on Charlie's arm. "Come on."

They filed down the narrow staircase to the musty room under the kitchen. One bare bulb lit the area.

Melinda followed. Conrad grabbed Vicki's arm. "What about her?"

"She'll find out sooner or later," Vicki whispered. "Maybe she'll trust us if we let her see."

"It came from over there," Shelly said, pointing to a stack of wooden pallets.

The kids moved the pallets to the other side of the room. Spiders and bugs scampered away. Conrad inspected the wall but found no door. He tapped, but the wood was solid.

"Look at that," Vicki said.

On the floor, barely visible under all the dirt and dust, was an old rug, about four feet square.

"This is interesting," Conrad said.

He jerked it away, and everyone coughed. When the dust cleared, Vicki knelt and inspected the floor. As she looked closely, Vicki saw the outline of a trapdoor. Conrad pulled out a pocketknife, but the wood was too heavy to pry open. Mark brought a crowbar and managed to lift it.

Vicki turned on the flashlight and peered into the darkness. Another set of rickety stairs led to an area about the size of a large bedroom. Vicki climbed down. There were no windows. They were well below ground level.

In the corner was a table with an oil lamp. A dusty book lay beside it. Vicki brushed it off, and flakes of leather crumbled in her hands. It crackled when she opened it.

"It's a Bible!" Vicki said. The pages were so brittle she closed it for fear of tearing them.

"Look at this," Conrad said. On the far wall was a door with a padlock that looked exactly like the door at the end of the tunnel. Mark used the crowbar again but couldn't open the lock. Finally, the hinges gave way, and the kids pushed the door open a few inches.

"The passage," Conrad said.

Vicki explained how she and Conrad had walked the length of the tunnel. "It goes all the way to the river," she said.

"What do you think it's here for?" Shelly said.

"Somebody must have needed a quick getaway," Conrad said, "but why would a school—"

Phoenix barked. The kids stared at one another. Mark

ran up the stairs. Vicki heard a rumbling. Pieces from the leather Bible danced on the table in front of her.

Mark stuck his head back into the room and whispered, "Somebody's coming."

5

"**DON'T** panic!" Vicki said. "They won't find us down here."

"I'll look through the hole in the tunnel and see who it is," Conrad said.

"Whoever it is, they sure are big," Charlie said. "Listen!"

The earth rumbled. Mark looked hard at Melinda. "Did you tip somebody?"

Melinda scowled. She looked at Vicki. "Is that what you think?"

"Tell us," Vicki said. "We need to know now."

Conrad returned, out of breath. "I can see a GC insignia on the side of the truck! I'm going back."

Melinda walked to the other side of the room, her head down.

Mark closed the doors leading to the basement and gently brought the trapdoor down on the secret passage. The rumbling increased.

Minutes passed. Finally, Vicki whispered, "Where's Conrad?"

Mark put a finger to his lips. His eyes darted. Footsteps above them. Doors opening. Voices.

"How could they have found us so fast?" Vicki said.

"Quick," Mark said, "everybody into the tunnel."

But it was too late. Vicki looked back and saw the trapdoor swing open.

———————————

The airstrip in Tel Aviv was a narrow lane of newly poured concrete. A woman in a brown jumpsuit approached and waved Taylor to a metal building. When they were inside the hangar, Taylor got out and hugged the woman.

"These are my friends," Taylor said, introducing Mr. Stein, Lionel, and Judd.

The woman was slender with dark hair and deep brown eyes. "Hasina Kamen," she said, extending a hand to each of them. She pushed a button and closed the hangar.

"I suppose you are all tired and hungry," Hasina said. She had a heavy Arabic accent, but she spoke English well. She led them into a conference area, where a tray of food was waiting.

"Is this who will paint your plane?" Mr. Stein said as he grabbed some pita bread and sauce.

"Hasina knows her stuff," Taylor said. "Max Stahley and I were working on a case in the Middle East when we met. I tried to get her to marry me."

Hasina blushed. "That is not the way I remember it."

Taylor laughed. "You can trust her with your life, which is what we're doing. Her dad was—"

Hasina held up a hand and asked Mr. Stein, "Why have you come to Tel Aviv with such a dangerous man?"

Mr. Stein explained that they were attending the Meeting of the Witnesses in Jerusalem. Hasina nodded. "There are many who have come in the last few days. Thousands. Do you consider yourselves followers of the rabbi?"

"Yes," Mr. Stein said. "Both Rabbi Ben-Judah and the rabbi named Jesus."

Hasina smiled. "Then you are no friend to the Global Community. Nicolae Carpathia has tried to postpone the conference many times."

"Dr. Ben-Judah will not stand for another delay," Mr. Stein said.

"There is a rumor that the potentate himself will make an appearance," Hasina said.

Taylor sat up straight. "Where'd you get that info?"

"Increased security at the largest airport in the city," Hasina said. "My sources say Carpathia will be here tomorrow."

"Why would Carpathia do that?" Taylor said.

Mr. Stein took more pita bread and smiled. "Perhaps he is on our side. Or he may foolishly think he can gain more followers."

"Tsion would never let Carpathia speak," Judd said.

"What if he's trying to kill the witnesses?" Lionel said.

"Where will you be staying?" Hasina said.

"God has brought us here by his own will," Mr. Stein said. "We are trusting him to provide."

"Your God will have to work a miracle if you hope to find hotel rooms," Hasina said. "Even Tel Aviv is booked."

Judd gave Mr. Stein a knowing look.

"Then we will have to pray," Mr. Stein said.

Hasina made a phone call and scheduled a driver. "You will stay here tonight. The driver will take you to Jerusalem in the morning."

Vicki watched the trapdoor open. Conrad stuck his head inside. At first, Vicki thought someone had forced him to betray the group. Then she saw a longhaired man with tattoos standing behind Conrad.

"Z!" Vicki shouted in relief.

Z knelt and peered into the dimly lit space. "Incredible." Then he laughed. "You guys don't have to hide from me. I use mouthwash."

Melinda pushed her way past Vicki and slammed the door at the top.

Vicki explained the situation to Z.

He frowned. "Having a GC Morale Monitor in your hideout's probably not the best idea I've heard all day. If she finds out who I am, that's worse."

"There wasn't much we could do," Vicki said. "I don't think she'll be a problem."

Mark scratched his head. "It's a pretty big risk."

Vicki rolled her eyes. *He's just like Judd,* she thought.

Vicki led the kids and Z upstairs. "What's that place down there?" she said.

"We've been looking for that a long time," Z said. "Let's unload and I'll tell you."

The kids eyed the huge truck parked in the front yard. On the side of the trailer was a Global Community insignia. Z explained that the gas station was nearly full of supplies. "My dad found this trailer a couple weeks ago. You should see everybody get outta the way when they see it coming."

"How'd you get past the logs in the driveway?" Conrad said.

Z pointed to the chains hanging on the front of the truck. "Took me a while, but I got through."

"What's in there?" Shelly said.

"Food mostly. And a couple surprises."

The kids spent the rest of the day unloading, organizing, and storing the canned food. They filled the storage area on the main floor and then moved to the basement. Z had them put water and fuel in the shed.

In the back of the truck, there was a stack of furniture. There were beds, mattresses, and even a kitchen table. Vicki was excited to see two couches. "I know exactly where those are going, but why did you take such a chance? Somebody could have followed you."

"I made sure they didn't," Z said. "The truck not only has a Global Positioning System—you know, those satellite things that can show you which turn to make—it also has something like radar that helps me watch for cars behind me."

"You can tell if you're being tailed," Mark said.

"You got it," Z said. "Plus, I knew you guys could use the stuff. This is basically a trial run. If things go okay, I'll be back every few weeks. You'll need to figure out where to stash it all."

Conrad showed Z the generator. Z looked impressed. Melinda locked herself in her room. When evening came, they all ate heartily, then set up the couches in the room with the fireplace. They talked late into the night.

"What are you going to call this thing where you move food around the country?" Mark said.

"I have no idea," Z said. "I'm just getting the materials in place. Doesn't matter what we call it as long as it works. The way I figure it, there are believers all around the world who will need what we have. I just pray God brings the right people together."

"Tell us about the tunnel," Vicki said.

"Like I told you, this land's been in my family for years. The first house was built in the 1850s. The boarding school came along after that. My grandfather always said this was part of the Underground Railroad."

"Railroad tracks ran by here?" Charlie said.

"No," Darrion said. "I studied this. The Underground Railroad was a network of safe houses and paths that slaves used to escape."

"I didn't know Illinois was part of that," Shelly said.

"A lot of slaves from the deep South went through Ohio or Pennsylvania," Darrion said, "but a lot came through Illinois. Usually, the safe houses were near rivers—"

"Which has got to be why the tunnel ends near the water," Conrad said.

"My dad and I searched for hiding places," Z said. "We found a door in a wall upstairs that led down to that cellar, but we could never find any outside entrance."

"They must have hidden down there and escaped to the river," Vicki said.

Conrad pulled the piece of cloth from his pocket and handed it to Z. "I found this in the tunnel."

Z held the cloth like it was a work of art. "This looks like a dress for a rag doll. I always heard that women gathered to sew clothes for the runaways. They'd make dolls for the kids to make them feel better. One of the children must have dropped this on the way out."

The kids sat, stunned. Vicki thought of the brave men, women, and children who had been through the house, searching for freedom.

Finally, Z said, "My grandfather also told us he thought there was a safe hidden in or near the house. We never found it, but this makes me think he was probably right."

Early the next morning, Judd awoke and found Hasina in her office. Mr. Stein and Lionel agreed that someone should talk with her about God. Judd volunteered.

Hasina turned the volume of a news station down when Judd walked in. "Did you sleep well?"

Judd nodded. "I'm anxious to get to Jerusalem. And I'm curious. Did Taylor really ask you to marry him?"

Hasina smiled. Judd thought she looked a little sad. "Taylor Graham will never marry. I suppose I came as close as any woman ever has."

Silence followed. Judd bit his lip. "Taylor mentioned something about your father."

Hasina closed the book she was writing in and sat back. She put both feet on the desk and looked squarely at Judd.

"I worshiped my father," Hasina said. "I was very young when my mother died. He could have shipped me off to any number of relatives, but he chose to keep me. He had great status as a pilot, but he gave that up to become a maintenance worker so he would have regular hours. He sacrificed everything for me."

"What happened?"

Hasina looked away. "Is *your* father still alive?"

"He was taken in the disappearances," Judd said.

"I'm sorry," Hasina said. "My father joined the Egyptian resistance. He helped plan the attack that led to World War III. He was shot down by Global Community planes near London. He called me the day before the bombings and told me he loved me. Over and over he said it. I never heard his voice again."

"And that's why you're against the GC?" Judd said.

"With every ounce of strength I have, I will avenge my father's death. That is what I live for."

Judd let the words sink in. After a few moments he stammered as he tried to tell Hasina about God.

"Whatever it is, just say it," Hasina said.

"We're here for the meeting, and its purpose is to

teach people to tell everyone how much God loves them. It would be awful if nobody talked with you about how much God cares for you."

Hasina smiled. "In the years before the disappearances, I worked as a guide in Israel. I came into contact with many Christians who tried to convince me of God's love."

"You didn't buy it?" Judd said.

Hasina shook her head. "I have seen the meteors, felt the earthquake. Most of my friends are dead. Whether there is a God of love out there somewhere, I do not know. I have never seen him. But I know you are against Nicolae Carpathia." Hasina looked at Judd without blinking. "Never get in my way. I will not rest, and I will let no one keep me from the sacred pledge of avenging my father's death."

Vicki was tired. She handed Z a pillow and some blankets.

"That's okay," Z said. "I sleep in the truck. Probably more comfortable anyway."

Mark said, "What about the surprise?"

Z stood and headed for the kitchen. In the doorway he turned. "How do you keep up with the news?"

"We don't have a TV," Mark said. "We get some stations on the Internet. That's our main link to the outside world."

Z returned with two boxes. As he opened the first, he said, "I got to thinking about the meeting and how much you will want to see what's going on." Z pulled out an ultrathin computer. "This oughta be faster and more powerful than what you have."

"The screen is so big!" Shelly said.

"Got it from a GC shipment. It's connected to the Internet by satellite. You don't have to dial up anything. Just turn it on and you're connected. And the best thing is, it's secure. The Global Community can't trace it."

"How'd you get it?" Mark said.

"Can't tell you," Z said. He pulled out a smaller box and handed it to him. "This is the phone that goes with it. It's hooked up to Carpathia's Cell-Sol system. They can't trace it. You should be able to keep in touch with the outside world. And the best thing is, they pick up the tab."

The kids laughed.

Shelly rushed into the room and grabbed Vicki. "Come quick! Melinda's gone."

6

VICKI rushed to Melinda's room. Cool air blew through the open window. Vicki grabbed Phoenix by the collar and let him sniff at the blankets. "Go get her, boy!"

Phoenix jumped through the window and bounded across the wooden walkway. Vicki followed. Phoenix headed toward the road, then turned and ran into the woods.

Mark caught up to Vicki. "If she gets away—"

"Let me handle this," Vicki said.

Mark threw both hands in the air. "I was just trying to help."

Vicki looked for Phoenix. He sniffed and ran through leaves in the distance. Someone whimpered. Vicki found Melinda near Felicia's grave. Phoenix licked the girl's hand. Vicki sat beside her.

Melinda spoke through tears. "When you heard that truck, you assumed I had told someone. I can't stay here."

"I'm sorry," Vicki said. "Mark thought you'd alerted the GC."

"You did too! Admit it."

"I don't know what I thought," Vicki said.

"I have to get out of here. I can't live with you people."

Conrad ran up the hill. Vicki waved him away.

"Who's the guy with the truck?" Melinda said.

"A friend with supplies," Vicki said.

Melinda started to leave, but Vicki grabbed her arm. "It's not going to be easy for us, but we have to admit we need each other."

Melinda wiped her eyes and stared at Vicki. "What do you mean?"

"We need you to keep quiet about us, and you need us for protection. From the GC and the judgments on the way."

"Protect me?"

"We saved you from the poisoned water," Vicki said. "I just wish we could have gotten to Felicia before she drank it."

"I'm out of place," Melinda said. "I feel guilty for staying with you and not turning you in. At the same time . . ." Melinda's voice trailed off.

"What?" Vicki said.

"There's something I haven't told you."

Judd tried to talk more with Hasina, but her hatred for the Global Community kept her from listening. Lionel rushed in. "You should see this."

Mr. Stein watched a report about Nicolae Carpathia.

The news conference was held at the main airport in Tel Aviv. Leon Fortunato, Carpathia's right-hand man, stood dutifully in the background as Enigma Babylon's Peter Mathews introduced the potentate.

"I cannot tell you what a pleasure it is to be back in Israel," Carpathia said with a broad smile. "I am eager to welcome the devotees of Dr. Ben-Judah and to display the openness of the Global Community to diverse opinion and belief."

"Right," Judd said sarcastically.

"I am pleased to reaffirm my guarantee of safety to the rabbi and the thousands of visitors from all over the world," Carpathia continued. "I will withhold further comment, assuming I will be welcome to address the honored assembly within the next few days."

"Surely Tsion won't let him," Judd said.

Mr. Stein stroked the stubbly beard he had grown. "I'm wondering how the witnesses will respond."

"The people in the stadium?" Lionel said.

"Eli and Moishe," Mr. Stein said.

Taylor Graham walked into the room and flipped off the television. "You guys want a little company at that meeting of yours? I hear the big guy is making an appearance."

Judd knew from reading Tsion's views of the book of Revelation that Nicolae Carpathia would be killed. But Judd thought it was too soon. They had just passed the two-year mark of the beginning of the Tribulation, and from what Judd could remember, Nicolae wasn't supposed to die for another year and a half.

While Lionel and Mr. Stein talked with Taylor, Judd slipped into Hasina's empty office and pulled up Tsion's Web site. Judd gasped when he saw Tsion's travel schedule. Everyone, including the Global Community, could see it!

Between Tsion's directions to the witnesses and what Buck Williams wrote in his Web magazine, *The Truth*, Judd couldn't wait for the meeting to begin. One thing was sure. Buck's days as the editor of Nicolae Carpathia's global magazine were over. Judd wondered whether Buck would attend the conference with Tsion or play it safe.

Later, a car pulled up outside. Judd and the others thanked Hasina for her kindness. "Perhaps I'll see you before you leave?" she said.

The drive to Jerusalem went quickly. Judd pointed out some of the historical sites as they drew closer. It was as if they had gone through a time warp. Tel Aviv was modern and fast paced. But as they neared the old city of Jerusalem, it looked thousands of years old. Mr. Stein watched in amazement. "I feel God has me here for a reason."

Tens of thousands crowded the streets. Many were no doubt converted Jewish witnesses from around the world.

"Can you drive us by the Temple Mount?" Mr. Stein said.

The driver wound his way through the jammed streets. "You should see it at night," the driver said. "It is spectacular."

The new temple gleamed in the morning sun. The Global Community had spent millions creating this

structure to honor Nicolae Carpathia. Judd figured
when the Dome of the Rock was moved to New Babylon,
animal sacrifices wouldn't be far behind. He was right.
Peter the Second had welcomed the Orthodox Jews into
the Enigma Babylon faith. Tsion Ben-Judah wrote in
disgust about the structure. He said the new building
and the sacrifices were an affront to the true God of Israel.

The driver of the car turned and, in a heavy Israeli
accent, said, "I will not be able to get you close to Teddy
Kollek Stadium. Too many people."

"We can walk," Mr. Stein said. "We are looking for
a room for the week. Can you help?"

The driver shook his head. "If you do not have a place
to stay, may God help you."

Mr. Stein smiled. "He will."

Mr. Stein paid the driver, and the three began their
walk.

"Who is Teddy Kollek, anyway?" Lionel said.

"I believe he was the mayor of Jerusalem for many
years," Mr. Stein said. "He helped develop the city."

"How many people will the stadium hold?" Lionel
said.

Mr. Stein looked around. "Not this many. Tsion's
Web site said they would transmit the signal to other
areas, but I must be where Dr. Ben-Judah is."

Global Community guards patrolled the area around
the stadium. "The meeting starts tomorrow night," a
guard said. "Come back then."

Judd pointed out several hotels as they continued, but
all were booked. Mr. Stein pleaded with manager after

manager, offering several times the amount of a single room. Each time, they were turned away.

"Does it strike you funny that there's no room at any of these inns?" Lionel said with a smile.

Melinda sat like a statue next to Felicia's grave.

"You want to go inside?" Vicki said. "It's late, and really cold."

"You asked about my mother," Melinda said.

"I figured you didn't want to talk about her," Vicki said.

"I didn't. But now . . ."

"What is it?"

Melinda took a deep breath. "My mom believed what you do."

Vicki couldn't speak.

"Not always. She used to be as wild as my dad. Even wilder. They'd go to cocktail parties and come home blasted. When my dad was on the road, she'd sneak out. She thought I didn't see her. I never told my dad, but I saw.

"I was out late one night. I came home and found her crying in the living room. There was a woman with her. We called her the preacher lady. She said my mother had something to tell me.

"I thought my mom had gotten some kind of disease the way she was crying. But that wasn't it. She said she was sorry for being a bad mother.

"Then the preacher lady said my mom had just asked

Jesus to forgive her. I couldn't believe it. I'd heard this
Jesus talk from a couple of kids at school. I thought it
was trash."

"What happened?" Vicki said.

"I told her I didn't want to hear it. She said she'd
waited up all night to talk with me. My dad had been
there and left. I started up the stairs, and my mom
followed. When I got to the top, she grabbed me by the
arm. She begged me to listen."

Melinda closed her eyes, as if she were watching the
scene again. "I yelled something awful at her and pulled
away. When I did, she lost her balance. I turned around.
There was nothing I could do. She fell the whole way
down those stairs.

"The preacher lady rushed to her and felt her neck.
She ran for the phone. I flew down the stairs to see if
I could help. Honestly, I didn't mean to hurt her."

Vicki nodded. "Was she dead when you got there?"

Melinda stared at Felicia's grave. "All that was left
at the bottom of the stairs were her dress and shoes. I
screamed and ran for the preacher lady. The phone was
hanging by the cord. Her clothes were in a pile on the
floor."

"You must have been so scared," Vicki said.

"I thought I'd killed her," Melinda said. "Killed them
both."

"Why did you tell me this story?" Vicki said.

"I've tried to get it out of my head for so long. I didn't
even tell my dad about it for a long time. When I did, he
said I was crazy. Accused me of being drunk." Melinda

sighed. "The way you looked at me tonight when you said you were sorry, it reminded me of my mom."

Vicki put an arm around Melinda. "If you want, I'll tell you exactly what happened to your mom."

When evening came and they still hadn't found a place to stay, Judd suggested they go back to the Temple Mount. "A lot of people stay there through the night."

"We can see the witnesses," Mr. Stein said, "Eli and Moishe!"

Mr. Stein darted into a store and brought back three heavy blankets. "These will keep us warm."

Judd hailed a cab. He recalled the terror the two witnesses had created the last time he had seen them.

A crowd gathered to watch Eli and Moishe thirty feet from the wrought-iron fence. Eli sat Indian style, his back to a stone wall. A slight breeze sent a chill through Judd and moved Eli's long hair and beard, but the prophet was unmoving, unblinking. Moishe stood near the fence, staring at the crowd.

"When's the show start?" a young man said, giggling, from the back of the crowd.

"Yeah, say something," another said.

"Come with me," Judd said. He led Mr. Stein and Lionel to a ledge overlooking the witnesses. Bushes blocked their view of the crowd.

"This will be a good place to rest," Mr. Stein said. They spread out their blankets and sat.

"I've seen them talk without moving their mouths,"

Judd said. "Everybody understands in his own language." Judd was exhausted. He put his head down and fell asleep.

Lionel shook him awake some time later. "Something's going on."

Judd rubbed his eyes and peered through the bushes. A disturbance in the crowd had caused some to back away from the fence.

"Carpathia!" someone shouted. "It's the potentate!"

"I don't believe it," Lionel said. "Those guys will eat him alive."

Judd recognized Leon Fortunato, Carpathia's right-hand man. He instructed the guards to keep the crowd away. The potentate boldly moved within ten feet of the fence. Someone shouted a greeting. Carpathia held a finger to his lips, and the crowd grew quiet.

The silence was shattered by the booming voice of Moishe. "Woe unto the enemy of the Most High God!"

Carpathia seemed startled but quickly collected himself. He smiled and spoke softly. "I am hardly the enemy of God. Many say I *am* the Most High God."

Moishe crossed his arms over his chest and spoke softly to Carpathia.

"What did he say?" Lionel said.

"I couldn't tell," Mr. Stein said.

Now Carpathia clenched his teeth and said, "Let me tell you and your companion something. You have persecuted Israel long enough with the drought and the water turned to blood. You will lift your hocus-pocus or live to regret it."

It was Eli's turn. He motioned Nicolae closer and spoke with great volume. Judd recoiled in fear. "Until the due time, you have no authority over the lampstands of God Almighty!" Eli said.

Carpathia seethed. "We shall see who will win in the end."

Eli stared at Carpathia. "Who will win in the end was determined before the beginning of time. Lo, the poison you inflict on the earth shall rot you from within for eternity."

Carpathia stepped back. He smiled. "I warn you to stay away from the charade of the so-called saints. I have guaranteed their safety, not yours."

Eli and Moishe spoke in unison. "He and she who have ears, let them hear. We are bound neither by time nor space, and those who shall benefit by our presence and testimony stand within the sound of our proclamation."

Leon Fortunato and the guards ushered the potentate away from the area. Mr. Stein was about to speak when someone moved back through the bushes. When it was clear they were safe, Lionel spoke.

"I got everything except the last statement," Lionel said. "What was all that 'benefit by our presence' jazz?"

Mr. Stein shrugged and looked at Judd.

"I don't know either," Judd said, "but this is the first time I've ever heard them say, 'He *and she* who have ears, let them hear.'"

7

VICKI took Melinda to the house and told her own story. Vicki's parents had changed overnight. They wanted Vicki to attend church, but Vicki wouldn't. Then came the awful morning when Vicki realized her whole family had disappeared.

"Would you let me show you verses from the Bible?"

Melinda frowned. "Don't think I'm ready for that."

Someone knocked on Melinda's door. "Can I see you a minute, Vicki?" Mark said.

"I'm kind of in the middle of something—"

"It's important."

"Go ahead," Melinda said. "I'm tired. We can talk tomorrow."

Vicki joined Mark in the kitchen. The others had gone to bed.

"We had a meeting while you were out looking for her," Mark said, "and most of us think it's time to set some rules about who gets to stay."

"Most of us?" Vicki said.

Mark shrugged. "Darrion and Conrad think I—*we* might be going a little too far."

"What do you propose?" Vicki said.

"If this is going to be a training ground for the Young Trib Force," Mark said, "the people who stay here ought to have the mark of the believer. If they don't, we can't trust them."

"Melinda just told me—"

"I'm not talking about just Melinda," Mark said. "Charlie's a threat to us too."

"How?"

"He could walk out of here anytime he wanted," Mark said. "Even if he doesn't mean to, he could bring trouble."

Vicki held up a hand. "I understand about safety. I don't want the GC to find us any more than you do, but for some reason, God brought three people here who aren't believers. One of them is buried up on the hill. I don't want the same thing to happen to the other two."

"That's not the point," Mark said.

"It is the point," Vicki said.

"Then this isn't the place for me," Mark said.

Vicki sat, exhausted. She thought her troubles with the group were over when Judd had left. "Can we talk about this in the morning?" she said.

———————————————

Judd, Lionel, and Mr. Stein slept near the witnesses until Global Community guards found them and shooed them away. They spent the rest of the night wandering the streets of the old city. Before dawn, Mr. Stein led them through a gate and past a cemetery. They found a peaceful place to watch the sunrise. Judd asked Mr. Stein what they were going to do, but the man didn't seem upset. As they drank the last of their water, Lionel wandered off. A few minutes later, he returned.

"Do you guys know what this place is?" Lionel said. "It's the Garden of Gethsemane. This is where Jesus was betrayed. Where he prayed on the night of his arrest."

Mr. Stein looked around the garden in awe.

A man approached. He was short, with stooped shoulders. He wore a wide-brimmed hat that hid his eyes. With a powerful voice he said to Mr. Stein, "Are you one of the witnesses?"

Judd put a hand on Mr. Stein's shoulder. Being in Israel didn't mean they were out of danger.

"Why do you ask?"

"Are you one of those called by God?" the man said. He drew close and lifted his hat above his forehead. Judd saw the telltale mark of the believer.

"I can see it in your eyes," the man said. "You have the fire of God in you."

"Are you a witness?" Lionel said.

The man turned and motioned for them to follow him.

"Where are you taking us?" Judd said.

"Where you are supposed to be," the man said.

Mr. Stein followed. Judd hesitated. Lionel shrugged, and they jogged to catch up. The man's car was parked a few blocks away. The three squeezed into the tiny backseat.

"Where are we going?" Mr. Stein said.

"You will see. When did you get to Israel?"

Mr. Stein told him when they had arrived and that they had slept outside the previous night.

"The foxes have holes," the man said, shaking his head. "You will not sleep outside again."

The man wound past the old city and into a newer section. The streets were already congested with traffic and people on foot. The man pointed out the Knesset, Israel's Parliament.

Mr. Stein introduced himself, then Judd and Lionel. "What is your name?"

"I am Yitzhak Weizmann, and God told me to expect you."

Mr. Stein looked at Judd and Lionel. "What do you mean?"

"The Lord God of Israel impressed upon me to make room for you. I have done as he suggested."

"God spoke to you and told you we would be coming?" Judd said, his mouth open.

Yitzhak ignored the question. They drove near Teddy Kollek Stadium. "That is where you will be tonight, along with thousands of other witnesses. I cannot wait until the rabbi speaks. I was watching the day he announced his findings on television."

They stopped in a huge parking lot near what looked like a school. "This is Hebrew University," Yitzhak said. "You are in the building on the far side. You will be able to walk to the stadium tonight." Yitzhak laughed. "If you leave early enough."

Yitzhak led them along a concrete path to a back entrance. Before he opened the door he said, "In the name of Jesus, our Lord and Savior, our provider, I welcome you." He opened the door.

What Judd saw next would stay with him the rest of his life. The gymnasium had been transformed into an emergency shelter for witnesses. Hundreds of cots filled the room. People gathered in small groups to pray. Others ate sack lunches and watched one of several monitors positioned throughout the room.

"Incredible," Judd said.

Yitzhak smiled. "When I read Tsion's messages about the meeting, God gave me this idea. I knew there would not be enough room in hotels for all of the witnesses, so I approached the administration of the university. They allowed me to rent five buildings like this."

"And they knew what you were using them for?" Mr. Stein said.

"They only know that I was willing to pay twice what they are worth," Yitzhak said, smiling.

"So you didn't really know *we* were coming," Judd said.

"Our God knows the number of hairs on your head. This morning I have found fourteen witnesses who spent the night sleeping on the ground. I must look for more."

Yitzhak showed them where to register for a cot. Mr. Stein asked the cost. "The money has already been paid," Yitzhak said. "Enjoy your stay."

Yitzhak left them, and they spent the rest of the morning meeting other witnesses and sharing stories. Mr. Stein couldn't stop talking. He went from one person to the next, trying to find out more about how to spread their message.

Judd and Lionel found their cots and collapsed.

Vicki awoke the next morning with a pain in her stomach. She felt such pressure to hold everything together. She stared at the ceiling and listened to the sounds coming from the kitchen. The kids were saying good-bye to Z.

Vicki dressed quickly and ran to the truck.

"Sounds like you had an interesting night," Z said.

Vicki got into the truck and closed the door. "This seemed so perfect for us, but even all the way out here we don't feel safe."

Z scratched his head. "Here's what I know. God wanted you here. That's pretty clear, right?"

Vicki nodded.

"If you know that, you know he's gonna work out the rest."

"I just don't know what to do. . . ."

Z started the big rig, and the whole truck shook. "I put a box for you in the kitchen. Hang on to your dream and don't give up."

Vicki and the others watched Z drive off. Conrad and Mark helped with the logs at the end of the road. Vicki looked in on Melinda, but she was still asleep.

When they were all gathered, Vicki asked Charlie to take Phoenix outside. Vicki briefly explained Melinda's story. "We can pull together on this, or we can pull apart. But I don't think we're as strong if we split up.

"God's given us this place. With the Meeting of the Witnesses starting, I think we should use this next week to study and pray that God would use us how he wants."

No one spoke. Vicki looked at each person and recalled what they had been through together. Though Mark was outspoken, she knew he loved God and wanted to do the right thing. Shelly had been with her almost from the start. Darrion had seen so much loss, she looked like a shell.

Finally, Conrad spoke. "None of us knows how much longer we have. I think Vicki's right. If we can help people like Melinda and Charlie know the truth, I think we ought to do it."

"There's risk in everything," Shelly said. "I say we open the place up and let God bring whoever he wants, believer or not."

Everyone spoke in support of Vicki except Mark. He stared at the floor. "I lost a lot of friends when the Global Community attacked the militia base. Now I've lost my cousin, John. Ryan's gone. Chaya's gone. The people we knew at the church. I don't want to hold you guys back. Maybe if I take some time . . ."

Mark's voice trailed off. Vicki could tell he was hurting.

"I'm thinking of going back to find my aunt," Mark said. "She'll want to know about John. She's the last of my family, as far as I know."

69

"There are two cycles left," Conrad said. "Take one."

"How will you see the Meeting of the Witnesses?" Vicki said.

"Can I take Judd's laptop?"

Vicki nodded.

Mark gathered some supplies later that morning. He said good-bye to everyone. When he got to Vicki, she said, "I hope you'll come back."

Mark pursed his lips. "Yeah."

When Judd awoke that afternoon, the room was crowded with witnesses. People stood shoulder to shoulder around Judd's cot. Judd stood on his cot. Lionel did the same.

A deep-voiced man spoke through a megaphone at the front of the gym. Judd recognized the hat and the stooped shoulders. It was Yitzhak. He stood on a stepladder and spoke in Hebrew, then translated into English. Around the room small groups who spoke other languages gathered for the translation.

"Last night, I met with others in the local committee for a final walk-through of the program," Yitzhak said. "You will be happy to know that Tsion Ben-Judah is here and alive and well!"

A cheer went up from the group. Some shouted, "May God be praised!" Others spoke in their own languages.

A chill went down Judd's spine. *This is what heaven is going to be like*, he thought.

When the cheering died down, Yitzhak said, "But there has been a disturbing development. The reports we have heard have been confirmed. Nicolae Carpathia has asked to address the meeting tonight."

A murmur rose from the crowd. Yitzhak held up a hand. "I do not know whether Dr. Ben-Judah will allow it, or if he refuses what will happen. But I do know that God is in control of this meeting!"

Another cheer arose.

"And now, I urge you to pray with me. What we will learn over the next few days will be vital. But our hearts must be right."

For the next fifteen minutes, Judd heard the sound of voices praying in different languages. Yitzhak gently interrupted them by saying, "My friends, there will be some in the stadium and many watching and listening via satellite who do not know our Messiah. Let us pray earnestly for God to open their eyes."

Again, voices swirled in prayer. Judd moved toward Lionel. "Can you believe this?"

Lionel shook his head.

As the prayers of the people wound down, Yitzhak said, "In the spirit of these prayers, O God, we commit ourselves to you. We ask that you give us clear minds to understand your teaching. In Jesus' name, amen."

Yitzhak led the group out the back door. There was no shoving, no pushing, no trying to get the best spot in line. Everyone slowly followed the little man across the parking lot toward the stadium.

"Where's Mr. Stein?" Lionel said.

Judd shrugged. "I guess we'll find him later."

Judd had never seen such traffic. Every road to the

stadium was jammed with cars and pedestrians. Every person he saw seemed happy. People carried satchels and notebooks and water bottles. Most of those on foot made it to the stadium faster than those in cars and buses.

"This looks like a lot more people than that stadium could ever hold," Lionel said.

Judd saw two jeeps with flashing yellow lights. Each vehicle carried four armed Global Community guards. Between the jeeps was a Mercedes van. Someone shouted, "The rabbi!"

With that, people broke from the line and rushed to the van. They waved and shouted and joyfully pounded on the doors and windows. Judd and Lionel tried to get close, but they were pushed back by the trailing GC jeep.

Suddenly, the van cut to the left and flew toward the median. The GC vehicles followed, blowing their sirens and bouncing crazily behind the van.

When they made it to the stadium, Judd noticed monitors outside the stadium for those who couldn't get in. Judd and Lionel squeezed their way through the crowd. Judd remembered his first trip to Wrigley Field with his dad and the sight of the green grass and white lines and the ivy on the outfield wall. It had filled him with awe. That was nothing compared to this. Men and women from around the world filled the stands and the infield. They shouted praises to God in many languages. Some huddled in groups to pray. Others sang and swayed as they wrapped their arms around each other.

A line of people appeared through an opening at the

back of the stage. "Interpreters," Lionel whispered. The crowd grew quiet.

At exactly seven, a man strode to a simple wood lectern and said, "Welcome, my brothers and sisters, in the name of the Lord God Almighty. . . ."

8

JUDD felt a chill down his spine. Before the translators could speak, the stadium erupted in cheering. When the applause faded, the man at the podium nodded to the interpreters, but the crowd shouted, *"Nein!" "Nyet!"*

"What's going on?" Lionel said.

The man continued. ". . . maker of heaven and earth . . . and his Son, Jesus Christ, the Messiah!"

The crowd went wild again. Someone hurried onto the stage. Judd leaned close to Lionel. "I think the same thing that happened at the Wailing Wall is happening here."

"What do you mean?"

"Everybody understands in their own language," Judd said. "They don't need the interpreters. That's why everybody's shouting no!"

The translators walked away from their positions. The crowd thundered. The man held up his hands and asked them to pray.

Many knelt in front of their seats. "Father, we are grateful for having been spared by your grace and love," the man prayed. "You are indeed the God of new beginnings and second chances. We are about to hear from our beloved rabbi, and our prayer is that you would supernaturally prepare our hearts and minds to absorb everything you have given him to say. We pray this in the matchless name of the King of kings and Lord of lords. Amen."

A huge "Amen!" echoed through the stadium. The massive congregation began to sing, "Amazing grace! how sweet the sound— that saved a wretch like me! I once was lost but now am found, was blind but now I see."

Judd remembered his mother singing that song. He had hated it because he didn't think he was such a bad person. But now, knowing the truth about himself and what God had done, Judd choked through the words. The sound of twenty-five thousand believers singing from their hearts, plus the thousands outside joining in, overwhelmed him.

"When we've been there ten thousand years, bright shining as the sun, we've no less days to sing God's praise than when we'd first begun."

The man at the podium asked the crowd to sit. "The vast majority of us know our speaker tonight only as a name on our computer screens," he began. "It is my honor—"

Before he could finish, people rose to their feet as one, cheering, clapping, shouting, whistling. Tsion Ben-Judah was nudged from the edge of the stage. He hesitated, looking embarrassed. The noise was deafening. Finally, the crowd settled.

"My beloved brothers and sisters, I accept your warm greeting in the name that is above all names. All glory and honor are due the triune God." As the crowd began to respond again, Tsion quickly asked that they withhold their praise until the end of the teaching.

Vicki and the others gathered in a meeting room to watch the opening session at 11:00 A.M. their time. After Mark had left, Vicki found Z's box in the kitchen. Inside was a note: *Every school needs supplies. I hope these help.*

Underneath were stacks of spiral notebooks, pens, colored pencils, and other materials. Vicki handed out the notebooks before Tsion began his message. "Z thought of everything," Vicki said.

Tsion's voice filled the room. "Ladies and gentlemen," he said, leaning over his notes, "never in my life have I been more eager to share a message from the Word of God. I stand before you with the unique privilege, I believe, of speaking to many of the 144,000 witnesses prophesied in the Scriptures."

The camera panned the crowd. Vicki was overcome by the size of the gathering and the anxious faces of people who hung on Tsion's every word.

"Let me review the basics of God's plan of salvation so we may soon leave this place and get back to the work to which he has called us. You have each been assigned a location for all-day training tomorrow and the next day.

On both nights we will meet back here for encouragement and fellowship and teaching."

Tsion outlined the evidence from the Old Testament proving Jesus was the Messiah. He recited the many names of God and finished with the powerful passage from Isaiah 9:6: "For unto us a Child is born, unto us a Son is given; and the government will be upon His shoulder. And His name will be called Wonderful, Counselor, Mighty God, Everlasting Father, Prince of Peace."

The crowd could not contain itself, leaping to its feet. Tsion smiled and encouraged them. "Jesus himself said that if we do not glorify God, the very stones would have to cry out."

Cheers went up around the room. Vicki jotted something down in her notebook. Someone moved near the doorway. It was Melinda. "What's going on?" she said.

"We're watching the opening session," Vicki said, as the kids fell silent. "Watch with us."

Melinda stepped back. "I don't want to interrupt."

"Please," Vicki said. "It might be good for you to hear it from a different perspective."

Conrad stood and offered Melinda his chair. She shook her head and stood in the back.

Tsion walked through God's plan from the beginning of time, showing that Jesus was sent as the spotless lamb, a sacrifice to take away the sins of the world.

"We are sinful from the day we are born and because God is holy, there is nothing we can do to restore our relationship to him. God had to restore it himself. That is why Christ died. Anyone who accepts the fact that they are a sinner and Christ died for them can be born again spiritually into eternal life.

"In John 14:6, Jesus himself said he was the way, the truth, and the life, and that no man can come to the Father except through him. This is our message to the nations. This is our message to the desperate, the sick, the terrified."

Vicki glanced at Melinda. The girl was deep in thought.

Tsion continued. "There should be no doubt in anyone's mind—even those who have chosen to live in opposition to God—that he is real and that a person is either for him or against him. We should have the boldness of Christ to aggressively tell the world that its only hope is in him.

"The bottom line is that we have been called as his divine witnesses—144,000 strong—through whom he has begun a great soul harvest. This will result in what John the Revelator calls 'a great multitude which no one could number.' Before you fall asleep tonight, read Revelation 7 and thrill with me to the description of the harvest you and I have been called to reap."

Vicki turned to Revelation 7 and read along as Tsion spoke. "John says it is made up of souls from all nations, kindreds, peoples, tribes, and tongues. One day they will stand before his throne and before the Lamb, clothed with white robes and carrying palms in their hands!"

Judd rose with the crowd at Teddy Kollek Stadium as Tsion's voice thundered. "They will cry with a loud voice, saying, 'Salvation belongs to our God who sits on the throne, and to the Lamb.'

"The angels around the throne will fall on their faces and worship God, saying, 'Amen! Blessing and glory and wisdom, thanksgiving and honor and power and might be to our God forever and ever. Amen.'" Tsion stepped back.

The crowd roared. Judd was overwhelmed. He leaned forward, trying to picture that scene. He saw that Tsion had moved back to the microphone. The standing thousands quieted again, as if desperate to catch every word.

"John was asked by one of the elders at the throne, 'Who are these arrayed in white robes, and where did they come from?' And John said, 'Sir, you know.' And the elder said, 'These are the ones who come out of the great tribulation, and washed their robes and made them white in the blood of the Lamb.'"

Tsion waited for another cheer to subside, then continued: "'They shall neither hunger anymore nor thirst anymore.' The Lamb himself shall feed them and lead them to fountains of living water. And, best of all, my dear family, God shall wipe away all tears from their eyes."

Tsion raised a hand before they could cheer again. "We shall be here in Israel two more full days and nights, preparing for battle. Put aside fear! Put on boldness! Were you surprised that all of us, each and every one, were spared the last few judgments I wrote about? When the rain and hail and fire came from the sky and the meteors scorched a third of the plant life and poisoned a third of the waters of the world, how was it that we escaped? Luck? Chance?"

The crowd shouted, "No!"

"No!" Tsion echoed. "The Scriptures say that an angel ascending from the east, having the seal of the living God, cried with a loud voice to the four angels to whom it was given to hurt the earth and the sea. And what did he tell them? He said, 'Do not harm the earth, the sea, or the trees till we have sealed the servants of our God on their foreheads.' And John writes, 'I heard the number of those who were sealed. One hundred and forty-four thousand of all the tribes of the children of Israel were sealed.'"

———

Vicki and the others jotted notes furiously. It felt good to study again. Tsion's words were like water on dry ground. Vicki knew people around the world were watching this very meeting.

Tsion moved close to the microphone and spoke softly. "And now let me close by reminding you that the bedrock of our faith remains the verse our Gentile brothers and sisters have so cherished from the beginning. John 3:16 says, 'For God so loved the world that He gave His only—'"

Tsion stopped talking. Vicki leaned forward. There was a faint noise coming from the speakers. She turned to the doorway and noticed Melinda was gone.

———

Judd heard the rumble behind them and turned. A helicopter slowly came into view over the lights of the stadium. The *thwock thwock thwock* of the gleaming white

81

helicopter drew every eye. Tsion stepped back from the podium and lowered his head, as if in prayer.

Judd recognized the GC insignia on the side of the chopper as it slowly descended. The wind whipped Tsion's hair and clothes.

"Is that who I think it is?" Lionel said.

"I'm afraid so," Judd said, staring at the chopper as the engine shuddered and stopped. A murmur rose from the crowd as Leon Fortunato bounded from the craft to the lectern. He nodded to Tsion, who did not respond. "Dr. Ben-Judah, local and international organizing committee, and assembled guests," he said loudly.

Thousands murmured in different languages. Finally, Judd understood. "Translators," Judd said to Lionel. "They need translators to understand Fortunato!"

Someone in front repeated what Judd had said at the top of his lungs. Others shrugged, looked puzzled, and began jabbering.

Fortunato looked at Tsion. "Dr. Ben-Judah, is there someone who can translate?"

Tsion did not look at him.

Fortunato then called for the interpreters to come forward. Judd stretched to see the interpreters who sat near the front row on the infield. They looked to Tsion, but Tsion stared straight ahead.

"Please," Fortunato continued, "it isn't fair that only those who understand English may enjoy the remarks of your next two hosts."

"*Two* hosts?" Lionel said. "Who else is with Carpathia?"

Tsion raised his head slightly. The interpreters hurried

to their microphones. Fortunato apparently expected applause when he mentioned Nicolae Carpathia's name, but no one moved. Fortunato cleared his throat and said, "First, I would like to introduce the revered head of the new Enigma Babylon One World Faith, the supreme pontiff, Pontifex Maximus, Peter the Second!"

Judd looked at Lionel and raised an eyebrow.

"They've got to be out of their minds, bringing him here," Lionel said.

Judd knew this was the former archbishop of Cincinnati, Peter Mathews. He was now the head of a mixture of nearly every religion on the globe except for Judaism and Christianity.

Peter the Second stepped out of the helicopter in an outfit that surprised even Judd. He wore a huge, pointed hat and a long, yellow robe with puffy sleeves. Several garments, inlaid with brightly colored stones, draped over his body. The supreme pontiff lifted his hands in a circle as if to bless everyone. When he turned to bless the people sitting behind him, Judd saw signs of the zodiac on the back of his robe.

"Looks like he wore the wrapping paper from his Christmas presents," Lionel said.

Peter stretched out his arms and spoke dramatically. "My blessed brothers and sisters in the pursuit of higher consciousness, it warms my heart to see all of you here, studying under my colleague, Dr. Tsion Ben-Judah!"

Peter waited for the applause and cheers. None came.

"I confer upon this gathering the blessings of the universal father and mother and animal deities who lovingly guide us on our path to true spirituality. In the spirit of harmony, I appeal to Dr. Ben-Judah and others in your leadership to join Enigma Babylon One World Faith, where we affirm and accept the beliefs of all the world's great religions."

The stadium was deathly silent. Fortunato announced, "And now it gives me pleasure to introduce the man who has united the world into one global community, His Excellency and your potentate, Nicolae Carpathia! Would you rise as he comes with a word of greeting."

No one stood. Lionel whispered into Judd's ear, "Nicolae's always been able to win over his audience. Think he'll be able to do that here?"

Carpathia appeared on the steps of the helicopter, a frozen smile etched on his face. He nodded toward Fortunato and Peter the Second.

Someone moved to Judd's right. A man was making his way along a back wall of the stadium. Lionel saw him too and slipped out. Just before Carpathia made it to the microphone, Lionel returned.

"You're not going to believe this," Lionel said. "That's Taylor Graham!"

9

AS NICOLAE Carpathia stepped to the podium, Judd
slipped from his seat. "If I'm not back before this ends,
stay here," Judd said to Lionel. Taylor Graham was still
moving when Judd caught up to him.

"What are you doing?" Judd whispered.

Taylor whirled, ready to fight. When he recognized
Judd, he rolled his eyes and put a finger to his lips.
"I came to hear Carpathia."

"Fellow citizens of the Global Community,"
Carpathia began, "as your potentate, I welcome you to
Israel and to this great arena, named after a man of the
past, a man of peace and harmony and statesmanship."

Judd knew what Nicolae was doing. He was trying
to win the crowd by talking about a well-known Israeli.
Judd tried to talk with Taylor, but he motioned for Judd
to keep quiet. An armed Global Community guard
approached them. "Take it outside," he said sternly.

Judd nodded. Taylor followed Judd through the gate.

Vicki couldn't believe Nicolae Carpathia would interrupt the Meeting of the Witnesses. The kids groaned when they saw him arrive.

"Do we have to watch this?" Shelly said.

"He's going to schmooze them all he can," Conrad said.

Carpathia pledged his protection and support of those who followed the teachings of Dr. Ben-Judah. "As a famous teacher of Israel once said, 'Blessed are the peacemakers, for they shall be called sons of God.'"

Carpathia paused. When the stadium remained silent, he said, "We in the Global Community wish this kind of peace, not as a slogan but as a living reality."

Vicki turned. Melinda stood in the doorway again, listening.

Judd and Taylor walked away from the stadium. They could still see the huge monitors and hear Carpathia's powerful voice.

"Why did you come here?" Judd said.

"You know why," Taylor said. "Saint Nick."

"You're not thinking of—"

"Only a fool would try to get a weapon past those guards." Taylor smiled. "I just wanted to make sure that was Nick in the white chopper."

Taylor opened the trunk of his car. He put on a

Global Community uniform and zipped it quickly.
"This is where you check out, okay?"

"Don't do this," Judd said.

Taylor glanced around, then opened a huge, black
box inside the trunk. In several pieces lay the biggest
gun Judd had ever seen. Beside it was a shell the size
of a loaf of bread.

"No!" Judd said.

"As soon as he takes off, that chopper's falling from
the sky."

Judd's mind reeled. He knew Rayford Steele was
Nicolae's pilot. Was he flying the chopper? And if the
potentate was assassinated, the Global Community
would blame the witnesses. Judd couldn't let Taylor
shoot it down.

Lionel was captivated by Carpathia and wondered
whether he would try his mind-altering techniques.
Buck Williams had described the potentate's ability to
sway people, but Lionel didn't know if it would work
on a crowd filled mainly with believers.

"And so, my beloved friends," Carpathia said,
"you do not have to join with the One World Faith
to remain citizens of the Global Community. There
is room for disagreement on matters of religion.
But consider the advantages and benefits that have
resulted from the uniting of every nation into one
global village."

Nicolae gave a list of his achievements: everything

from the repair of cities, roads, and airports to the rebuilding of New Babylon into the most magnificent city ever constructed. "It is a masterpiece I hope you will visit as soon as you can."

Lionel closed his eyes in thought. *One day Carpathia is going to declare himself god. With this kind of technology, Nicolae will be able to rule the world!*

As Lionel listened, he noticed something strange about Carpathia's voice. In the past, he had been always in command, never making a mistake, never struggling to remember a name or a date. Now he had grown hoarse. He turned away and cleared his throat. "Pardon me," he said, his voice still raspy. "I wish you and the rabbi here all the best and welcome you, . . . *ahem, ahem,* . . . excuse me—"

Nicolae turned to Tsion. "Would someone have some water?"

Dr. Ben-Judah didn't respond. Lionel saw someone in the front pass a bottle to the stage. Nicolae nodded and smiled. He unscrewed the cap, tipped it back for a long gulp, then gagged and spit it out. The crowd gasped. Nicolae's lips and chin were covered with blood. He held the bottle at arm's length, staring at it in fear.

Carpathia cursed at Tsion. "You and your evil flock of enemies! You would disgrace me like this for your own gain? I should have my men shoot you dead where you stand!"

Lionel saw two figures pass in the aisle near him. Both had long hair and wore tattered clothes. In unison Eli and Moishe spoke without any microphone. The crowd fell back from around them, and the two stood in the eerie light of the stadium, shoulder to shoulder, barefoot.

"Woe unto you who would threaten the chosen vessel of the Most High God!"

Carpathia threw the bottle to the ground. Clear, clean water splashed everywhere.

Lionel looked around. Other people carried water bottles containing clear liquid. *Eli and Moishe caused his throat to parch,* Lionel thought. Nicolae pointed at the two and screamed, "Your time is nigh! I swear I will kill you or have you killed before—"

"Woe!" Eli and Moishe thundered, silencing Carpathia. "Woe to the impostor who would dare threaten the chosen ones before the due time! Sealed followers of the Messiah, drink deeply and be refreshed!"

A man beside Lionel took a long drink from a small bottle of water. He wiped his mouth and handed it to Lionel. "You drink now," he said.

The bottle was ice-cold and full. Lionel took a long drink. He handed it back to the man. Again, it was full. Throughout the stadium people sighed with pleasure at the taste. A few others tried to drink, but like Nicolae's bottle, the water turned to blood.

Lionel glanced at the stage. The chopper blades whirred to life, and Tsion was again alone. His notes flew around the stage like a tornado, then settled. People leaped to retrieve them. Tsion remained motionless, having ignored the entire episode with Carpathia.

Lionel looked around for the two witnesses, but they were gone.

Judd pleaded, but when the helicopter prepared for lift-off, Taylor picked up his weapon and placed it against his shoulder. The white chopper appeared over the top of the stadium and flew directly overhead.

Taylor aimed. Judd started to rush him, but before he did, Taylor dropped to the ground with the gun.

"It's them," Taylor gasped, his mouth hanging open.

Judd turned and saw Eli and Moishe walking toward them. They didn't say a word or even glance up as the helicopter passed. When they were gone, Taylor said, "I thought I was dead."

Judd helped him up. "You have to understand who you're dealing with. If you shot Carpathia down, the GC would blame the followers of Ben-Judah. They'd make us all martyrs tonight."

"I don't care. If that chopper returns, it's going down."

"Then I'll have to do what I have to do," Judd said, walking away.

"Which is what?" Taylor said.

The crowd around Lionel took their seats. Tsion was back at the lectern. As if nothing had happened since he began quoting John 3:16, Tsion continued:

"'—begotten Son, that whoever believes in Him should not perish but have everlasting life.'"

Tsion stepped back and repeated the verse louder as the helicopter flew away. "'For God so loved the world that He gave His only begotten Son, that whoever believes in Him should not perish but have everlasting life.'"

A man near Lionel fell to his knees. The man was holding a bottle filled with blood. Tsion said, "There may be some here, inside or outside, who want to receive Christ. I urge you to pray after me: 'Dear God, I know I am a sinner. Forgive me and pardon me for waiting so long. I receive your love and salvation and ask you to live your life through me. I accept you as my Savior and resolve to live for you until you come again.'"

As the man near Lionel repeated the prayer, the blood in the bottle changed to ice-cold water. The man stood. Lionel pointed at the bottle. The man raised it over his head, laughing, and let the liquid pour over him.

"I can see it," the man yelled, looking from one face to the next. "The cross on your foreheads. I see it!"

Others shouted, "Praise God!" and embraced one another.

Tsion stood at the lectern, his eyes brimming with tears, his hands clasped in front of his face in a posture of prayer.

Judd knew he had to tell someone about Taylor's plan. He pushed his way into the stadium and found a young guard with "Kudrick" on his name tag.

At first the guard told Judd to move along, but when Judd mentioned the high-powered weapon, the man radioed other guards and followed Judd outside. When they reached the area, Taylor was gone.

The guard pulled out a handheld computer and entered some data. Judd was sketchy about Taylor. "All I know is that this guy had a bazooka ready to fire at the potentate's helicopter, and the thing that stopped him was those two fire-breathing guys from the Wailing Wall."

The guard studied Judd. "Why are you here?"

"Curious," Judd said.

The guard put his computer away. "Do you know anything about the teaching of this Ben-Judah?"

"Are you asking for your report or because you're interested personally?"

The guard crossed his arms. "Does it matter?"

Suddenly an alarm went off on the guard's communication device. The guard plugged in his earphone, then pulled out his pistol and released the safety lock. He gave Judd a frantic look and ran back toward the stadium.

"Meet me right here tomorrow night," Judd yelled.

Judd wondered if he had just hurt the Young Trib Force by giving the GC information. Or had he made contact with a future follower of Christ?

———————————

Lionel waited for Judd. Though Dr. Ben-Judah had left the stage, people stood at the front, weeping, kneeling, and praying. As he watched, Lionel saw Mr. Stein walk across the stage and jump to the infield.

Lionel got Mr. Stein's attention, and the two embraced. Mr. Stein glowed with excitement. "I am overwhelmed. I had hoped you and Judd would be able to get inside."

"What happened to you?" Lionel said.

"You will not believe it. Yitzhak asked me to accompany him backstage as the group met for prayer before the message. I actually met Tsion Ben-Judah face-to-face."

"I bet he was surprised you were here in person."

"Very," Mr. Stein said. "I saw Buck and Chloe Williams backstage as well."

Nicolae Carpathia's helicopter appeared again. Judd rushed up and explained what had happened with Taylor Graham.

"You did the right thing," Mr. Stein said. "Taylor must be stopped."

"Something's wrong," Judd said. "The guard took off with his gun drawn."

"You don't think they're going to kill people, do you?" Lionel said.

Mr. Stein grabbed their arms. "Let's not give them the chance." The three raced for the nearest exit.

Above them, Leon Fortunato's voice boomed over the helicopter's loudspeakers. "We have been asked by Global Community ground security forces at the stadium to help clear this area! Please translate this message to others if at all possible! We appreciate your cooperation!"

Lionel ran ahead of Judd and Mr. Stein. The crowd did not obey. Hundreds of people moved to the corner of the stadium where the helicopter hovered.

As Lionel reached the stairs that would lead them outside, a machine gun fired outside the stadium. People screamed and dived for cover. Lionel kept moving, stepping over those on the ground. As the three made it outside, more shots filled the air.

10

VICKI switched the laptop to the sleep mode and sat back.

"I wonder how Carpathia's going to work this to his advantage." Conrad said. "I can't believe he lost his cool and cursed like that on live television."

"Can you imagine what the press will do with the water-to-blood thing?" Shelly said. "It's going to be plastered all over the headlines."

"Yeah, but the publicity will make everybody want to watch," Vicki said. "The meeting will be the biggest thing in TV history."

"If they let them continue," Conrad said.

Vicki sighed. An idea had been brewing since the beginning of Tsion's message. "I think we should change our clocks to Jerusalem time."

"What for?" Shelly said.

"The all-day meetings will begin just after midnight," Vicki said. "I know it's the middle of the afternoon, but if we get some sleep now, we can get up and watch the whole thing live."

The kids all agreed to try it. Vicki went to the kitchen to prepare what would be a midnight breakfast. Conrad said, "I want to see what Carpathia says about all this."

Vicki looked in on Melinda. Her door was slightly open. Vicki knocked and entered. "What did you think?"

Melinda shrugged. "Interesting. I've never seen the potentate that upset."

"What about the rabbi?" Vicki said.

"I guess he made some sense. A lot more than that Peter guy. But there's a lot I don't understand."

"Like what?"

"The stuff about the sheep," Melinda said.

"You mean the lamb?"

"Whatever."

Vicki sat on the bed. She explained that Jesus was the Lamb of God. "In the days before Jesus, God asked for a sacrifice for sins. I don't understand everything about it, but basically the people had to take a perfect lamb, kill it, then sprinkle its blood on an altar."

Melinda scowled. "That sounds weird. Why does God have to kill something? Can't he just look the other way?"

"The sacrifice reminded the people how bad sin is. Because God is holy, there has to be some kind of payment. That ceremony was sort of a picture of Jesus' sacrifice. He was the perfect Lamb who gave his life for us."

"I got it," Melinda said, "but I still think it's pretty weird."

Conrad knocked at the door. "You oughta come see this."

"We'll talk later," Vicki said.

The voice of Leon Fortunato echoed down the hall. "The supreme commander's introducing Nicolae," Conrad said.

"I don't believe this," Shelly groaned as Vicki came into the room. "This is the ultimate setup guy."

Fortunato looked calm and collected. He said there were still pockets of resistance to the progress of the Global Community. "One of those movements revealed its true nature earlier this evening before the eyes of the world."

"Yeah, they turned his drinking water to blood," Darrion said.

"His Excellency has the power to use extreme measures because of this action, but in the spirit of the new society he has built, His Excellency has a different response he wishes to share with you.

"Before he does that, however, I would like to share a personal story."

"Uh-oh," Conrad said, "here it comes."

Fortunato told the world that after the earthquake, Nicolae Carpathia had raised him from the dead. He finished with, "And now, without further ado, your potentate and—may I say, my deity—His Excellency, Nicolae Carpathia."

"My deity?" Shelly said. "He thinks Carpathia's God?"

"Tsion said this would happen," Vicki said.

Fortunato bowed deeply and tried to make way for

Carpathia, but he stumbled on a light cord and tumbled out of range of the camera. The kids laughed. Carpathia seemed flustered by the distraction, then quickly recovered.

"Fellow citizens, I am certain that if you did not see what happened earlier this evening at Teddy Kollek Stadium in Jerusalem, you have by now heard about it. Let me briefly tell you my view of what occurred and outline my response.

"One of my goals as a strong leader is tolerance. We can only truly be a global community by accepting our differences. It has been the clear wish of most of us that we break down walls and bring people together. Thus there is now one economy highlighted by one currency, no need for passports, one government, eventually one language, one system of measurement, and one religion."

Carpathia described Enigma Babylon One World Faith, which brought different religions under one banner. "Your way may be the only way for you, and my way the only way for me, but all religions of the world have proved themselves able to live in harmony."

Carpathia frowned. "All religions except one. You know the one. It is the sect that claims its roots in historic Christianity. It holds that the vanishings of two and a half years ago were God's doing. Indeed, they say, Jesus blew a trumpet and took all his favorite people to heaven, leaving the rest of us lost sinners to suffer here on earth."

Carpathia crossed his arms and squinted. "This is not the truth of Christianity as it was taught for centuries. That wonderful, peace-loving religion told of a God of love and of a man who was a teacher of morals. His example was to be followed in order for a person to one day reach eternal heaven by continually improving oneself."

"This is too much," Vicki said. "If we reach heaven by improving ourselves, why did Jesus have to die?"

Carpathia continued. "Following the disappearances that caused such great chaos in our world, some misguided people looked to the Christian Bible for an explanation. They created a belief that said the true church was taken away."

"You think people are actually buying this?" Darrion said.

Carpathia referred to the followers of Dr. Ben-Judah as a cult. "I come to you tonight from the very studio where Dr. Ben-Judah turned his back on his own religion. While in exile, he has managed to brainwash thousands who are desperate. Dr. Ben-Judah has used the Internet for his own gain, no doubt taking millions from his followers. He has invented an us-against-them war."

"He hasn't taken a penny," Vicki shouted.

"For months I have ignored these harmless holdouts to world harmony. When Dr. Ben-Judah invited his converts to meet in the very city that had exiled him, I decided to allow it."

"Here comes the payoff," Conrad said. "He's about to bring the hammer down."

Carpathia held up his hands in a gesture of peace. "In a spirit of acceptance, I gave my public promise for Dr. Ben-Judah's safety. I believed the only right thing to do was to encourage this mass meeting. I wanted his followers to join us. But the choice was theirs. I would not have forced them.

"And how were my actions rewarded? Was I invited to the festivities? Allowed to bring a greeting or take part in any of the pageantry? No. I traveled to Israel at my own expense and dropped in to say a few words.

"My supreme commander was met with the rudeness of utter silence. The most revered Supreme Pontiff Peter the Second was received in the same manner, even though he is a fellow clergyman. This was obviously a well-planned mass response."

"A vast conspiracy," Conrad said.

"Shh," Vicki said. "Here's his explanation."

Carpathia accused Dr. Ben-Judah of controlling the minds of his audience. "I had the clear feeling that the crowd was with me. They wanted to welcome me. Dr. Ben-Judah somehow gave a signal to release an invisible dust or powder that instantly parched my throat and resulted in a powerful thirst.

"I should have been suspicious when I was immediately presented with a bottle from someone in the crowd. But as a trusting person, I assumed an unknown friend had come to my aid."

Carpathia gritted his teeth. "I was ambushed by a bottle of poisonous blood! It was such an obvious assassination attempt that I accused Dr. Ben-Judah right there. He had hidden in the crowd the two elderly lunatics from the Wailing Wall who have murdered several people. With hidden microphones turned louder than the one I was using, they shouted me down with threats.

"My doctor says if I had swallowed what they gave me, I would have died instantly."

Judd, Lionel, and Mr. Stein had fought their way through the crowd of frightened people to the safety of a nearby building. When the GC emergency vehicles left, the three headed for the university gymnasium.

Judd was exhausted. He lay on his cot, listening to the prayers and conversation around him. Before he drifted off to sleep, Mr. Stein touched his shoulder and asked him to follow. "You'll want to see this."

A small group gathered around a television in an office near the front. Yitzhak sat with his feet on a desk. Judd recognized the man who had introduced Tsion onstage. His name was Daniel. Other members of the local committee stared at Nicolae Carpathia on TV.

Lionel brought Judd up to speed about Nicolae's speech. "He just said the assassination attempt is an act of high treason, punishable by death."

"Who are they going to execute, all of us?" Judd said.

Lionel shrugged.

Carpathia clenched his jaw. "There is no doubt that this ugly incident was engineered and carried out by Dr. Ben-Judah. But as a man of my word, I plan to allow the meetings to continue for the next two nights. I will maintain my pledge of security and protection."

"We do not need either from you," Daniel muttered.

Carpathia continued. "Dr. Ben-Judah, however, shall be exiled again from Israel within twenty-four hours of the

end of the meeting. As for the two who call themselves Eli
and Moishe, let this serve as public notification to them as
well. For the next forty-eight hours, they shall be restricted
to the area near the Wailing Wall. They are not to leave
that area for any purpose at any time. When the meetings
in the stadium have concluded, Eli and Moishe must leave
the Temple Mount area. Their appearance anywhere but
near the Wailing Wall for forty-eight hours or their showing their faces anywhere in the world after that shall be
considered reason to kill. Any Global Community officer
or private citizen is authorized to shoot to kill."

Yitzhak shook his head. "You will not kill the Lord's
anointed until the due time."

"I know you will agree," Carpathia concluded, "that
this is a most generous response to an ugly attack. Thank
you, my friends, and good night from Israel."

As the news anchor recapped the story, Yitzhak turned
off the television. "God is at work, my friends. Now we
must rest. The next two days are very important."

Mr. Stein followed Judd and Lionel to their cots.
"Before you sleep, you must know what has happened.
There was an attempt on Tsion's life tonight."

"What?" Judd said.

"Somehow Tsion and the others found out that the
guards were preparing to attack."

Judd gasped. "The guard I met was probably after
Tsion! I'm hoping to meet him before tomorrow night's
session."

Lionel scowled. "I don't know if we should get that
close to a GC guard."

Judd asked how Tsion got away.

"He hid with Chloe in a utility room until a friend created a diversion with gunfire," Mr. Stein said.

"So that's where the shots came from," Judd said. "Where are they now?"

"Tsion, Buck, and Chloe are staying at the Chaim Rosenzweig estate." Mr. Stein leaned close to the boys. "I am almost convinced I am a true witness of God. I am going to see Eli and Moishe now. I must talk to them."

Judd sighed. "I can hardly keep my eyes open."

"I'll go," Lionel said.

Mr. Stein smiled. "I would be honored to have you with me." He looked at Judd. "I may not be able to spend much time with you over the next two days. Drink in as much of the teaching as you can."

Mr. Stein led them in a prayer. Judd fell back on his cot and was asleep in minutes.

11

LIONEL rode with Mr. Stein in Yitzhak's car. They took a wrong turn and drove through a shabby part of Jerusalem. Drunks staggered about the streets. Bars, fortune-telling shops, tattoo parlors, and strip clubs advertised in glaring lights.

"Yitzhak told me about this," Mr. Stein said, turning the car around. "The new religion welcomes any belief system. Hedonism is rampant."

"Hedonism?" Lionel said.

"Pleasures of the flesh. Whatever feels good. This is what happens when people buy into the lie that God is whoever we want him to be."

Mr. Stein found the right road and made it to the Wailing Wall. When they arrived, a GC guard was making an announcement.

"Attention, ladies and gentlemen! I have been asked by the Global Community supreme commander to remind citizens of the proclamation from His Excellency,

Potentate Nicolae Carpathia, that the two men you see before you are under house arrest. They are confined to this area until the end of the Meeting of the Witnesses Friday night. If they leave this area before that, any GC personnel or private citizen is within his rights to detain them by force, to wound them, or to kill them. Further, if they are seen anywhere, repeat, *anywhere*, following that time, they shall be put to death."

A huge crowd near the fence cheered wildly, laughed, and jeered at the witnesses. Eli and Moishe seemed not to notice the guard or those nearby who spat at them.

Gigantic lights lit the area. The witnesses were bathed in a glaring spotlight, but they didn't squint or blink.

"So much for a quiet conversation," Lionel said. "Since Carpathia's new law, the media's crawling everywhere."

Mr. Stein took Lionel to the bushes where they had been before. The crowd cheered when a man suggested he wanted to kill the witnesses.

Barely moving his lips, Eli spoke at the top of his lungs. At the force of his voice, the crowd stumbled back. "Come nigh and question not this warning from the Lord of Hosts. He who would dare come against the appointed servants of the Most High God, the same shall surely die!"

When the crowd inched forward, taunting again, Eli erupted a second time. "Tempt not the chosen ones, for if you come against the voices crying in the wilderness, God himself will consume your flesh!"

A man held up a high-powered rifle and laughed. The GC guards spoke to the man, but Lionel couldn't hear them. Mr. Stein tugged on Lionel's arm. "They're moving!"

Eli and Moishe disappeared behind the slope. Mr. Stein stood. "If we can make it to the other side of the hill, I may be able to speak to them."

Lionel ran through the dewy grass, following Mr. Stein to the bottom of the hill. Behind them the GC guard spoke urgently. "Search the area behind the fence! If the two are not there, they are in violation of the potentate and may be shot!"

"The Mount of Olives!" Mr. Stein whispered.

Lionel gasped for air as they climbed. Finally they spotted the two at the top of a knoll beside a lone olive tree. Mr. Stein bent double, his hands on his knees. They were ten feet from the two witnesses.

"Please," Mr. Stein gasped. "I am a Jew. I believe Jesus is the Messiah. Can I know if I am truly a witness of the Most High God?"

Moishe didn't speak but motioned for them to get behind a tree. Crowds ran up the hill, shouting murderous threats.

Eli and Moishe spoke at the same time. They looked directly at Mr. Stein and said, "Harken unto us, servants of the Lord God Almighty, Maker of heaven and earth!"

The witnesses were suddenly bathed in light, not from the news cameras or anything earthly, but from a heavenly glow. The sight was awesome.

Eli and Moishe warned the mob that they would be devoured by fire if they tried to hurt God's servants. "We have been granted the power to shut heaven, that it rain not in the days of our prophecy. Yea, we have power over waters to turn them to blood and to smite the earth with all plagues, as often as we will.

"And what is our prophecy? That Jesus of Bethlehem, the son of the Virgin Mary, was in the beginning with God, and he was God, and he is God. Yea, he fulfilled all the prophecies of the coming Messiah, and he shall reign and rule now and forevermore, world without end, amen!"

Lionel looked down the hill. The people ignored the warnings. "I don't like the looks of this."

"It is ours to bring rain," the witnesses shouted. A freezing gush of water poured from the skies and drenched the ground.

"Yitzhak said it has not rained here in twenty-four months!" Mr. Stein said, shivering.

The rain stopped a moment later.

"And it is ours to shut heaven for the days of our prophecy!" the witnesses proclaimed.

Lionel heard the murmurs and threats of the crowd. They were a hundred yards away and tramping through the mud.

"You got your answer when they called you a servant of God," Lionel said. "We should get out of here."

Before Mr. Stein could move, the prophets stopped the crowd with their booming voices. Eli and Moishe spoke against the new temple. They called it blasphemy. "Your sacrifices of animal blood are a stench in the nostrils of your God! Turn from your wicked ways, O sinners! Advance not against the chosen ones whose time has not yet been accomplished!"

Lionel peeked from behind the tree. Two GC guards rushed up the hill, weapons raised. They slipped on the wet hillside and fell to the ground.

"Woe unto you who would close your ears to the warnings of the chosen ones!" the witnesses shouted. "Flee to the caves to save yourselves! Your mission is doomed! Your bodies shall be consumed!"

The guards crawled on their bellies. The crowd shouted to the guards, "Kill them! Shoot them!"

Gunfire exploded. Lionel heard a *ping* and looked up. A bullet left a gash in the tree just above his head. The witnesses remained steady, unmoving, unhurt. They stood, still illuminated on the hill. The guards reloaded and fired again. Lionel and Mr. Stein huddled together.

A flash of light and a *whooshing* sound surrounded them. The air was filled with an intense heat. The gunshots were replaced with a sizzling fire. Lionel looked down the hill and saw the two guards engulfed in flames. They had no time to react. Within seconds the white heat turned their rifles to puddles of boiling liquid and their bones to ash. The crowd fled, screaming, cursing, and crying.

"Let's go," Mr. Stein said.

Lionel looked back only once more. The witnesses were walking slowly down the hill toward the Wailing Wall.

Vicki awoke at 11 P.M. Midwest time. It was pitch-black outside, and there wasn't a sound in the rest of the house.

She went to the meeting room and searched the Web to find coverage of the all-day training. It would begin at midnight her time.

The numbers reported by the media were staggering. Twenty-five thousand had been in Teddy Kollek Stadium the night before. More than fifty thousand had gathered outside. Another report said the two preachers at the Wailing Wall had violated the potentate's directive. Two guards had been murdered trying to apprehend them. Eyewitnesses on the Mount of Olives accused the two of hiding flamethrowers in their robes. The weapons had not been recovered, and the preachers were reported back in their usual spots.

Vicki scoffed at the report and wondered what the real story was. She opened her Bible and went through the passages Tsion had read during the first meeting. She wrote out a prayer in her notebook: *God, show us what you want us to do. I put myself and all of the Young Trib Force in your hands. Amen.*

Listening to the meeting the day before had given Vicki an idea. The evening sessions seemed mainly for encouragement, motivation, and Tsion's teaching. She could only imagine the feeling of worshiping God with thousands of other believers, hearing the words of their earthly leader firsthand. But the bulk of the training to evangelize the world would occur during the all-day sessions. Vicki and the others could memorize that teaching and train other kids.

She quickly sketched out a plan of action. They would record the sessions onto the computer's hard drive, just as they were recording Tsion's messages. The kids would then write out the lessons in a way anyone could understand.

At 11:30, Vicki set out the food and awakened the others. Conrad nodded when he heard Vicki's plan. "This could help us answer some of the e-mail Tsion is getting from kids."

Judd awoke, refreshed, and found his way to the morning session. Lionel was still asleep. The meetings were open on a first-come, first-served basis. When one location filled, participants moved to the next site. The teacher at Judd's seminar was Yitzhak. Judd was amazed that such a humble man was actually one of the leaders.

After a song and prayer, Yitzhak tackled the subject of speaking one-on-one with unbelievers. "Though many of us have come to faith via the Internet or watching the mass media, we must not underestimate the importance of talking with individuals."

Yitzhak outlined a series of questions. "Do not use these as a list to check off. If you are not interested in the other person, he or she will know it and will sense you are asking in a selfish way. If you can, get to know the other person. Many have gone through tragic circumstances. They have lost loved ones. They are separated from family members. Remember that the Good News must be accompanied by true compassion."

Judd believed each member of the Young Trib Force had already followed these principles. Their work on the

Underground and Judd's message at graduation proved how much they were willing to risk. Now Judd felt like being even bolder with people one-on-one.

"We only have a limited time," Yitzhak said. "If someone does not respond to the message, pray for that person. Then ask God to lead you to someone else who needs the hope of eternal life."

Speaker after speaker circulated through the meeting places. By the end of the day, Judd had taken in an incredible amount of information.

He met with Lionel for dinner at the gymnasium and found out what had happened with Eli and Moishe the night before. "Because of the death of the two guards," Lionel said, "security is supposed to be really tight tonight."

"I almost forgot," Judd said, looking at his watch. "I was supposed to meet the guard!"

Vicki and the others took turns taking notes during the early morning sessions. When she heard one man talk about speaking to people one-on-one, she thought of Melinda and Charlie. Melinda stayed away from the daytime sessions, but Charlie watched. He began to ask questions, and Vicki had to take him out of the room.

Charlie seemed upset. "I don't have that thing on my head," he said. Vicki questioned him once more about what he thought had happened during the disappearances.

"That's easy," Charlie said. "All the good people got taken up to heaven, and the bad people stayed down here."

She explained that afternoon and again at dinner that those who were raptured weren't better than those left behind—they had just been forgiven. "How much good stuff do you have to do to get into heaven?" Vicki said.

"Enough so that the good stuff is more than the bad?" Charlie said.

"No," Vicki said. "Even if you do only one bad thing, God has to reject you because he's holy."

Charlie nodded, but Vicki knew he still didn't get it.

Conrad rushed into the room. "You have to see this."

Vicki rushed to the meeting room and saw an urgent e-mail on the screen. "Is it from Judd?"

Conrad shook his head. "This is really weird."

Vicki scanned the message. It simply said, *Need to talk to Mark immediately. Let me know how I can find him. A friend.*

"Who could it be from?" Vicki said.

"Look at the return address," Conrad said.

Vicki gasped. It was from a GC military post.

As thousands streamed toward the stadium, Judd and Lionel looked for the guard. GC guards looked threateningly at the growing crowds. Judd could tell by the conversation of those around him that many were skeptics, curious about the meeting.

"Let's separate," Judd said as the meeting time approached. "He might think I'm up to something if he sees somebody with me."

"It's your funeral," Lionel said, walking away.

A few minutes later the guard approached Judd, his rifle ready.

"I'm glad you came," Judd said. "I wanted to talk to you about—"

The guard interrupted. "You heard about the two who were killed last night?"

Judd nodded.

"I was supposed to be on duty there," the guard said. "My friend took my place and now he's dead."

Judd thought of the guards who had been burned alive.

"You and your kind are the reason he's dead."

"You've had a terrible loss," Judd said, "but don't blame us. God loves you and wants to get your attention."

The guard pushed Judd away. "If I get the okay, the people onstage are dead."

12

VICKI and the others tried to figure out who had written the e-mail and what they should do. As difficult as it was to put it out of their minds, they decided to leave the e-mail unanswered until after the Meeting of the Witnesses was over.

After the early sessions were complete, the kids ate. Some slept, while others went outside to walk or get some fresh air. Conrad had found an old baseball and a tree limb about the size of a bat. He tried to get others to join him, but no one seemed interested.

The meeting began at 11 A.M. with cheers and applauses for Tsion. He smiled and raised his hands for silence.

"You have learned much today," Tsion began, "and I have warned you of many judgments. I will tell you now what to expect next. When it occurs, let no man deny that he was warned and that this warning has been recorded in the Scriptures for centuries."

Tsion explained that God doesn't want anyone to die without being forgiven of their sin. "That is the reason for this entire season of trial. In his love and mercy God has tried everything to get our attention. Is there doubt in anyone's mind that all of this is God's doing?

"Repent! Turn to him. Accept his gift before it is too late. It is likely that three-fourths of everyone left behind at the Rapture will die by the end of the Tribulation.

"I want to tell you tonight of the fourth Trumpet Judgment that will affect the look of the skies and the temperature of the entire globe. Revelation 8:12 reads, 'Then the fourth angel sounded: And a third of the sun was struck, a third of the moon, and a third of the stars, so that a third of them were darkened. A third of the day did not shine, and likewise the night.'"

Tsion explained that this judgment would cause great distress on the earth. "Prophecy indicates this darkening and cooling is temporary. But when it occurs it will usher in—for however long—winterlike conditions in most of the world. Prepare, prepare, prepare!"

"It's a good thing we have a generator that works," Conrad said. "We'd freeze out here."

"The glorious appearing of Jesus Christ is fewer than five years away," Tsion said. "I believe the greatest time of harvest is now, before the second half of the Tribulation, which the Bible calls the Great Tribulation.

"One day the evil world system will require the bearing of a mark in order for its citizens to buy or sell. You

116

may rest assured it will not be the mark we see on each other's foreheads!

"You must begin to store food and other provisions for what is to come. Above all, we must trust God. He expects us to be wise as serpents and gentle as doves.

"Tomorrow night I'm afraid I have a difficult message to bring. You may get a preview of it by reading Revelation 9."

It was afternoon in Illinois, but the kids were exhausted. Vicki and the others went to their rooms. She couldn't get the e-mail out of her mind. Had the GC found them? Was Mark in some kind of trouble?

Before she went to sleep, Vicki opened her Bible. Her hands trembled as she read.

Judd awoke early Friday and spent the day in a blur of activity. The all-day meetings focused on the importance of the message and gave specific texts of Scripture to memorize. "These are the words of God," one speaker said, "and God's words are effective. Use them well."

Late in the afternoon, Judd and Lionel walked to the stadium early to make sure they got seats. At the east entrance they were amazed to see the crowds already standing shoulder to shoulder. Most were Jewish believers, but many were also skeptics and seekers who had seen the coverage and wanted to view Dr. Ben-Judah themselves.

"Can you believe Carpathia's news media has covered this whole thing?" Lionel said.

"Probably Nick's way of keeping track of everything they say," Judd said.

Again, Judd looked for the GC guard but couldn't find him. He and Lionel made their way into the already packed stadium. As darkness fell, Judd spotted the guard near the stage. "Save my seat. I'll be right back."

"I can't talk to you," the guard said as Judd approached, his eyes darting toward the stage.

Judd turned his back and kept talking. "Why not?"

"Get out of here—"

"Just answer this," Judd said. "You've listened the last two nights. Does Tsion's message make sense?"

"I'm telling you, I can't talk," the guard said.

"Tell me, is any of it getting through?"

The guard looked down and whispered, "Last night I listened and wondered what would have happened . . . if those two preachers had zapped me instead of my friend."

Judd felt a ray of hope for the guard.

"At first, I thought you people were crazy, all the praying and singing. Last night I was ready to kill everyone on the stage. Now, I don't know. I wonder if I've done something wrong."

"We all have," Judd said. "That's the point. But God's trying to get our attention. Let me tell you what we believe. I can help."

The guard stole a glance around the stage. "You have to go. The other guards will see us."

"If you ask God to forgive you, he will," Judd said. "You can become one of us."

"How would you know I wasn't a GC spy?"

Judd smiled. "Trust me, I'll know." Judd quickly explained what it meant to be a believer. The guard listened. Suddenly the man's radio squawked.

"I have to go," the guard said, "but I want to talk again afterward. Meet me here by the stage when everyone is gone."

Judd walked away. He prayed Tsion would say something tonight to get through to the guard.

Judd made it back to his seat as Daniel announced a rally at the Temple Mount the following day. "What's that about?" Judd said.

"A thank-you to the local committee," Lionel said. "We ought to go."

A few moments later Daniel said, "And now I invite you to listen to a message from the Word of God."

As Tsion Ben-Judah walked to the podium, the crowd rose and clapped. There was no shouting, cheering, or whistling. The response overwhelmed Tsion. He put his notes on the lectern and waited for the applause to end.

"God has put something on my heart tonight," Tsion said. "Even before I open his Word, I feel led to invite seekers to come forward and receive Christ."

Immediately, from all over the stadium and even outside, lines of people, many weeping, began streaming forward, causing another burst of applause. Judd couldn't believe how many were coming. He wondered if those watching over the Global Community's outlets were praying as well.

Tsion said, "You do not have to be with us physically

to receive Christ tonight. All you need to do is tell God you are a sinner and separated from him. Tell him you know that nothing you can do will earn your way to him. Tell him you believe that he sent his Son, Jesus Christ, to die on the cross for your sins, that Jesus was raised from the dead, and that he is coming again to the earth. Receive him as your Savior right where you are."

After nearly an hour, the people who had come forward headed back to their seats. Tsion looked tired. His shoulders sagged. When he spoke, his voice was weak.

"My text tonight is Revelation 8:13." Tens of thousands of Bibles opened around the stadium. "This passage warns that once the earth has been darkened by one-third, three terrible woes will follow. These are so horrible that they will be announced from heaven in advance."

Lionel grabbed Judd's arm. "Look!"

Emerging from the shadows of the stage behind Tsion were Eli and Moishe. They walked to the front as the crowd pointed and leaned forward to hear them.

Moishe said, "My beloved brethren, the God of all grace, who hath called us unto his eternal glory by Christ Jesus, after that ye have suffered a while, make you perfect, stablish, strengthen, settle you."

Then Moishe loudly quoted Tsion's passage for everyone to hear. "'And I beheld, and heard an angel flying through the midst of heaven, saying with a loud voice, "Woe, woe, woe, to the inhabiters of the earth by reason of the other voices of the trumpet of the three angels, which are yet to sound!"'"

GC guards engaged their rifles, but no one fired. Judd wanted to run to the guard he knew and hold him back. Judd closed his eyes, ready for the gunfire, but when he opened them he saw Eli and Moishe were gone. Guards scrambled everywhere.

Tsion shook. Whether from fear or excitement, Judd couldn't say. To Judd's surprise, Tsion said, "If we never meet again this side of heaven or in the millennial kingdom our Savior sets up on earth, I shall greet you on the Internet and teach from Revelation 9! Godspeed as you share the gospel of Christ with the whole world!"

The Meeting of the Witnesses was over. Tsion disappeared into the shadows. Judd leaped to his feet, while the aisle was clear, and ran toward the front.

"They're ending early," Vicki said as the kids watched the wrap-up of the final session.

Conrad was deep in thought. "If Tsion's right, we're going to spend the rest of our lives as criminals. We won't be able to trust anyone."

"With the GC in control of everything," Shelly said, "we'll have to scramble just to stay alive."

Vicki heard a noise. Scratching. She opened the front door but didn't see anything. The noise was coming from the back of the house. She rushed into the kitchen. The noise got louder. She checked the back door.

Nothing.

Then Vicki realized the noise was coming from Melinda's room.

Before Judd could get past, the crowd filed into the aisles. He pushed his way around the last person and rushed toward the front.

"Let's figure out a place to meet," Judd said as he made it to the guard. The man turned. It was a different guard. "Sorry," Judd said.

Judd moved along the front of the stage. People craned their necks to get a glimpse of Tsion. Others knelt and wept.

Judd finally located the guard, but he could tell something was different. The guard held his gun high, his helmet pulled low. When he saw Judd he put a finger to his lips. He touched his earpiece and said something into the microphone on his shoulder.

"You have to leave," the guard said.

"I'm not going until I talk with you," Judd said.

"You don't understand," the guard said. "People are going to be killed here tonight. Leave!"

"What people?" Judd said. "Who?"

The guard lowered his voice. "My job is to keep everyone away from the backstage area. You're not safe here. Meet me at the east entrance in an hour."

"Tell me—"

The guard pushed his helmet up so Judd could see his forehead. Judd gasped as he saw the mark of the true believer.

"Go now," the guard said.

Judd rushed back to Lionel and told him about the guard. "I have to hear his story!" Lionel said. They looked for Mr. Stein but couldn't find him. Slowly they filed out behind the thousands who would take the message of the gospel to the ends of the earth.

As they reached the top of the stairs, Judd looked down on the infield. The guard was talking to someone. Suddenly, the man bolted onto the stage. The guard yelled, "Wait! Stop! Assistance!"

"That's Buck Williams!" Lionel shouted.

The guard aimed his rifle and fired.

"He's going to kill him!" Lionel shouted.

At the sound of the gunfire, frightened people pushed toward the exit. Some fell in the panic. Others tried to help them but were pushed along with the crowd.

"I've got to get down there," Judd yelled.

Vicki opened Melinda's door. Phoenix whimpered on the floor, his legs taped together. Around his snout was another wide band of tape.

"How long have you been here, boy?" Vicki said as she struggled to free the dog.

Vicki looked out the window. She had been so engrossed in the teaching of Dr. Ben-Judah that she had forgotten about Melinda.

Vicki shook her head. "Where's she going?"

Judd led Lionel toward the infield, walking on the backs of seats. Several times Judd nearly lost his balance, but they finally made it to the infield and sprinted toward the guard. The man's gun was still smoking. Judd shouted. The guard turned, saw Judd, and waved his hands. "Get down!" the guard yelled.

Judd and Lionel hit the ground just as another round of gunfire erupted. People screamed as the *pop pop pop* of shots rang out near the stage.

On his knees, Judd looked for the guard. The man lay in a pool of blood. Three bullet holes had pierced his chest. Judd lifted the man's head.

The guard gasped for air. "I prayed tonight. I asked God to forgive me. Thank you for helping me see the truth."

"Why did you shoot at that man?" Judd said. "He's one of us!"

"I know," the guard choked. "We had orders to shoot the rabbi. I shot over Mr. Williams's head to distract the other guards. They must have figured it out and turned their guns on me."

The guard closed his eyes. "What happens to me now? Where will I—"

"You'll see God," Judd said. "When you wake up, you'll be in heaven."

The guard smiled. He grabbed Judd's arm. "Get out while you can."

Judd felt for a pulse. The guard was dead. Above them came the pounding of footsteps. The other guards were on the stage searching for Tsion Ben-Judah.

13

JUDD gently lowered the guard's head to the ground, knowing the man had died trying to protect Buck Williams and the others in the Tribulation Force. Footsteps continued to pound on the stage above them.

Lionel grabbed the guard's walkie-talkie. "Come on. We have to get out of here!"

Judd and Lionel rolled under the stage and held their breath. The radio squawked in Lionel's hand. He turned it down.

Two guards jumped from the stage and felt for a pulse on the downed guard. One barked into his radio, "He's dead, sir."

A voice shot back, "Find the rabbi and those others. I want them dead before they get out of the stadium!"

Judd whispered to Lionel, "We've got to stop them!"

But before Judd could move, another voice blared on

the guard's radio. "We've spotted them in a Mercedes a few blocks from the stadium, sir."

"Probably headed to the Rosenzweig estate," another voice said. "After them!"

Judd sighed. "Nothing we can do now."

The stadium was nearly empty. A few stragglers knelt near the stage, praying. Medical personnel attended to the injured.

Judd and Lionel watched from the shadows as GC peacekeepers dragged the dead guard away. A cameraman flipped on a light, and a reporter stepped in front of it. "We are live at Teddy Kollek Stadium," the reporter said. "Just moments ago, this Global Community peacekeeper was murdered at the conference called the Meeting of the Witnesses. Those in the audience listened to a message of love and peace, but it seems someone did not follow their leader's teaching."

"No way one of the witnesses shot that guard," Lionel said.

Judd gritted his teeth. "Carpathia will make Tsion look—"

"What?" Lionel said.

Judd spied a heavyset boy near the front row. "I know that kid," he said.

When the Global Community guards were gone, Judd and Lionel crept from under the stage and approached the boy.

The boy's mouth dropped open. "Judd," the boy said, "what are you doing here?"

"How do I know you?" Judd said.

"I'm Samuel. Nina and Dan Ben-Judah were my neighbors." Samuel had given Judd the video of the murders of Tsion's family.

"I wondered what happened to you," Judd said. "They took the video you gave me and—"

"We should not stay here," Samuel interrupted. "Come with me."

"We have to find our friend," Lionel said.

"You can find him later," Samuel said. "The followers of the rabbi are in danger. Come to my house."

Judd told Samuel their things were at the university. Samuel said, "We will go there on the way. Quickly! My father must not see you."

"Why not?" Judd said.

"He is working with the Global Community!"

Vicki ran to the others to tell them about Melinda. Phoenix ran beside her, clearly glad to be free from the tape Melinda had wrapped around his legs. When Vicki entered, Darrion held up a hand.

"Just a minute," Vicki said, "I need to talk to you all."

"But something terrible's happened!" Darrion said.

Vicki yelled. "Please! Melinda's gone! She taped Phoenix up and left."

Conrad said, "How long ago?"

"I can't tell," Vicki said. "Let's search the house and the woods."

"I'll check the shed for the motorcycle," Conrad said.

"Sorry, Darrion," Vicki said, "but this is important."

127

Darrion hung her head. "I thought you'd be concerned about Judd and Lionel and Mr. Stein."

"What do you mean?"

"Shots were fired at the stadium."

Vicki put a hand over her mouth. "The GC is shooting at the witnesses?"

Darrion shook. "I'm scared, Vick."

"Judd and Lionel can take care of themselves," Vicki said, hugging Darrion.

The kids found no trace of Melinda in the house. Conrad said, "At least she didn't take the last motorcycle. She has to be on foot."

Vicki looked at her watch. "Plenty of daylight left, but we have to spread out."

Conrad and Darrion roared off on the motorcycle toward the main road. The others split up on foot. Vicki prayed as she ran into the woods.

GC emergency vehicles stopped traffic as Judd walked with Lionel and Samuel to the university. Lionel turned up the walkie-talkie and heard peacekeepers relaying information.

"They must be checking every car," Judd said.

"The GC are very upset about the rabbi and what he has done," Samuel said.

Judd turned. "Why are you helping us? You're not a follower of Dr. Ben-Judah."

"How do you know?" Samuel said.

Judd glanced at Lionel. "We can tell."

"Nina and Dan were my friends," Samuel said. "I feel terrible about what happened to them. I would not want to see the same thing happen to you."

Hundreds of witnesses gathered outside the gymnasium. A commotion at the front caught Judd's attention. GC guards led a dozen people from the building.

"What's going on?" Judd asked a man nearby.

"They are arresting the local committee," the man said.

Yitzhak Weizmann, the man who had given them shelter before the meetings began, was being led away in handcuffs. Behind him stood other committee members, including the meeting emcee.

The man next to Judd said, "They suspect the group is hiding the rabbi."

Judd gasped. The last man out the door was Mr. Stein. Judd shouted and waved and pushed his way to the front, but a uniformed officer appeared at the door with a bullhorn. "Attention, everyone who was using this gymnasium for shelter!" The officer passed the bullhorn to another man, who repeated his statement in several different languages.

"This is a crime scene," the man continued. "We have your belongings, and we will keep them until this situation is resolved."

"Mr. Stein's money!" Lionel whispered. "That's the only way we're getting home."

"Form a single line to register for your belongings," the officer said.

People lined up, but Samuel pulled Judd and Lionel away. "Do not give them your names. Come with me."

"We have to help Mr. Stein," Judd said.

"I can help you get him out," Samuel said, "but you must come with me."

Judd and Lionel followed Samuel back into the traffic near the stadium. They got in a cab, but the driver yelled at Samuel in Hebrew, and the three got back out.

"What did he say?" Judd said.

"He cursed at us," Samuel said. "Because of the traffic, he cannot move."

They walked through the congested streets. "You have heard about the meeting at the Wailing Wall tomorrow?" Samuel said.

"We'll be there," Judd said.

"Don't," Samuel said. "The GC are planning to execute Dr. Ben-Judah."

"Carpathia promised he wasn't going to hurt anybody," Lionel said.

"They're going to make it look like a terrorist attack," Samuel said.

"You know this because of your father?" Judd said.

Samuel nodded.

"Why did he let you go to that meeting?" Lionel said. "He didn't know," Samuel said. "I came on my own."

They passed a crowded bar, and a photo of the guard Judd had met flashed on a big-screen television inside. Beneath his photo were the years of his birth and death.

"Wish I could hear this," Judd said.

"We're not far from my house," Samuel said. "We can watch there."

Lionel pulled Judd aside. "His father's working with the GC!"

"He trusted me with the videotape. He's okay. He wants to help."

"But he doesn't have the mark."

"Maybe we can change that," Judd said.

———

Conrad and Darrion returned and met Vicki and the others near the shed to discover that still no one had seen Melinda.

"I say we head toward town," Darrion said.

Vicki's weird friend Charlie walked up. "What are you guys going to do with her after you catch her?"

Vicki looked at the others and shrugged. "Drag her back here?"

Conrad scratched his chin. "I don't care. I just want to find her."

"Maybe she doesn't want to rat us out," Vicki said. "Maybe she just wants to get away."

Shelly agreed. "Tsion's message could have been too much for her. She might just need time."

"And she might run into the GC," Conrad said, "which would be the end for her. Let me at least stay on the road awhile."

———

Judd and Lionel crept to the back door of Samuel's house and followed him in. Emergency vehicles screamed by, sirens blaring. Samuel answered the ringing phone. "My father," he mouthed.

"Did he tell you what's happening?" Judd said as Samuel hung up.

"He told me to stay inside. The crazy zealots are killing people."

Samuel turned on the television, and the photo of the guard flashed on the screen again. Another photo appeared beside the guard.

"It's Buck!" Lionel shouted.

The news anchor looked grim. "Global Community forces believe this videotape reveals this man as the murderer at Teddy Kollek Stadium. The suspect has been identified as American Cameron Williams, former employee of the GC publishing division. Williams is reportedly staying with Rabbi Tsion Ben-Judah at the home of Israeli Nobel Prize–winner Dr. Chaim Rosenzweig."

Lionel's radio squawked. "Proceeding to the Rosenzweig estate," a man said.

"That is only a few blocks from here," Samuel said.

Leon Fortunato, Nicolae Carpathia's right-hand man, appeared on the screen at a news conference. "We will do what we must to bring these criminals to justice. We have witnesses to the act, a videotape recording, and several of the local committee members in custody. Rest assured, we will bring to justice the man or woman who did this."

"Buck was running away when the guard was shot," Lionel said. "The videotape has to show that."

"The truth never stops these people," Judd said.

Samuel brought snacks, and Judd and Lionel ate as they watched the news and monitored the guard's radio.

"Has your dad always worked for the GC?" Lionel said.

Samuel shook his head. "Only since the murder of Dr. Ben-Judah's family. My father had helped them in the past, but that changed when the rabbi abandoned his faith. My father went totally for the Global Community and Nicolae Carpathia. He works—"

A roar went over the house. Judd ran to the window and saw a brilliant flash.

"A GC chopper," Samuel said.

"Closing in on Buck and Tsion, I bet," Judd said. "We have to help."

"You can't go there," Samuel said.

"These are our friends," Judd said. "We might be able to do something."

Samuel told them how to find the Rosenzweig estate, then turned on a light at the rear of the house. "If this light is off when you return, tap on my window and I'll let you in."

The night air was cool and the streets almost deserted. Judd and Lionel rounded a corner and saw two squad cars parked in front of a huge gate. They could hear the chopper nearby.

Lionel listened to the banter of the GC peacekeepers on the walkie-talkie. Chaim Rosenzweig wasn't letting them inside.

The chopper hovered over the estate, then put down on top of the house.

133

"They're going in through the roof," Lionel said.

Judd peered through the darkness at the GC insignia on the side of the chopper. Three figures leaped into the helicopter just before it lifted off and headed north, a few feet above the rooftops.

Another chopper approached from the south and hovered directly over them. The frantic voice of the pilot came over the radio, trying to communicate with the other chopper.

"Tsion and Buck have to be in the first chopper," Judd said.

"Who else was with them?" Lionel said. "Chloe?"

Judd shrugged. "Let's head back to Samuel's house before they spot us."

Just after 1 A.M. Judd and Lionel found the light off. Judd tapped lightly on Samuel's window. A light came on over the door. Judd and Lionel climbed the steps and waited.

Something moved behind them.

Samuel opened the door and smiled. "I knew it! I told you they'd come back!"

Judd turned. A man stood behind them, holding a gun. "Good work, Son."

14

"YOU LIED!" Judd said as the man shoved him and Lionel inside. Samuel led them to two chairs in the living room.

"You were trying to help Ben-Judah escape," Samuel said. "Doesn't matter what I did to catch you."

"He won't escape," Samuel's father said.

"You can't hold us here," Judd said. "We didn't do anything."

"Shut up," Samuel's father said. He turned to his son. "How'd you find them?"

"You know I felt guilty about shooting that video. Then, when it was stolen—"

"Stolen?" Judd said.

"Be quiet!" Samuel's father said.

"Tonight I went to the meeting to see if I could expose some of the zealots." Samuel glared at Judd. "They preach hatred. They think their way is the only way. Then I saw Judd, the very one who had taken the video. I knew if I could get him to come back here, you would know what to do."

"I told you to stay away from the stadium," Samuel's father said. "You could have been killed." The man sighed. "But finding these Americans might help us."

"They knew some of the men arrested at the university tonight," Samuel said. "And they are friends with Ben-Judah and the others staying with Rosenzweig."

Judd said, "So the potentate was lying when he promised protection for the witnesses?"

"Carpathia does not lie," Samuel's father said. "You saw what the zealots did to him and the supreme pontiff. They were completely—"

"I was there," Judd said. "Why are you working with the GC? Were you afraid they'd find out you helped Ben-Judah's family?"

"How did you know—"

"Your son told me before he gave me the video of the murders," Judd said.

"I did not!" Samuel shouted. "I tried to help you, and you repay me by stealing?"

"The question is how much you know," Samuel's father said, "and whether you can help us capture the fugitives."

"Never," Lionel said, "even if we knew where they were."

The phone rang. Samuel's father handed his gun to Samuel and hurried into the next room to answer it. "This is Goldberg," Judd heard him say. "I had to leave . . . no, I did not realize that, sir . . . how many?"

Samuel turned on the television to more reports of the killing at the stadium. Finally, Mr. Goldberg returned.

"Your friends are gone," he said. "They stole a Global Community helicopter and flew to Jerusalem Airport. All of them escaped onto a plane except one. He's dead."

The phone rang again.

"Who's dead?" Lionel said.

Judd shook his head. "He might be lying."

Samuel turned up the television. Lionel whispered, "My ID says I'm Greg Butler, but if they find out I'm a Morale Monitor . . ."

"Did they fingerprint you?" Judd said.

"Yeah," Lionel said. "And they printed you when you and Taylor Graham were arrested, right?"

Judd sighed. "Our IDs won't do us any good if they check the prints. We have to get out of here."

From the next room Judd heard Mr. Goldberg say, "I may have more answers after I question these two."

Samuel glanced at Judd and moved toward the door. "What's the matter, Father?"

Judd rushed Samuel and knocked him to the ground, the gun clattering to the floor. Before Judd or Lionel could reach it, Mr. Goldberg ran in and grabbed it. "Stop!"

Judd flung open a door just as the gun went off. Wood splintered above his head as he and Lionel dove for cover.

Judd swung the door shut, leaving him and Lionel in darkness. The room smelled musty. Mr. Goldberg jiggled the doorknob and put his weight against the door.

"Good choice," Mr. Goldberg said, laughing. He

locked the door from the outside. "That should keep you until the GC arrive."

Judd felt along the wall for a light switch. He flipped it on and saw that they were at the top of a landing. Stairs led to the basement.

"Find a way to block the door," Judd said.

"But they locked it from the other—"

"Just block the door. Hurry!"

Judd raced down the stairs and got his bearings. In one corner he found a large dresser. He pulled out the drawers and moved it away from the wall. Behind the dresser he found a doorway that had been nailed shut. He quickly located a toolbox and found a hammer.

Lionel came down the stairs, out of breath. "I did the best I could," he gasped. "How did you know about this door?"

"Dan and Nina led me through here once," Judd said.

Judd pried off the wood, trying to be quiet. He had two corners free when he heard a siren outside. "That's the GC," he said, and he and Lionel attacked the door. As they pried the last plank away, footsteps sounded overhead. Someone tried to open the door at the top of the stairs, then smashed it, splintering the wood. Judd felt the chill of the night air as he and Lionel pried open the secret door.

He threw the hammer and burst the lightbulb that lit the room. Someone yelled, "They've got a gun!"

Judd and Lionel rushed out into the night and nearly ran Samuel over. "I knew you'd find the passage," he whispered.

Judd braced for a fight. "Stay out of our way!"

Samuel slipped them a piece of paper. "Go to this address. They will take you in, no questions asked."

"What?" Lionel said. "No way we'll trust you."

"Go," Samuel said. "I will explain later."

They ran to a main street, where many of the witnesses still milled about. A helicopter passed, its light scanning the crowd. Judd and Lionel blended with the others. Judd read the address Samuel gave them.

"You're not—," Lionel said.

"What choice do we have?" Judd said.

Lionel sighed. "A hotel?"

"How much money do you have?" Judd said.

Lionel emptied his pockets. Not enough.

"The GC will check the hotels anyway," Judd said. He held up the paper to the light. "This is our only good option."

Judd asked for directions several times before they found the right street. As they moved farther from the Old City, fewer people passed them. Finally they were alone outside a tall apartment building. Judd rang the buzzer, but there was no answer. He rang again.

"We have company," Lionel said.

Judd glanced around. A Global Community squad car sat across the street.

"Let's run for it," Judd said. "You go to the right—"

But the door buzzed and they slipped inside to find a dark elevator. Someone stood in the shadows. A gun clicked.

"Face forward," a man said.

He was short with dark hair, a large nose, and a

mustache. He pointed the semiautomatic pistol at Judd. "I said face forward."

Judd turned. The man told him to punch the top button. The rickety elevator slowly climbed to the twelfth floor.

"Who sent you?" the man said.

"Samuel," Judd said. "Don't know his last name. He was friends—"

"Were you followed?" the man interrupted.

"Not that we know of," Lionel said. "But this GC squad car—"

"We saw," the man said. "A routine check. But your timing was not exactly perfect."

"Who's *we*?" Judd said.

The elevator opened. "To your right," the man said.

Judd and Lionel stepped onto faded brown carpet. The hallway was dark. Several sockets had no lights. At the end of the hall was a stairwell. "Keep going," the man said.

Judd and Lionel climbed the stairs to what looked like a janitor's room. The door opened, and they were greeted by a woman wearing a veil.

The large room they were in led to several smaller rooms and a hallway that looked as if it ran the entire length of the building.

The man locked the door behind him. "Sit," he said.

Lionel and Judd sat on a shabby couch. Stuffing showed at the edges of the cushions. The woman left the room and quietly closed the door. She came back a moment later and whispered something to the man.

"There are people sleeping," the man said.

Judd sat forward. "Who are you, and where are we?"

The man turned on a lamp and leaned close. He pulled back his thick, black hair and showed them the sign of the believer on his forehead.

"Why didn't you tell us?" Judd said.

"I wanted to make sure you were not followed," the man said. "My wife just told me the squad car is gone. I am Jamal. I run the apartment complex."

"You're the manager?" Lionel said.

"I would love to claim that title, but I'm afraid janitor would be closer to the truth. I will explain more, but you must first tell me what kind of trouble you are in."

Judd told the man about the Meeting of the Witnesses and going to Samuel's house. "How does Samuel know you?" Judd said. "He's not a believer."

"I do not know," the man said. "Perhaps the Global Community has set a trap. It troubles me to think a GC employee's son has our information."

"Are there other believers here?" Judd said.

"We kept many of the witnesses here throughout the meetings," Jamal said. "As many as a hundred per night. Most of them are gone, but a few are leaving tomorrow."

"We had a friend taken by the GC," Lionel said. "Mr. Stein is our only way back to the States."

"They will likely question and release him, unless they uncover something," Jamal said. "Contacts will keep us informed."

Judd had more questions, but Jamal held up a hand.

"It is almost dawn. You are safe. That is all you need to know right now."

Jamal showed them a room with four beds. "Sleep, and may God watch over you and your friends."

Mark's mind reeled as he drove the motorcycle through the old neighborhood. He wanted to tell his aunt about John's death and see if he could help her, but after tracking her through various GC emergency shelters, Mark discovered she had been transferred to the same furniture store, which had been converted to a makeshift hospital, where Ryan had died. The man at the front wouldn't let him through, but Mark found a back entrance and searched a filing cabinet filled with patients' names. He found his aunt's name on a list of patients. She had died four days earlier.

Mark found the morgue and asked to see his aunt's body. "I'm sorry, son," the attendant said, "but a person unclaimed for that long is cremated."

Mark drove back to his aunt's house. There, he watched the Meeting of the Witnesses on Judd's laptop. It was hard to concentrate. He felt guilty for not being with his aunt when she needed him.

Not knowing what to do next, Mark decided to visit Z at the gas station. Z fed Mark and gave him a place to sleep. They talked.

"You haven't always seen eye to eye with Judd and Vicki, have you?" Z said.

"They don't see eye to eye with each other."

"But you were hooked up with the militia," Z said.

"I should have listened to them," Mark said, "but this is different. I don't feel like I've got a place there."

Z nodded. "I've been reading in the Bible about Paul and Barnabas. They disagreed and had to separate, and there were bad feelings, I guess. But later they worked it out."

Mark tried to sleep but couldn't. He joined Z early the next morning to watch the coverage of the meeting in Israel. By Friday night he had made his decision.

"I'm going back to see if I can hash it out with them," Mark said.

Early Saturday morning Mark headed back to the schoolhouse. At 9:00 A.M. he wound through the small town near the access road. He noticed a GC security vehicle and several officers.

Mark rode as close as he could without drawing attention. Several townspeople stood watching.

"What's going on?" Mark said to an older man.

"They caught some girl," the man said. "Been talking on the radio for quite a while. They got her in the back of the squad car."

Mark rode past the officers and stole a glance at the car. The door was slightly open. Mark gasped. Melinda sat in the backseat, crying. Her hands were cuffed.

15

MARK parked his cycle and walked past a few stores. He wondered if Melinda had told the peacekeepers about the Young Trib Force and their hideout. He studied shop-windows as he listened to the squawking radios.

"Still waiting for the fingerprint ID," one officer said.

"She sure looks like the photo," another said. "Wonder how she wound up here?"

Mark walked into a small grocery store and watched the GC officers through the window. He bought a pack of gum and asked the girl at the cash register what happened.

"She ran in here out of breath," the girl said. "Real dirty. Looked like she'd spent the night in the woods. I figured it was one of those women who escaped from the GC prison I've been hearing about on the news."

"There was a breakout?" Mark said.

"Yeah. One of those reeducation camps or whatever

you call them. When that girl saw the squad car go by, she freaked. Hid behind one of the aisles back there. I went outside and flagged 'em down."

"You're pretty much a hero," Mark said.

The girl blushed. "I didn't do nothin'. Just figured she had to be guilty of something, the way she acted."

Mark thanked the girl and left. A small bell rang as he opened the door, and the Peacekeepers glanced at him. Mark walked the other way.

The radio squawked. "Here's the report," a man said. "We have a negative on the downstate facility. Your girl is MM-1215, Melinda Bentley." The man read off more information about Melinda. "You're instructed to interrogate, then carry out GC order X-13."

The peacekeepers looked at each other. "Can you repeat that?"

"Interrogate and carry out an X-13. Over."

The peacekeeper sighed. "Ten four, we copy. Out."

Mark didn't know what an X-13 was, but it didn't sound good for Melinda. He turned the corner and walked his motorcycle closer. He wanted to hear the GC question Melinda.

"We know who you are," a peacekeeper said. "Who's been hiding you?"

"I was staying with some friends," Melinda said.

"Who?"

Her handcuffs clinked as Melinda pushed the hair from her eyes.

"I don't know their names."

"Where?"

Melinda shrugged. "Talking to you isn't going to do me any good. I know what's going to happen."

Mark darted into the grocery store and handed the girl behind the counter a large bill.

"What's this for?" she said.

"You'll see," Mark said. He walked into the street and faced the squad car. The peacekeepers leaned against the open door. Mark got Melinda's attention and motioned for her to get out of the car. She seemed to understand. Mark returned to the cycle.

"I'm tired of sitting here," Melinda said.

"Answer our questions and we'll take you for a long walk," a peacekeeper said, chuckling.

"Let me at least stretch my legs," Melinda said. "Then I'll tell you anything you want to know."

As soon as she was out of the car, Mark started the cycle. He grabbed a loose brick and pulled into the street. As the peacekeepers turned, he threw the brick through the front window of the store.

"Hey!" one of the peacekeepers shouted. Both moved toward Mark.

"It slipped," Mark yelled.

"We saw you! Now get off your bike!" the second peacekeeper said, unlocking his gun holster.

Melinda inched around to the other side of the squad car. Mark gunned the engine and raced past the peacekeepers, who shouted at him and drew their weapons. He barreled around the car, and Melinda jumped on behind him.

Mark shot down an alley as gunfire erupted.

"I can't hold on!" Melinda shouted.

"Put your hands over my head," Mark shouted.

With the cuffs still on, Melinda slipped her hands over Mark's head and worked them down to his waist.

"Did you tell them about us?" Mark shouted.

"No!"

The GC squad car's siren blared behind them.

"Hang on," Mark said. "This is going to be some chase!"

Judd awoke late in the afternoon in Israel. Jamal stood in the doorway. "You have a visitor."

Judd woke Lionel. From a tiny monitor mounted near the door Judd saw someone pushing the buzzer on the first floor.

"Do you know him?" Jamal said.

"That's Samuel," Judd said. "His dad works for the GC."

Jamal shook his head. "I cannot allow him here. It is too great a risk."

"If he's the one who sent us, why can't we trust him?" Judd said.

Jamal studied the screen as Lionel said, "Maybe it was their plan to let us escape Samuel's house. To find this place. They may want you more than they want us."

Judd had to admit it was a possibility. "Still, something tells me Samuel's okay."

"Can we get outside some other way and meet him on the street?" Lionel said.

"There is a way," Jamal said, "but I can't let you endanger the lives of those we are hiding."

"We'll get outside and follow him to make sure it's safe," Judd said.

Jamal handed Judd a key, then took them through a corridor to the freight elevator. "This comes out at the back of the building. Go to the bottom floor, the garage. You can walk around to the front from there, but I warn you, watch out for anyone who looks like they're with the Global Community. If they catch you, you must never tell them about this place."

The garage was dingy and dark. Judd and Lionel hid behind bushes as they approached the front. No one was at the door.

"Guess he gave up," Lionel said.

Judd glanced both ways. "Want to split up?"

"Let's stick together," Lionel said.

They ran north three blocks. Lionel grabbed Judd's arm. Samuel stood in a nearby phone booth. Judd and Lionel approached slowly and listened.

"Please pick up the phone," Samuel said. "I sent two people to you yesterday. I need to talk with them. Their names are Judd and Lionel. They think—"

Samuel turned and saw them. He hung up the phone. "I am so glad to see you. We must talk."

"Where's your dad?" Judd said.

"At work," Samuel said. "He let me stay home from school because of last night."

"Do you ever go to school?" Judd said skeptically.

"I know a café nearby," Samuel said.

Samuel led them to the café. The waiter seated them in a secluded spot inside. Judd and Lionel kept an eye on the street. "We're almost out of cash," Judd said as he glanced at the menu.

"Don't worry. I will pay for this," Samuel said.

"One more favor," Judd said. "Unbutton your shirt."

"What for?" Samuel said.

"Just do it," Judd said.

When Judd was sure Samuel was not wearing a bug, he relaxed a little. The waiter came with their food, and Lionel and Judd ate hungrily. Samuel described what had happened after the two had escaped.

"They questioned me for an hour," Samuel said. "They wanted to know everything I knew about you. I told them the truth about meeting you the first time, but I lied about the video. I'm sorry."

"Did they connect us with Mr. Stein?" Lionel said.

"That is why I risked coming here," Samuel said. "I had to tell them enough so they would believe me. They have interrogated Mr. Stein about you."

"They're still holding him?" Judd said.

"I overheard my father's phone call. Mr. Stein admitted he knew you both, but would say nothing further. The GC have beaten him severely."

"They beat him?"

"He is still in custody, but you must not try to help him escape. They are expecting you. I will get word to you when he is released."

"We can't tell you about the place we're staying," Lionel said.

Samuel nodded. "But I must know how to get you if something should happen."

Judd worked out a code with Samuel to use when calling Jamal's apartment. If Mr. Stein was freed or if he needed Judd and Lionel, Samuel would leave a message in code.

"We also need to know who was killed last night at the airport," Judd said.

"My dad will know," Samuel said. "I don't think the information has been released to the media."

As they finished their meal, Samuel grew quiet. Judd still didn't know whether to trust him, but so far, his story checked out. "What's the matter?" Judd said.

"There's another reason I came to see you," Samuel said. "It's about the meeting last night and some things the rabbi said."

Mark didn't want the GC squad car to follow him to the hideout, so he backtracked to the expressway. Most of the highway still had large gaps in it from the earthquake. Cars poked along.

The squad car was close when they first made it to the highway, but Mark rode on the edge of the pavement and dodged the slower cars.

"Where are you going?" Melinda shouted over the noise of the bike and the honking cars around them.

"Just hang on," Mark said.

Suddenly, Mark veered left and into the median. The bike slid sideways, but Mark regained control. The squad car followed, mud flying into the air behind it. Mark shot over the median and across the oncoming cars on the other side of the highway. Melinda screamed. A semi-trailer swerved to miss them and hit another car, sending it careening toward the squad car.

Mark slowed as they went over an embankment he had seen earlier in the day. He drove through the edge of a cornfield and onto a small, country road.

"Are they still following us?" Mark yelled.

Melinda glanced back. "Not yet. I think the truck's blocking them."

Mark pushed the bike to its limits, screaming around curves. Three miles later, he turned off the engine and coasted down a hill to a small stream. "This is where we get off," Mark said. "Hurry."

Melinda struggled to get her hands over Mark's head. "We'll get those cuffs off you when we get back to the schoolhouse," Mark said.

Mark pushed the motorcycle to a stream that ran under the road. They found a dry place under the bridge and waited.

Finally, Mark whispered, "Why'd you leave the group?"

Melinda explained that she had heard Tsion's message. Coupled with the clear lies of Nicolae Carpathia, it was too much for her. "I had to get away."

"You don't believe what Tsion says?" Mark said.

"He has to be right," Melinda said, "but after all I've staked my life on . . . it's hard."

Mark nodded. "You went straight to that little town?"

"I hid from Vicki and the GC during the night,"

Melinda said. "They came pretty close a couple of times, but I got under some brush.

"This morning I made it as far as the town when I spotted those peacekeepers. I tried to play it cool, but the girl in the store ratted me out."

"What's an X-13?" Mark said.

Melinda pursed her lips. "That's the order to eliminate a prisoner."

"They were going to kill you?" Mark said.

"If you hadn't come along, they would have," Melinda said.

Cars passed overhead. Dust and debris fell from the bottom of the bridge. Mark stuck his head out and quickly returned. "GC squad cars," he said.

Judd and Lionel talked with Samuel about Tsion's message. Samuel wanted to know what the people were doing who came to the front of the stadium. Judd told him.

Lionel jumped in with questions about what Samuel believed about God. Judd was impressed with the way Lionel showed Samuel the truth about Jesus.

"The Bible shows us that Jesus is more than just a good teacher," Lionel said. "He's God."

Samuel glanced at his watch and gasped. "My father! He will be home soon."

"You shouldn't put off this decision," Lionel said.

"I will relay information when I can," Samuel said. "I must go."

Lionel handed Samuel a piece of paper. The boy took it, put money on the table, and quickly walked away.

"What was that?" Judd said.

"A verse I found that might make him think," Lionel said.

Judd wondered if they would ever see Samuel again.

16

JUDD and Lionel told Jamal what had happened. Jamal winced when he heard they had met with Samuel in a public place. Jamal turned on a videotape from the GC network that showed Buck Williams talking to the guard who had been killed.

"The news has been running this to show that Mr. Williams is guilty," Jamal said.

"Buck's not even carrying a gun," Lionel said.

"Exactly," Jamal said. "After Buck leaves, the guard fires over his head. Then, the guard is hit."

"How could they say Buck killed him?" Judd said.

Jamal shook his head. "The Global Community will cover up the truth. I'm afraid of what might happen to Mr. Williams and the others. Especially since the pilot is dead."

"What?" Judd said. His heart raced. "Rayford Steele is dead?"

Mark and Melinda kept quiet as the squad cars passed again. Clouds rolled in and the light grew dim.

"How long did it take you to get to the town?" Mark whispered.

"I'm not sure," Melinda said. "I had to hide so many times. Maybe a couple of hours. Why?"

"We're going to have to ditch the motorcycle," Mark said. He glanced at her. "That's assuming you want to go back."

Melinda looked away. "You sure you want to risk being seen with me?"

Mark smiled. "I risked getting you out this morning, didn't I?"

"Why do you people keep helping me?" Melinda said.

Mark picked up a rock and tried to break the chain between the cuffs. "We can't leave the cycle here. It's too close to the schoolhouse."

"What do we do?" Melinda said.

"Wait here until nightfall."

The two listened to the stillness of the countryside. An occasional car passed, but the GC had apparently moved their search. Finally, Melinda broke the silence. "Why did *you* leave the schoolhouse?"

Mark told her about his fight with Vicki and his search for his aunt. "I don't see eye to eye with everybody in the group," he said, "but they're all the family I have now."

Melinda stared at Mark. "I'm sorry about your aunt."

Judd put his face in his hands. He couldn't believe Rayford Steele had been killed. Jamal rewound the tape.

A news reporter dramatically walked the runway at Jerusalem Airport. "One of the American terrorists was shot and killed here," he said. "It happened late last night, after the final session of the so-called Meeting of the Witnesses." The reporter walked near a Global Community helicopter. "The daring escape included hijacking Potentate Carpathia's own helicopter."

"That's what we saw last night!" Lionel said.

Chaim Rosenzweig's estate flashed on the screen. "Dr. Rosenzweig had hosted Ben-Judah, murder suspect Cameron Williams, and Williams's wife. According to Global Community Supreme Commander Leonardo Fortunato, the escape was well calculated."

A disgusted Leon Fortunato was shown at a press conference. "We were assured that the prisoners were under house arrest. Upon further investigation, we found a door to the roof clearly broken from the inside. This shows conclusively how the Americans escaped."

The reporter knelt on the runway, pointing at a red stain. "When the helicopter landed here, an American terrorist opened fire on GC forces nearby. A sniper killed terrorist Ken Ritz with a single shot to the head."

"Do you know this Ritz?" Jamal said.

Judd shook his head. "He must have been working with Buck and Tsion."

The reporter stood in front of the downed helicopter. "The other three fugitives—suspected murderer Cameron

Williams, his wife, and Tsion Ben-Judah—have escaped and are at large internationally. It is assumed that Williams is an accomplished pilot."

"What?" Lionel said. "Buck's smart, but he's never flown a plane before in his life."

"Somebody else had to help them get away," Judd said.

The reporter concluded by showing photos of Ben-Judah and Buck Williams. "These men are considered armed and extremely dangerous. If you have any information about their whereabouts, please contact your nearest Global Community post."

Vicki and the others tried to stay busy throughout the day, but each sound, every crack of a twig made them nervous. Finally, Vicki called a meeting.

"I've been reading a lot in Philippians," Vicki said. "Paul was a prisoner and was writing to encourage a church he helped start." Vicki opened the Bible. "Toward the end he said, 'I have learned how to get along happily whether I have much or little. I know how to live on almost nothing or with everything. I have learned the secret of living in every situation, whether it is with a full stomach or empty, with plenty or little. For I can do everything with the help of Christ who gives me the strength I need.'"

Vicki closed her Bible. "He was content even in prison. God had a purpose for him wherever he was. It's the same with us. Maybe God wants us to stay here. Maybe he wants us in some GC jail so we can talk to the people there. Whatever the situation, we need to be content."

"So you're saying we shouldn't be nervous about Melinda?" Darrion said. "Well, I am nervous. I don't want the GC to come in here and arrest us."

"Neither do I," Vicki said, "and we need to do everything we can to keep them from finding us. But at some point we have to trust God to protect us."

"I see your point," Conrad said. "I think the best thing we can do right now is pray that Melinda will come to her senses and return."

The kids gathered in a circle and joined hands. Each took a turn praying that God would bring Melinda back, or at least keep her from the Global Community.

As night approached, the kids ate dinner together. Vicki and Darrion answered some of the messages that had come in after the Meeting of the Witnesses. Kids around the world still begged to know God.

Conrad volunteered to take the first watch. While he put Phoenix on a chain in the front yard, Vicki gathered some blankets. Conrad climbed a narrow staircase that led to the old bell tower. As he settled in for the night, Vicki and the others tried to sleep.

Mark worked on Melinda's handcuffs throughout the day with several rocks he found by the stream. When one broke, he picked up another. Mark had rubbed blisters on his hands trying to break the cuffs. Once he missed and hit Melinda's wrist.

159

The chain between the two cuffs was nearly broken when something moved nearby. Mark looked at Melinda. He could barely see her face in the dim light. He put a finger to his lips and cautiously moved from his hiding place under the bridge.

As he stuck his head out, someone jumped into the water nearby. "I found you!" a girl shouted and nearly knocked Mark into the water. "I've heard that knocking sound all day."

The girl peered under the bridge and spotted Melinda. "Why's she got handcuffs on?"

Mark ignored her. "Who are you?"

"You first," the girl said.

Mark noticed the girl was wearing a jumpsuit that looked like it had come from a prison. But he couldn't keep from studying her face, which looked somehow familiar.

"Those are GC clothes," Melinda said.

The girl scowled. "I've been staying with my uncle on his farm for a few days. He gave me these."

Finally, Mark remembered. "Janie!"

"How'd you know my name?" Janie shouted.

"You were being held at the GC reeducation camp," Mark said. "What are you doing out here?"

"A few of us got out last night," Janie said. "I got separated this morning. Then I saw all those GC cars. Decided I'd stay put until tonight." Janie eyed the motor-cycle. "Is that yours?"

Mark nodded.

"Let me have it, and I won't tell anybody you're down here," Janie said.

"You won't get very far—," Melinda said, but Mark interrupted her.

"We were going to leave on foot anyway," Mark said. "You headed to Chicago?"

Janie nodded. "I got some friends back there who might help me."

Mark handed her the keys to the cycle. Janie turned. "You look familiar to me, too. How do I know you?"

"I went to Nicolae High," Mark said. "You were staying with a girl I knew."

"Vicki?" Janie said.

Mark nodded.

"She's the one I'm looking for," Janie said. "Best friend I ever had. I've changed a lot since I last saw her."

"How?" Mark said.

"I've gotten more religious," Janie said. "You know where I can find her?"

Mark strained to see Janie's forehead, but couldn't. He wasn't sure Janie could be trusted. She had lied about staying with her uncle, but he might have done the same thing talking to strangers. He was going to let her take the cycle and lead the GC away from their hideout, but since she was looking for Vicki, he felt guilty letting her go.

"I can take you where she is," Mark said, "but we'll have to ditch the cycle." Mark explained their run-in with the GC and that Melinda was wanted by the GC as well.

"I hate to lose good wheels," Janie said, "but if you can help me find Vicki, let's go."

Mark rolled the motorcycle to a hill near a lake and pushed it over the edge. The cycle splashed into the water and disappeared. The kids stole into the night, staying close enough to follow the road, then hiding when a car passed.

In the distance they saw the lights of the small town. Dogs barked. A squad car drove by on the interstate, its lights flashing. Mark motioned for the girls to follow as they entered the woods.

Judd and Lionel had slept so late in the day that they couldn't get to sleep that night. They sat in their room talking about Mr. Stein and wondering what had happened.

They had eaten dinner with several other witnesses and heard their fantastic stories of how God had convinced them that Jesus was the Messiah of the Jewish people. They talked about the Meeting of the Witnesses, how encouraging it had been, and what a fool Nicolae Carpathia had made of himself.

When Judd explained about Mr. Stein, several of the witnesses gathered to pray. Others came from the nearby rooms, and soon people were praying in different languages for Mr. Stein's safety.

Later, while Judd and Lionel went over the day's events, a beautiful girl with dark skin and brown eyes knocked on their door and entered. "Are you Judd?" she said.

Judd nodded.

"There is a phone call for you."

Judd went into the next room and found Jamal and

his wife. Jamal looked sternly at Judd. "I do not like calls in the middle of the night."

Judd nodded and picked up the phone. It was Samuel.

"I called as quickly as I could," Samuel said, out of breath.

"What's wrong?" Judd said.

"Your friend, Mr. Stein," Samuel said. "Something has happened. I think he may have been released."

"Where can we find him?" Judd said.

"I don't know," Samuel said. "My father rushed from the house, very upset. I came to this pay phone immediately."

Judd thanked Samuel and told Jamal what had happened.

"Tomorrow I will call my contacts about him," Jamal said. "Get some rest."

Judd nodded. As he closed the door he noticed the girl smiling at him.

17

CONRAD sat in the tower, watching for any sign of the Global Community. He used a flashlight to read a printout of Tsion Ben-Judah's latest teaching. The teaching was so interesting, he had to be careful not to get too absorbed.

Late that night he took a break and closed his eyes for a moment. He ran his hand along the floor and felt a weird bump. A piece of wood stuck up about an inch. He placed his hand on the other side of the plank and pushed. The board gave an inch or two, and Conrad was able to get his fingers underneath.

As he pulled, other boards lifted. Conrad put his flashlight near the hole. Some sort of box fit perfectly inside.

Conrad tried to lift the board, but it wouldn't budge. The box was decorated with fancy etchings. He shifted his weight to try again, but just then something moved in the woods.

Phoenix growled below. Conrad peered into the darkness and took out his pistol. He quickly ran downstairs and woke Vicki. Vicki let Phoenix loose, and the dog headed for the road, then quickly darted into the woods, barking.

Conrad listened closely. The barking stopped. Footsteps. Had something or someone killed Phoenix? Conrad cocked his pistol and waited.

Three figures moved out of the woods. Conrad lifted the gun and pointed it as he clicked on the flashlight.

"Don't shoot!" Mark said, squinting into the light.

"Mark!" Vicki screamed. "You're back!"

Conrad shone the flashlight on the other two. Melinda and another girl were right behind Mark.

The girl raced toward them. "Vicki!" she shouted.

Vicki stepped back, then hugged the girl and yelled, "Janie!" Vicki looked at Mark. "How did you—?"

"Let's go inside," Mark said, "and we'll tell you all about it."

———————————————

When Judd awoke the next morning, Lionel was talking with the girl he had seen the night before. Jamal was on the phone speaking in a different language.

"This is Jamal's daughter, Nada," Lionel said.

Judd nodded. Nada smiled and shook his hand.

"Any news on Mr. Stein?" Judd said.

"Haven't been able to understand a word," Lionel said.

Nada spoke with an Arabic accent. "My father still searches for your friend. If anyone can find him, he can."

"How did you become believers?" Judd said.

"My mother was first," Nada said. "When people disappeared around the world, she began reading the theories. Then, when the rabbi spoke on television, she was convinced that Jesus had returned for his true followers."

"Did you know much about Christianity before that?" Lionel said.

Nada shook her head. "We had read the Old Testament that spoke of Abraham. But to us, Christians were unbelievers. When my mother predicted a great earthquake would strike and it happened, my father finally read the rabbi's Web page and received the mark of the believer."

Jamal hung up the phone and quickly dialed another number.

"Who is he calling now?" Lionel said.

Nada listened. "It is a funeral home."

Vicki talked with Janie while Conrad and Mark worked to get Melinda's cuffs off. Melinda seemed happy to be back, but cautious. Vicki hoped to talk with her later. Mark's return was a miracle to Vicki. She was dying to talk with him but knew that would best be done in private.

Vicki looked closely at Janie's forehead. Mark had brought someone who wasn't a believer. She would have to ask him why, but first she wanted to hear Janie's story.

"The last I heard from you," Vicki said, "you'd been taken downstate."

Janie nodded. "I know I gave you and your adoptive dad a hard time after you took me in. I'm really sorry. Where is Bruce?"

Vicki sighed and told Janie that Bruce had died just as the bombs started falling during World War III. "He may have died from a virus he caught overseas, or it could have been the bombing."

"No matter how it happened," Janie said, "he's dead. I'm sorry."

"What happened after you left Chicago?"

Janie said the Global Community had treated her harshly at the first facility, then moved her to one with less security. There she came in contact with the nurse who had helped Vicki take Ryan's body from the makeshift hospital.

"They had her on some kind of charge," Janie said. "We talked a lot about you and religion."

"Religion?" Vicki said.

"Enigma Babylon is what they taught us, and it really turned me around."

Vicki frowned.

"I don't know how I'd have gotten through it without my faith guide," Janie said.

"Your what?"

"We had our own faith guide at the reeducation facility," Janie said. "He taught us that God's within us and we have the power to do anything we want to do."

"What did he say about the Bible?" Vicki said.

Janie shrugged. "We didn't talk about it that much. I guess there are some good stories in there, and some nice teachings, but you really have to follow your own heart if you want to be happy."

Vicki decided not to go further into the Enigma Babylon teaching, but Janie drew close. "That's one reason I wanted to find you. I know you and that Bruce guy, God rest him, follow the Bible. Our faith guide told us how the thing about Adam and Eve, the Flood with Noah, all that stuff's just a myth."

Vicki bit her lip. "What about the prophecies?"

Janie squinted. "What's that?"

"The predictions in the Bible that there would be a worldwide earthquake. The meteors. Wormwood. All that's in the Bible."

"Like I said, we didn't talk much about it," Janie said. "We just learned that God is an idea that lives inside all of us."

"What about heaven and hell?" Vicki said.

"We get what we deserve right here," Janie said. "Heaven's in your head. Besides, why would a God who's supposed to care about us cause all these bad things?"

"Because he wants to get your attention," Vicki said.

"Well, I let my god guide me, and he got me out of that prison."

Vicki got Janie a hot drink and asked Mark to step into the next room. Mark explained what had happened with his aunt and finding Melinda. "I couldn't tell whether Janie was a true believer, but when she mentioned she was trying to find you, I couldn't let her fall into the GC's hands."

Vicki nodded.

"I did a lot of thinking while I was away," Mark said. "I want to stay if you'll let me."

Vicki smiled. "I'm glad you're back."

Judd shuddered when he heard Jamal was talking to someone at a funeral home. When Jamal hung up Judd said, "Is he dead?"

"I must hurry," he said. "One of you goes with me; the other stays here."

"But if he's dead—," Lionel said.

"I cannot discuss it further," Jamal said. He pointed at Lionel. "You come with me."

Judd protested, but Nada put a hand on his arm and shook her head. "You will be here in case there is trouble."

As Jamal put on a hat he said, "Yitzhak is still being questioned. We must pray for him."

When Lionel and Jamal left, Judd and Nada prayed for Yitzhak and the other members of the local committee. Judd then logged on to the Internet to see the latest teaching by Dr. Ben-Judah. Nada noticed an e-mail that looked like it had come directly from the rabbi.

The e-mail was directed to those on the Tribulation Force. *We have another martyr from our midst,* the rabbi wrote. *Ken Ritz was a pilot who helped Buck Williams locate Chloe. He came to faith in Jesus Christ after talking with Buck.*

Ken flew the helicopter that rescued Buck, Chloe, and me from the Rosenzweig estate in Israel. He was not an American terrorist. He was a hero. While Rayford Steele waited for us at

Jerusalem Airport, Ken expertly flew us to the plane. He was shot to death by a Global Community peacekeeper. We will miss him greatly.

Tsion went on to describe some of the ideas Ken Ritz had about feeding believers who would need to go underground after the Global Community required a mark to buy and sell.

"That's exactly what Z was talking about," Judd said. "I hope they get together."

"Z?" Nada said.

Judd explained what he and the Young Trib Force had been through. Nada listened carefully and wiped away a tear when she heard about Bruce, Ryan, Chaya, and John.

Judd hung his head. "And now, Mr. Stein's gone."

———————————

Lionel rode in the backseat of Jamal's small car. They wound through the Jerusalem streets that seemed deserted compared to the time of the Meeting of the Witnesses. Lionel wanted to ask questions, but each time Jamal would hold up a hand. "Very dangerous. Must concentrate."

They parked in the back of the funeral home. A hearse was parked with its back door open. Jamal knocked twice at the building, waited, then knocked a third time. A face appeared at the window.

A tall, thin man pointed toward Lionel. The man had circles under his eyes, and his wispy hair was combed over his forehead. "Who is he?"

Jamal explained that Lionel was a friend of Mr. Stein.

The man showed them to a nearby room with a wooden coffin.

"You spared no expense," Jamal said.

"This will be lighter for you," the man said as he helped them carry the coffin to the waiting hearse.

"How much for the . . . burial?" Jamal said.

"Get the hearse back this afternoon and we'll call it even," the man said.

Lionel jumped in the back with the coffin. Jamal shook hands with the man and climbed in behind the wheel.

"What about your car?" Lionel said.

"I will pick it up when I return the hearse," Jamal said.

Lionel looked at the coffin. "I appreciate you doing this, but what are we going to do with the body?"

Jamal ignored Lionel's question and said, "Open the lid and see what kind of shape he is in."

"What?" Lionel could see Jamal's eyes in the rearview mirror.

"They said he was badly beaten at the station," Jamal said. "Open it and tell me how he looks."

Vicki wanted to speak with Melinda about why she had left the kids, but Janie kept talking about Enigma Babylon One World Faith. She didn't seem to think of anyone but herself. When Conrad and Mark cut through the handcuffs, Melinda went to her room to sleep.

"I broke out two days ago," Janie continued. "I slept

in a barn the first night and then I found your friends. Lucky break, huh?"

"Yeah," Vicki said. "I'm going to set up your room, but we have to get some things straight first."

"Shoot," Janie said.

"The stuff that got you into trouble when—"

"The drugs?" Janie said. "I'm clean; you don't have to worry about that."

"Good," Vicki said. "Everybody pitches in with the work here. We take turns with chores and cleaning."

"Yeah, I can handle that," Janie said.

"And we're starting a school in the next few days. We'd like you to try it out as part of our first group of students."

"School for what?" Janie said.

"It'll mostly be studying the Bible. We have material we think will help you. We'll all be studying it."

Janie scowled. "I already have my religion. Don't know what good the Bible will do me."

"Let's give it a week and see what happens," Vicki said.

Lionel took a deep breath. He had seen dead bodies before, but it was different looking at someone he knew and loved.

"Can't it wait till we get . . . to wherever we're going?" Lionel said.

"Open it," Jamal said.

Lionel slowly opened the coffin. Mr. Stein lay

peacefully, his eyes closed, his hands folded together. Lionel thought the funeral director had done a good job making him look as lifelike as possible. Mr. Stein had bruises around his eyes and a gash in his lower lip. The funeral director had even put a hint of a smile on the man's face.

"How does he look?" Jamal said.

Lionel shook his head. "I hate to think of what they did to him."

"If you could say one thing to your friend that you didn't get to say, what would it be?" Jamal said.

Lionel closed his eyes and took a deep breath. "I guess I never told him how much I appreciated him. He hadn't been a believer that long, but he motivated all of us to study harder. I'm gonna miss him."

When Lionel opened his eyes, Mr. Stein was sitting up in the coffin, his face inches away.

"And I would say the same to you," Mr. Stein chuckled.

18

JUDD couldn't believe it when Mr. Stein walked through the door of the apartment. Mr. Stein hugged him, then moved to Nada. "I have heard from Yitzhak what women of faith you and your mother are."

"Yitzhak talks too much," Nada said, blushing.

All Lionel could do was shake his head. "I thought he was dead."

The witnesses who had remained in Jamal's apartment eagerly greeted Mr. Stein. Some spoke in other languages, but Judd could tell they were thanking God their prayers had been answered. As they sat down at the evening meal, Mr. Stein explained what had happened. Nada and Jamal interpreted for the others.

"When the meeting ended that final night, I accompanied Yitzhak behind the stage to greet Dr. Ben-Judah," Mr. Stein said. "We all thought it might be our last time to express our gratitude to him. The rabbi seemed agitated,

like something was wrong. I overheard him talking to
Mr. Williams. He said, 'I have a terrible feeling I can only
assume is from the Lord.' He wanted to leave quickly, but
Mr. Williams could not find his wife and Dr. Rosenzweig.
We all looked for them.

"Buck ran away, then a few moments later rushed
at Tsion. They hit the ground just as gunfire erupted."

Judd broke in and told them what had happened with
the Global Community guard. The witnesses all praised
God when Judd told them the guard had become a
believer.

Mr. Stein picked it up from there. "GC guards ran to
the stage as the gunfire began," he continued. "Buck
grabbed Dr. Ben-Judah and ran for their car. The local
committee provided a few obstacles."

"What do you mean?" Lionel said.

"We stood in front of the exits and blocked the
guards," Mr. Stein said. "We thought it was the least
we could do for Tsion."

Witnesses laughed. "What happened then?" Lionel said.

"They shot their guns in the air to frighten us, but we
were not about to allow them to shoot at our leader."

"Did that stop them?" Judd said.

Mr. Stein smiled. "We gave the rabbi and the others
a few extra moments to get away. The guards finally got
through us, but not before Tsion and the others escaped."

"Is that when you were arrested?" Judd said.

Mr. Stein nodded. "I have never been treated so
roughly in my life. They held their guns to our heads
and led us to a GC van parked near the entrance to

the stadium. We sang praises to God and encouraged each other with verses we had memorized. I said to Yitzhak, if Paul and Silas can pray all night in prison, so can we."

The witnesses seated around him sent up another cheer.

"Daniel stood in the van as it careened around the streets. He shouted, 'We are pressed on every side by troubles, but we are not crushed and broken. We are perplexed, but we don't give up and quit.' Another said, 'We are hunted down, but God never abandons us. We get knocked down, but we get up again and keep going.' And Yitzhak finished the passage, saying, 'Through suffering, these bodies of ours constantly share in the death of Jesus so that the life of Jesus may also be seen in our bodies.'

"When we stood before the Global Community officers, each of us was asked why we were a follower of Dr. Ben-Judah. I learned later that each of us answered with the apostle Paul's words, 'I believe in God, and so I speak!'"

The witnesses around the room lifted their hands and praised God. Some whispered; others shouted.

Mr. Stein held up a hand. "I had no idea the enemy would inflict so much punishment on us. They knocked us down and made us suffer greatly. They beat me again and again, asking me where they could find the rabbi and the others. But I do not know, so how could I tell them?"

Mr. Stein smiled, then grew serious. "At one point

yesterday, I believe they planned to kill me. They knew I was the only American in the group and believed I had to know more than I had told them, which was nothing. They had treated me so badly they knew there was nothing they could do to make me give them information about my friends.

"So I waited and prayed. Yitzhak was in the next cell. We prayed together for courage and strength. We were both so exhausted, so spent from the mistreatment.

"And then, at our lowest point, we heard a noise. Faint, down the hallway. I went to the front, pressed my ear between the iron bars, and heard a sound I will take with me to the Glorious Appearing of our Great God."

Judd leaned closer. Mr. Stein stopped, overcome with emotion. "What was it?" Judd said.

Mr. Stein looked up, tears in his eyes. "Singing," he whispered. "I heard a dear brother—I cannot tell you who he was—but he began the little song I have never heard, but I will never forget."

Mr. Stein softly sang the words Judd knew were from the Doxology. They had sung it at his church at least once a month when he was a kid, and it had meant nothing to him then. Now the words sent a chill throughout his body.

"Praise God from whom all blessings flow. Praise him, all creatures here below. Praise him above, ye heavenly host. Praise Father, Son, and Holy Ghost. Amen."

Witnesses wept as they quietly sang along with Mr. Stein. "Forgive my voice," he said. "The only place my wife would let me sing was in the shower."

Everyone laughed.

"But I am sure that sound brought joy to our heavenly
Father. We were praising him in the midst of our trouble.

"We sang the song over and over, until I learned all
the words. Then, Yitzhak recited something from the
Psalms. I do not recall the entire verse, but it talked about
committing your way to the Lord. It was very powerful."

A barrel-chested man stood meekly in the corner. His
voice was strong and clear as he recited from Psalm 37.
"'Commit everything you do to the Lord. Trust him, and
he will help you. He will make your innocence as clear
as the dawn, and the justice of your cause will shine like
the noonday sun. Be still in the presence of the Lord,
and wait patiently for him to act. Don't worry about evil
people who prosper or fret about their wicked schemes.'"

"That's it!" Mr. Stein said. "And that is exactly what
we did. In the midst of suffering and possible death, our
hearts were knit together. The fear I had was gone. I knew
if I lived, I would give glory to God. If I died, I would be
with my wife and daughter, and with my Lord. Wherever
I was, I would give glory to God."

Mr. Stein wiped his eyes and sat. His shoulders shook
with emotion. Finally, he spoke. "I fell into a deep sleep.
It had nothing to do with the mistreatment by the guards.
I simply drifted off and slept like a little child.

"When I awoke, I discovered they had taken me into
a sort of doctor's office. There were beds around the room
and a huge, metal refrigerator with compartments for
bodies."

"The morgue!" Lionel said.

"Exactly," Mr. Stein said. "I had gone into such a deep sleep that somehow they believed I was dead."

"Didn't they check your pulse?" Judd said.

"I have no doubt that they did," Mr. Stein said, "but I do not know why they could not feel it. Either God blinded their eyes or he made it so faint that they could not detect it. How he did it, I do not know, but that the tall man did it I am sure.

"A tall man and his assistant wheeled me to a hearse. Once I almost sneezed, but I was able to control it. I kept my eyes closed until we reached the funeral home. That is when I opened my eyes and saw that the tall man had the mark of the believer on his forehead. When he came close, I reached out and grabbed his arm.

"I raised up on the bed and said, 'The Lord be with you, my brother!' and the man nearly fainted dead away."

Witnesses around the room laughed and shouted with joy.

"And here I am," Mr. Stein said, "a testimony to the grace of God, a picture of the goodness and provision of God. May he alone be praised."

With that, the people around the room clapped and commended Mr. Stein on his faith. Behind Judd, a small voice began the strain again. Judd turned and saw Nada, singing through tears, "Praise God from whom all blessings flow. . . ."

Vicki and Mark spoke briefly with Melinda the next morning. Melinda apologized for putting the group in danger and thanked Mark again. "If he hadn't helped me, I wouldn't be here right now."

"And if I hadn't gone to see about my aunt," Mark said, "I wouldn't have had any reason to be there."

"God works everything for good," Vicki said, "even disagreements." Vicki told Melinda about the school.

Melinda seemed hesitant but gave her word that she would attend classes at least the first week. "I'm not sure I buy into everything you guys believe," Melinda said, "but I'm pretty sure you're right about the Global Community."

Vicki and Conrad met with Mark to discuss the mysterious e-mail messages that had been coming in for Mark. The same message asking for him to respond immediately had appeared again, and it concerned Conrad.

"I think the safest thing we could do is delete the thing and not respond," Conrad said.

Mark studied the message. "It's definitely from a GC post. How would they get our e-mail address, and why would they want to write me?"

"Have you answered any of Tsion's e-mails?" Conrad said. "They could have gotten the address from that."

"Some, but not nearly as many as Judd," Mark said. "It just doesn't make sense."

"Unless it's from somebody who knew John," Vicki said.

Mark nodded. "That's a possibility, but how do we know they're friendly? Maybe whoever wrote met John and he ticked them off."

"What would it hurt to try?" Vicki said. "They can't trace our location from the e-mail, right?"

Mark nodded and read the message again. "Vicki's right. We ought to try." Mark wrote a quick reply that read: *I'm not sure I can trust you. Explain your intentions.*

Vicki asked, "What now?"

Mark sat back. "Wait to see what he says."

———————————

Judd stayed with Mr. Stein and listened to more witnesses share their stories. Some seemed as amazing as Mr. Stein's. One man described how he had walked a hundred miles, then traveled by camel, by boat, and finally by plane to get to the Meeting of the Witnesses. His food and water ran out the second day of his journey, but God had provided. At one point he thought he would pass out from thirst, but there came a downpour, and the man caught rainwater in his hat. When he had enough to drink, the rain stopped.

"Our God is awesome," the man said.

Nada touched Judd's shoulder. "You have a phone call from Samuel."

Samuel was still out of breath when Judd picked up the phone. "I'm very sorry about your friend, Mr. Stein," Samuel said. "He is dead."

Judd asked for more information, not letting Samuel know the truth about Mr. Stein. He didn't want Samuel to know more than he had to.

"My father is still very upset. He wants to catch Ben-Judah and the others who have made the GC look bad. They think you might be able to lead them there."

"We have no idea where the rabbi is hiding," Judd said.

"I believe you," Samuel said, "but you must be very careful. They have increased security at all the airports in the country. They suspect you will try to leave soon. And my father says they have a plan to catch you."

"Thanks for the info," Judd said. "You'd better be careful yourself."

"I do not think he suspects anything," Samuel said.

"Have you thought about what we talked about?" Judd said.

Samuel sounded agitated. "I think I see my father's car!"

"Go!" Judd shouted. "And call me back when you get the chance." Judd hung up.

Mr. Stein took him and Lionel aside. "I have been given a wonderful opportunity. I did not want to talk about it in front of the others."

"What kind of opportunity?" Judd said.

"Yitzhak and the others on the local committee want me to stay and learn from them. They have agreed to teach me about the Scriptures. It is exactly what I've been looking for."

Judd was excited for him but couldn't help wondering how he and Lionel would get home then.

"I know you want to return to your friends," Mr. Stein said. "I will arrange a commercial flight for you both."

Judd told them what Samuel had said about the airports.

183

"That will make it more difficult," Mr. Stein said.

"Do you still have your money?" Lionel said.

"I sensed there might be a problem, so I hid it at the university."

"So all we have to do is get it and find a way back," Judd said.

Mr. Stein nodded. "What about Taylor Graham's friend in Tel Aviv?"

"Hasina!" Lionel said. "She'd help us!"

Mr. Stein looked at the ceiling and wiped away a tear. "Call her first thing in the morning. Perhaps she will come through."

"What's wrong?" Judd said.

"Throughout this ordeal I thought of Chaya," Mr. Stein said. "She would have loved to see me at the Meeting of the Witnesses and hear Tsion speak."

"I bet she was watching," Lionel said.

Mr. Stein smiled. "It's clear we must retrieve the money, but we have a problem. Neither you nor I should be seen in public."

"I will go," Nada said.

Judd turned. He didn't know she had approached.

"I'm the same age as many of the students," Nada said, "and I blend in much better than you Americans."

"We'll talk about this in the morning," Mr. Stein said. He went to his room.

"I can do it," Nada said.

Judd nodded. "We'll run it past your dad in the morning. Maybe he has a contact who can get us in."

Nada said good night and returned to her family's

apartment. Judd grabbed Lionel's arm. "I can't wait till tomorrow to call Hasina. Let's try her now!"

Judd found her card and dialed the number. It rang several times before Hasina's answering machine picked up. Judd left a message about needing a flight home, but he thought it too dangerous to leave Jamal's number. He told Hasina he would call the next morning at 9 A.M. Judd wondered if she would be able to help them. She was their best chance to make it back to the States.

19

VICKI checked e-mail late that night in Illinois. She was relieved to see a message from Judd. He briefly explained what had happened at Teddy Kollek Stadium and how Mr. Stein had escaped a Global Community prison.

We're trying to get back as fast as we can, but there may be problems, Judd wrote. *I'll write again and tell when you can expect us. Lionel sends his best and so do I. Hope things have worked out with Melinda. Judd.*

Vicki frowned. When Judd was gone from the group she felt an emptiness that wouldn't go away. When he was there, he and Vicki fought. She still had feelings for him, still missed him, but she had no idea what to do with those feelings.

She pushed the thoughts from her mind and scanned the other messages. She sat up straight when she saw another e-mail to Mark. It was from the same person who had written earlier from the GC. She called out to Mark.

Mark came quickly. Vicki read over Mark's shoulder as he opened the message.

Dear Mark,

My intentions are pure. I'm at a GC outpost in South Carolina, recovering from injuries I received on the Peacekeeper 1. Your cousin, John Preston, saved my life.

I want to meet with you. I'd like to tell you what happened, since the GC has kept the story quiet. Can you come here? If not, I can come to you as soon as I'm released from the hospital.

Please write and let me know. You can trust me.

Sincerely, Carl Meninger

Mark scratched his chin. He opened a computer filing cabinet filled with other e-mails.

"What are you doing?" Vicki said.

"That name sounds familiar," Mark said. He did a search of the name *Meninger* and came up with nothing. Then he typed in the name *Carl*. A single e-mail appeared on the screen. It was John's last message.

"This is it," Mark said.

At the end of the message John had written, *Someday I hope you meet Carl. He can tell you what happened here. No time now. Just enough to say I love you all. Keep fighting the good fight. We'll be cheering you on. Never give up. John.*

"You think it's the same Carl?" Vicki said.

"Has to be," Mark said. "John says he hopes we get to meet him. That's enough for me."

"What if it's a GC trick?"

Mark raised his eyebrows. "Now who's the one being too cautious?"

Vicki smiled.

Mark answered the e-mail, saying that he would love to meet Carl, but he could not get to South Carolina any time soon. Mark suggested that Carl write about his experience with John or set up a phone call.

"I wonder how he survived the meteor," Vicki said.

When Judd awoke the next morning, he heard Mr. Stein and Nada talking in the next room. He called Hasina again but hung up when he reached her answering machine. By the time Judd joined them, Nada was gone.

Judd could tell that Mr. Stein was upset, and in the morning light he saw more clearly the bruises about the man's head. It was a miracle he had gotten out of the GC questioning alive.

Before Mr. Stein could explain what they had talked about, Jamal came in the room. He spoke through clenched teeth as he looked at Mr. Stein.

"Stay away from my daughter, and stop filling her head with these crazy ideas!"

"Believe me," Mr. Stein said, "I told her I couldn't put her life in danger—"

Jamal looked at Judd. "You put her up to this!"

"Is this about Mr. Stein's money?" Judd said.

"You care more about your own lives than you do hers," Jamal said.

Judd started to explain that Nada had volunteered to get the money, but Mr. Stein put up a hand. "Trust me; we will speak no more of this to her."

Jamal stared at them. "I will not lose another child." He slammed the door as he left.

"What was that about?" Judd said.

Lionel walked in. Mr. Stein offered him some breakfast. "Did Nada tell you how she became a believer?"

Judd nodded. "She said her mother believed first."

"Did she say anything about her brother?"

Judd was puzzled. "I didn't even know she had a brother. Jamal never said anything about him."

"Yitzhak told me their story while we were detained," Mr. Stein said. "Just as the rest of the family believed that Jesus is the Savior, Jamal's son, Kasim, believed that Nicolae Carpathia was the way to peace and happiness. They had many arguments about it."

"Just like in your family," Lionel said.

Mr. Stein nodded. "Except I finally agreed with my daughter. Kasim was killed before he came to the truth."

"What happened?" Judd said.

Mr. Stein sat back and folded his hands. "Yitzhak said Nada was very bold with her brother. Kasim was three years older, but she would not back away from telling him the truth.

"Kasim was so committed to Carpathia that he volunteered to become a GC guard. Even while he was training,

Nada would come into the Global Community compound and speak with Kasim openly about Christ."

"That girl knows no fear," Lionel said.

"Maybe she just loved her brother," Judd said. "Was he accepted into the GC?"

"He was assigned to security in New Babylon," Mr. Stein said, "to the main building where Nicolae Carpathia kept his office."

"The earthquake!" Judd said.

"Exactly," Mr. Stein said. "He was on the ground floor when the quake hit. Jamal and his wife received a letter of sorrow and thanks from the potentate just after the mass funeral. They never found Kasim's body."

"I'm sure Nick's letter meant a lot to them," Judd said sarcastically.

"You see why I did not challenge Jamal," Mr. Stein said. "He has been through much pain. I can understand him wanting to protect his only living child."

"We'll have to get the money ourselves," Judd said.

"How are we going to get inside the gymnasium?" Lionel said.

Mr. Stein pulled out a key. "Yitzhak gave me this. It is to the back entrance. Perhaps one of us should go, rather than all three."

They drew straws. Lionel's was the shortest. "Looks like I'm headed back to the university," he said.

In the excitement of Mark's return with Melinda and Janie, Conrad hadn't forgotten what he had seen in the tower. The next day he climbed to the top and inspected the board again. He put a foot on one end and tried to pry it loose, but when he did, he noticed something he hadn't seen the night before. Four boards were attached together.

Conrad inspected the others and found a tiny hook barely visible under the middle boards. He retrieved a screwdriver and tripped the hook. The boards lifted easily.

Conrad gasped when he saw the ancient box in the daylight. It was two feet square with fancy carvings on top. The box was made of thick metal, and a huge lock hung on the front.

Conrad knelt and strained to lift the box. It was almost more than he could carry. He struggled down the stairs into the meeting room and dropped it on the floor. It fell with such a crash that the kids came running from all over the house.

Vicki ran a hand over the ornate etchings on top. "You think this is what Z was talking about?"

Conrad shrugged. "When he talked about a safe, I thought it would be five feet tall. But this is sure old."

Mark looked closely. "This lock's going to take some time to open."

Janie stepped forward. "Are we gonna split what's inside evenly?" When Vicki didn't answer, Janie said, "I mean, if there's anything valuable inside. I just want to be fair."

"This isn't our house to begin with," Vicki said. "If there's anything of value inside, Z would need to make that call."

"Right," Janie said. "I didn't know this wasn't your house. Sorry."

Shelly, who had wandered off, called for the others from the next room. "Judd just sent a message. He asked us to pray for Lionel. He's evidently doing something pretty dangerous."

Lionel felt queasy about going to the university but glad that Jamal had agreed to drive him in his small car. In the afternoon, Lionel and Judd helped Jamal move large boxes up the freight elevator and into the hideout. Jamal spoke very little, clearly still upset about what he thought they had asked Nada to do.

"What are these for?" Judd said.

"You will see" was all Jamal would say.

Lionel put on a long robe and turban Nada had found. "One of the witnesses left it behind," she said. The outfit dragged the floor, and Lionel felt goofy.

"I don't care if it makes me look less American," Lionel said "If they catch me, they'll call the GC."

Lionel left the disguise and climbed into the tiny backseat of Jamal's car. He lay on the seat as Jamal wound through the Old City. Several times Jamal warned Lionel to keep down as he spotted Global Community squad cars.

Finally, they came near the university. Lionel sat up. Teddy Kollek Stadium was deserted. Yellow tape circled many of the university buildings where the witnesses had stayed.

Jamal pulled close to the gymnasium and handed Lionel his cell phone. "This is in case you have trouble finding what you're looking for," Jamal said. "I'll wait on the other side of the street until you give the signal."

Lionel felt inside his pocket for the flashlight. He hoped there would be no cameras or alarms in the building.

Judd and Mr. Stein prayed for Lionel as they waited for him to return. Nada handed Judd the phone. It was Samuel again.

"Did your father catch you outside last night?" Judd said.

"No," Samuel said, "but I don't have time to talk. I called to warn you."

"About what?" Judd said.

"The GC found something at the university where Mr. Stein was staying," Samuel said. "They have guards there in case someone shows up!"

"Thanks," Judd said. He hung up without saying good-bye and ran for Nada. "What's your dad's cell phone number?"

Lionel let his eyes adjust to the darkness and tried the key. Wrong door. He walked to the end of the building and tried again. This time the lock clicked, and he walked inside.

The cots had been removed from the gym floor.

Lionel tiptoed across the hardwood floor, but his footsteps still echoed. He scanned the door for anything suspicious.

Lionel pulled out the map Mr. Stein had drawn and found the hallway leading to a small office. He looked along the wall for the fire extinguisher but couldn't find it.

He pulled out the cell phone and dialed Jamal's house. The line was busy.

Something moved in the gym. Footsteps. Voices. Lionel turned off his flashlight and darted into an open doorway. He was in the men's room. He backed against a wall and listened, his heart pounding furiously.

"What did they say?" one man said.

"Get out your gun," the other man said. "Campus police said somebody was just at the back of the gym."

Lionel dialed Jamal's number again. Judd answered.

"Let me talk with Mr. Stein, quick!" Lionel whispered.

"No!" Judd said. "Get out of there! The GC has guards waiting for you."

The back door opened.

"I might as well try," Lionel whispered. "Let me talk with Mr. Stein!"

"Please, Lionel," Mr. Stein said, "get out now."

"Just tell me again," Lionel said. "I can't find the fire extinguish—"

"Do you see the office?"

"Yeah, I'm in the men's room across the hall."

"You are at the wrong end," Mr. Stein said. "Go the other direction down the hall."

"Got it," Lionel whispered. He hurried from the bathroom and down the hall, being careful not to make noise. He found the fire extinguisher behind a glass door.

The gym door closed. The guards were coming. Lionel heard Mr. Stein plead with him to get out. Lionel opened the door to the fire extinguisher slowly. Someone honked their horn. *Jamal,* Lionel thought. The guards took the bait and ran for the back door.

Lionel pulled the fire extinguisher out of the wall and felt behind it. Nothing. He switched on the flashlight and saw a small bag at the bottom. He picked it up and looked inside.

"The money's not here," Lionel said.

Suddenly an alarm sounded.

20

LIONEL knew the alarm was somehow attached to the empty bag. He dropped the fire extinguisher and ran into the gym. The guards rushed inside. Lionel had a head start on them, but not much.

He ran into a long hallway. He looked right, then left. At the left end was an Exit sign. He sprinted toward it, then realized as he got closer that the sign pointed down another hallway.

"There he goes," a guard yelled behind him.

Lionel didn't slow down. He rounded the corner and bounced off a row of lockers. Through light, then shadows, he careened down the hall. A red sign was posted over the door at the end of the hallway: ALARM WILL SOUND. PLEASE USE OTHER EXIT. He hit the red lever full force, and another alarm screamed over his head. He flung the door open and raced into the cool air.

He had hoped Jamal would be waiting, but the man

was nowhere in sight. Lionel cursed, then realized what he had said and shook his head.

He sprinted to the right and into the darkness beside the building. The door opened behind him, and both guards raced out. One fired his gun, but Lionel kept running.

"Go that way! I'll follow him," a guard said.

Lionel rounded the corner and was nearly hit by Jamal's car, its lights off. "Get in quickly!" Jamal yelled.

Lionel opened the back door and yelled, "Go!" He jumped inside, hitting his head against the other door as Jamal floored the gas pedal of the tiny car. As Jamal rounded the corner, he turned on his lights and blinded the guard running toward them. The guard threw a hand over his eyes and shot wildly at the small car, the bullet pinging off the hood.

"Stay down!" Jamal shouted.

Jamal zigged and zagged until they were out of the parking lot and into the street. The GC guards followed, but they were no match for Jamal's knowledge of the city. He took alleys and backstreets until he arrived safely in the parking garage of the apartment building.

Judd and Mr. Stein hugged Lionel when he returned. Lionel filled them in on what had happened.

"They must have found your money when they searched the building," Judd said. "What do we do now?"

"Maybe Hasina will take an IOU," Lionel said.

Mr. Stein said, "God will provide."

Judd tried Hasina's number again, and his eyes widened. "It's busy!"

"Keep trying," Lionel said.

Before dinner, Vicki had a chance to talk more with
Melinda. The girl seemed less angry and a little more
open since she had returned.

"I just couldn't stay here," Melinda said. "Listening to
all those prophecies, all the bad stuff to come, knowing
that it might be true. It just overwhelmed me."

"How do you feel now?" Vicki said.

"Afraid I'll be the one who leads the GC here."

"We have people watching around the clock," Vicki
said. "And we always have a way to escape if we have to."

Melinda pulled her hair from her face. "I want to go
to your classes and all that, but I'm still not sure if I can
believe the way you guys do."

"You mean you're not sure if what we're saying is
true?"

Melinda shook her head. "I'm pretty convinced you're
on the right track. I'm just not sure I can study the Bible.
Still feels a little weird to me."

"If you'll ask God into your heart, it won't feel weird.
I remember when I did it. It was a couple of years ago.
I'd never even thought of what would happen to me after
I died. Reading the Bible was for losers. Then I realized
it was true. Practical. What I read in the Bible every day
helps me. Every day is a new chance to really live."

Mark walked into the room holding a few sheets of
paper. He had a blank stare on his face.

"What's wrong with you?" Melinda said.

"I can't believe we missed it," Mark said.

"Missed what?" Vicki said.

"Tsion's message from the Meeting of the Witnesses. It's all right here, and we missed it."

Vicki took the paper and scanned the message. "I remember hearing this. Tsion said the sun, moon, and stars are going to be affected by the next judgment."

"Don't you see what that means?" Mark said.

"We'll have a third less light," Vicki said, "but that's what the generator's for."

"You don't understand," Mark said. "A third less solar energy means disaster. The whole planet's going into the deep freeze."

"We happen to be out in the middle of the woods," Melinda said. "If what's been predicted actually happens, we can just cut down some trees and throw another log on the fire."

Mark shook his head. "You still don't get it. I've worked it out on the computer. The temperature's not going down by a third. You cut direct sunlight like this and we're all in big trouble. People are going to die."

―――――――――

Judd dialed Hasina again and again. Finally, on the tenth try, the phone rang and Hasina picked up, out of breath. "Taylor, I'm not ready!" Hasina yelled.

"It's Judd Thompson! What's wrong?"

"Judd, the GC are chasing Taylor. He tried to take out another installation. He's on his way here. I have to get his plane ready."

Hasina took the cordless phone with her as she walked through the steps to start the plane.

"I know this is not the time to ask," Judd said, "but Lionel and I need a ride out of Israel. Our money is gone. The GC took it. Is there a chance—"

"Taylor wants me to go with him," Hasina said. "He believes the GC know about our operation. Perhaps we'll get set up in another city, and we can fly you from there."

Judd heard a clanking sound and figured Hasina was opening the hangar door. Seconds later, the plane's engine fired.

"Where do you think you'll go?" Judd said.

"Spain, perhaps," Hasina said. "Taylor has a friend there who has said he will help us." She gasped.

"What is it?" Judd said.

"I see Taylor's car! The GC are right behind him."

"Get out on the runway!" Judd shouted.

"I can't," Hasina said. "They already have it blocked."

"Is there a place you can hide?"

"Oh no," Hasina said, "they have him trapped."

Judd closed his eyes and listened. He could hear sirens blaring in the background. He thought of Taylor's escape from the earthquake. Judd had thought Taylor was dead when the raging waters had taken him over the edge of a chasm, but Taylor had survived. Was there any way he could survive this?

"Look," Judd said, "Taylor will never let them take him alive. He'll put up a fight. That should give you time to hide!"

A gun went off. Then another. Then a *pop-pop-pop* of automatic fire.

"It's no use," Hasina said, her voice full of despair. "They have him."

"What do you mean?"

"They shot him as he sat in the car, and they're coming this way."

"Hasina, get out of there!" Judd shouted. He turned to Lionel and Mr. Stein. "Pray, and pray hard!"

"I'm putting the phone in my shirt pocket so you can hear what happens," Hasina said. "If we do not make it, good luck."

Judd heard the door to the plane open. The phone was muffled for a moment as Hasina put the phone away. She breathed heavily as she ran. Someone shouted, "There she is!" A few shots rang out.

A door opened and closed. Hasina moved furniture to get to something. Keys jangled.

Judd turned on the speakerphone and turned it all the way up. Mr. Stein and Lionel leaned close. They heard Hasina open a door with the keys. It sounded like she was loading a weapon of some sort.

Then someone banged on the door. Something fell to the floor, and Hasina cursed.

"Open it now!" someone shouted.

"Shoot them!" Taylor Graham said from the other side.

Hasina was breathing hard and scrambling on the floor to pick up what had fallen. Two huge gunshots exploded, and the door banged open.

"Drop it now!" a voice boomed.

"Shoot them!" Taylor screamed, his voice louder now that the door was open.

"I said shut up!" a man yelled, and Judd heard a whack and a crunch of bone.

"Taylor!" Hasina shouted.

"Put the gun down," another man said.

Something clattered to the floor.

"Good, now step away from the desk, your hands in the air."

Hasina was breathing heavily now. She spoke with her teeth clenched. "Do you know what this is?" she said. "We rigged this just in case something like this happened."

"Put it down!"

"I push this button, and the whole place goes up. You shoot me, and I swear I'll take you all with me."

A GC officer clicked his radio. "There's a bomb. The girl's threatening to blow the whole place up. Everybody out!"

"Leave Taylor and get out of here, and I'll let you live!"

The radio crackled. "Confirm explosive!" someone said.

Hasina barked, "This is hooked to the underground jet fuel. Now unless you want to all go up with us, leave now!"

The GC officer spoke into his walkie-talkie. He ordered everyone to move a safe distance away. Hasina ran to Taylor Graham and spoke his name.

Judd felt almost guilty, listening. These were such private moments, and Hasina had either forgotten that Judd was on the line or didn't care.

"Taylor, I love you."

203

Taylor's voice was groggy. "I love you, too. Always have. If I'd have married you like I promised, we wouldn't be in this mess. We'd probably have five or six kids by now and be living on a beach somewhere."

Hasina laughed. Taylor sounded close to the phone. "We don't have to worry about what might have been," she said. "We both made our choices."

"Did you really rig the place to explode?" Taylor said.

"I control everything with this," Hasina said. She giggled. "It's my lipstick case."

"Pretty convincing," Taylor said, and then he cried out in pain. "I'm bleeding to death. I think they hit an artery in my leg."

Hasina moved. Judd heard a cloth ripping.

"It's no use," Taylor said. "They're going to figure out you don't have explosives in here."

Judd had a million questions. How had the GC discovered Taylor? Was Judd partly responsible since he told the GC guard about him?

"Try to make it back to the plane," Taylor gasped. "There's a chance you could get around them to the runway."

"You know that's not possible now," Hasina said. "Listen. More GC cars are on their way."

"We could ask for a personal audience with Nicolae Carpathia," Taylor said.

"Other than marrying you, that is the only thing I wanted to do in this life."

"Somebody else will have the privilege," Taylor said. "If that Thompson kid and his friends are right—"

"Judd!" Hasina said. She pulled the phone out of her pocket. "Are you still there?"

Judd picked up the phone on his end. "We're here."

"I guess you've heard we're in a pretty tight spot." She handed the phone to Taylor.

"I wish we could be there to help you," Judd said. "I'm sorry. I feel responsible—"

"I made more than one mistake trying to shoot that guy down," Taylor said. "It's not your fault I'm in this mess."

Mr. Stein asked to talk to them, so Judd flipped on the speakerphone again. "Taylor, you may not have much longer to live. We've told you about Jesus. If you die without him—"

"Save your breath," Taylor said. He passed the phone to Hasina.

"Hasina, I talked with you about Jesus," Judd said. "If you ask him to forgive you—"

"I'm sorry, Judd," Hasina said. "I appreciate your concern and your love, but a last-minute step of faith is not for me."

"The thief on the cross asked for forgiveness and received it," Lionel said.

Something banged in the background. The phone dropped to the floor. Guards were back. "We checked your tanks. They're not wired."

Judd heard a smack. Hasina cried out.

"It's lipstick!" the guard sneered.

"Don't hurt her!" Taylor shouted.

A gun went off.

"Taylor!" Hasina screamed.

"You were part of the plot to kill the potentate," the guard said.

"I would gladly pull the trigger," Hasina said.

The gun fired again. "You will not have the chance," the guard muttered. He clicked his walkie-talkie. "Both suspects are dead. They resisted arrest, and we were forced to kill them."

"Liar," Judd muttered.

Another guard entered. "What should we do with the crime scene, Commander?"

"Burn it."

The guard ran away. Someone picked up the phone. Judd heard breathing on the other end. "Who is there?" the man said.

"You won't get away with this," Judd said. He hung up the phone.

21

VICKI looked at Mark's prediction on the computer. Though she was never that good at math, his numbers seemed right. At dinner she announced an all-out effort to store fuel.

"We have enough food to keep us going a few months," Vicki said, "but if Mark is right about what's coming, we need to insulate the problem areas and get more fuel."

"What fuel?" Janie said.

"Firewood," Vicki said, "enough to last a couple months."

Janie sighed. "Thought I was done with grunt labor when I escaped the GC camp."

Vicki ignored her. "Conrad, I need you to coordinate the around-the-clock GC lookout from the tower."

"Already done," Conrad said. "We do three eight-hour shifts. Shelly's up there right now."

"Any luck with the box?" Vicki said.

Conrad shook his head. "I've broken three saw blades on it so far."

"It'll have to take a backseat to this," Vicki said. "As a matter of fact, we'll have to postpone classes, too."

"What happens if his predictions don't come true?" Melinda said. "We're already into spring. Summer's not far away. How's it going to get that cold this time of year?"

"Yeah," Janie said, "we could work our tails off for nothing."

Mark scowled. "Dr. Ben-Judah's been predicting stuff since the GC made their treaty with Israel. He hasn't been wrong yet."

Judd was crushed by the deaths of Taylor and Hasina. He wanted to call the media and tell them the truth about what happened, but he knew the media was controlled by Nicolae Carpathia. A sense of despair set in. Not only had they lost two friends, but they had also lost their best chance of getting home.

Judd went to his room and tried to sleep, but couldn't. He composed an e-mail and sent it to Conrad, then fixed a cup of coffee. His father had been a big-time coffee drinker, but his mother had warned Judd not to start. In his senior year he had pulled several all-nighters with nothing but sheer willpower and a thermos filled with coffee.

Now, as Judd held the hot cup and thought about his

family, it seemed like two different lives. Only a little more than two years had passed since the vanishings. In those two years his life had turned upside down. Nothing was constant. He seemed to always be on the run.

He longed for some kind of stability. He thought of Vicki. Maybe her idea about the school was best. Judd regretted his harsh words and disagreements with her. If he could start over again, things would be different.

A door opened behind him. Nada sat down. "Couldn't sleep?"

Judd shook his head.

"I heard about your friends. I'm very sorry."

"I knew Taylor would go too far sooner or later," Judd said, "but I really hoped Hasina would come to believe in Jesus."

"It is the same way I felt about my brother," Nada said. She tucked her feet under her and leaned back. "I talked with him the night before he died. He was so excited about seeing Leon Fortunato in the hallway."

Judd sighed in disgust. "Leon came to my school once. The guy's a weasel."

"He is worse than that," Nada said. "My father believes he is the false prophet." She waved her hand. "Enough about Fortunato. My brother could not stop talking about the lavish lifestyle the Global Community provided him. He was only a guard, but he said his apartment was like a palace compared to our house."

"It's hard for people to think about heaven when they feel like they have it here," Judd said.

"I think in his heart, he knew the truth. He told me he

had seen and heard things that troubled him. The potentate seemed loving and giving to the public, but behind the scenes he could be ruthless."

"So your brother was coming around."

"Not quickly enough. I told him about Dr. Ben-Judah and his teaching. My brother knew all about him. He said he was Public Enemy Number One with the GC."

"Had he read anything Tsion wrote?"

"He saw the news broadcast when Dr. Ben-Judah announced that Jesus was the true Messiah of the Jews," Nada said.

"Mr. Stein said you received a personal letter from the potentate after his death."

Nada went to a cabinet just inside the front door and found a photo album. She turned the pages carefully until she came to Kasim's picture. "This is us on holiday in Greece when we were kids." Standing beside a huge sand castle, Nada and Kasim smiled at the camera. Jamal and his wife knelt behind them, the Mediterranean Sea in the background.

Judd stared at the photo. He thought of his own family album and photos at their cottage on Lake Michigan or on vacation in Florida.

Nada flipped the pages and couldn't hold back the tears. "When I see my brother, I can only think of what might have been. What God might have done through him."

Judd put an arm around her. He wanted to say something, anything, but he could think of nothing. They spent the rest of the night looking through the album and telling stories of their families.

Vicki showed Conrad Judd's e-mail about Taylor. Conrad pursed his lips. "I knew it would happen if he didn't change, but it's still hard."

Vicki put an arm around him. "If you need to take some time, I understand."

Over the next few days, Vicki supervised the storing of wood near the schoolhouse while Mark, Conrad, and Charlie worked in the forest, gathering firewood. Each evening Mark would fill Vicki in on how much help Charlie had been.

"I know I complained about him coming here at first," Mark said, "but that guy can really handle an ax!"

Vicki's most difficult task was keeping an eye on Janie. She was constantly taking a rest and grumbling about doing so much manual labor. Melinda even commented in private about Janie's poor attitude.

As the temperature rose one day, Vicki went to the kitchen to fix some cool drinks. Vicki found Janie in the main meeting room, her feet on the table, watching a music video on the computer.

"What are you doing?" Vicki said.

Janie whirled, her feet hitting the floor hard. "You almost scared me to death!"

"Why aren't you outside helping?"

"Do you know how hot it is out there?" Janie said. "And we're stacking firewood like our lives depend on it."

"Our lives may very well depend on it," Vicki said.

Janie scoffed. "Even back at the camp, we got to watch videos and stuff. Here, all we do is work."

"You know this computer's not for entertainment," Vicki said, disconnecting from the Web site.

"I'm going to my room," Janie shouted. "I need a day off."

Vicki recalled how difficult Janie had been at Bruce's house. She wouldn't follow the rules there either. Nothing had changed in her life except her move toward the Enigma Babylon Faith. Vicki wondered if she would hang on to that belief after the next judgment hit.

———————

Lionel noticed Judd and Nada were spending more time together. They talked till late at night. Many afternoons they exercised together on the rooftop. Lionel asked Mr. Stein if he should say something to Judd.

"What would you say?" Mr. Stein said. "These things happen between males and females."

"I understand that," Lionel said, "but if he gets too involved here, he may not want to go back to the States."

"Perhaps that is what God wants," Mr. Stein said. "None of us knows what will happen in the future."

Jamal asked Mr. Stein, Judd, and Lionel to remain with them until they heard from Yitzhak. "As long as you're here, you should be safe," Jamal said. Lionel knew he and Judd would be on their own if Yitzhak were released.

Jamal kept quiet about the mountain of boxes Judd

and Lionel had carried to the apartment. Things were getting tight in many of the rooms, but Jamal wouldn't reveal the contents or his plan.

One afternoon while Judd and Nada were exercising, Lionel took a call from Samuel. "I have been thinking about what Dan and Nina said before they died, and the verse you gave me."

Lionel had almost forgotten about the words he had handed to Samuel. It was the strangest verse he had ever given a nonbeliever, but he thought it applied.

The words of Jesus were found in Luke 12. "From now on families will be split apart, three in favor of me, and two against—or the other way around. There will be a division between father and son. . . ." Lionel had finished the note by writing, *The truth may divide you and your father, but it's always best to stick with the truth.*

Samuel said, "I have read that verse over and over. I had always thought to obey my father was the best thing I could do as a son."

"You're supposed to honor your father," Lionel said. "But if your dad believes something that's wrong, or asks you to do something that goes against what God wants, you have to disobey him."

"I've always believed that if I do the right things I will someday get to heaven. But I have been reading this rabbi's writings on the Internet, and I have been reading the words of Jesus in the Gospels. I don't know how to get to heaven."

"There's only one way," Lionel said.

Lionel explained that Jesus was not just a good

teacher, but God in the flesh. "His mission was to live a perfect life and die as a sacrifice for your sins and mine. And he did that."

"Dan and Nina always said I could never earn my way into heaven," Samuel said.

"They were right," Lionel said. "The way to heaven is open right now. And God will show you what to do about your dad."

"Will I have to leave home if I pray this?"

"I don't know," Lionel said. "Becoming a believer doesn't make everything smooth. As a matter of fact, if your dad finds out, things will probably get worse. That's why I wrote what I did after that verse I gave you. It's better to find the truth and follow it than to live a lie."

Lionel paused. He could hear the street sounds in the background and pictured Samuel standing at the pay phone across from his house. "Are you ready to pray?"

Samuel hesitated. "Once I do this, I cannot go back, can I?"

"Once you ask God to come into your heart, you'll never want to live any other way. I wonder every day how we're going to get home. I've been through stuff that makes me doubt I'll live another hour. But in the middle of it all, God gives me peace. I know what'll happen after I die, and that I'll be with God and my family who disappeared."

"I wish I could have that confidence," Samuel said.

"You can," Lionel said.

"Tell me again how I should pray."

"Just tell God you've done bad stuff and you're sorry.

You believe that Jesus came to die for your sins and right now you accept his gift of salvation. Ask God to come into your life and make you a new person. Say you want him to save you and guide you for the rest of your life."

Lionel paused. All he could hear was the sound of the street behind Samuel. For a moment he thought the boy had left the phone off the hook and had walked away.

"Samuel?" Lionel said.

"I am here," Samuel said. "I just prayed and asked God to forgive me."

"That's great," Lionel said. "How do you feel?"

"I'm not sure," Samuel said. "Like I have finally found what I was looking for. Like Dan and Nina did not die in vain."

"I want you to do me a favor," Lionel said.

"Anything," Samuel said.

"Are there people walking on your street?"

"A few. And there are some at an outdoor café nearby."

"Get ready," Lionel said. "God has done something special to help you. Look at the people and see if any of them have a special mark on their forehead. It should look like a cross."

The phone clanked against the booth. A few seconds later, Samuel returned, out of breath. "I see someone! He just walked past."

"Go back and ask if he sees anything on your forehead," Lionel said.

Again, Samuel went away and came back overjoyed.

"He called me *brother!* He said I have the mark as well, but I don't see anything."

Lionel explained the mark and that you could not see your own. "We can use this to our advantage. We know who the other believers are, but no one can see the mark except us."

Samuel was thrilled. "I want to talk to my father. I want him to have this same peace."

"But you have to be careful," Lionel said. "And you have to be prepared for your father not to accept what you've said."

Lionel told Samuel to continue reading his Bible and Tsion's Web site. Lionel couldn't wait to tell Mr. Stein and Judd what had happened.

22

JUDD was elated when he heard the news about Samuel. Mr. Stein smiled broadly, then shook his head. "I'm afraid that boy is in for a difficult time if he tries to talk with his father about Christ. We should pray for him."

Judd could tell Mr. Stein was restless, but something else seemed to be bothering him. Judd brought it up one evening.

"I am concerned about Yitzhak," Mr. Stein said, "but even if he is okay, I do not think I should leave you two alone. I brought you here, and I should provide you a way home."

"Nonsense," Judd said. "We came because we wanted to."

"Still, I cannot abandon you simply because I have a wonderful opportunity."

Lionel leaned forward. "You keep talking about God providing. Don't you think he can provide for us just as easily as he can provide for you?"

"Of course, but—"

"God will provide for us," Lionel said.

The next evening Judd took a call from Samuel. He said he had been reading Tsion's Web site as much as possible, but his father had been home and he didn't dare risk reading it then.

"I overheard a conversation with headquarters," Samuel said. "They have released all the local committee members. After the death of your friend, the GC was concerned how it would look if that information leaked to the public."

Judd felt guilty keeping the information about Mr. Stein from Samuel. Judd felt it best that Samuel not know so he wouldn't have to lie to his father.

"Won't the local committee know Mr. Stein is gone?" Judd said. "Couldn't they leak the story?"

"They were told he was banished to his homeland to face criminal charges," Samuel said.

Judd couldn't wait to see Yitzhak's face when Mr. Stein walked into the room. He asked Samuel how it felt to be a believer in Christ.

"It feels wonderful! I am learning so much in such a little time. I hope to speak with my father soon."

"Choose your time wisely," Judd said.

———————————————

Vicki talked with Mark and Conrad about Janie. She was becoming increasingly difficult to work with. Vicki had threatened to withhold meals if Janie didn't pitch in, but Janie had complained about the food and said she didn't want it anyway.

"I feel responsible," Mark said. "I was the one who brought her here."

"I'm glad you did," Vicki said. "We want this place to be open to skeptics and seekers."

"We can't just kick her out," Conrad said. "She might get caught. Knowing her, she'd tell the GC about us just to get a half hour of TV privileges."

"I'd like to throw her in the tunnel and lock both doors," Vicki said.

"That would be an effective evangelism tool," Conrad said. "Convert or we'll starve you."

Vicki smiled. "Maybe we should just keep praying that God will cause her to come around."

"Any news from Judd and Lionel?" Mark said.

Vicki frowned. "They're stuck."

Judd walked beside Lionel, just behind Jamal. Mr. Stein wore a cloak over his head and held onto Jamal's arm. Judd couldn't tell what part of the Old City they were in, but he could imagine an upper room and frightened disciples waiting to be arrested by Roman guards.

They passed through a garden, then up a narrow alley. Clothes were hung out to dry on a wire strung between the buildings. The light was fading. Something about the scene filled Judd with sadness, but he couldn't figure it out. Then it came to him. *There should be children playing here, kicking a ball and laughing.* But there were no children.

Jamal cautiously led them through a doorway and up

two flights of rickety stairs. He knocked twice, waited, then knocked twice again. The door creaked open, and the group was waved in quickly.

Yitzhak sat in the corner with a blanket draped over his frail shoulders. His voice was weak and he had bruises about his head. He welcomed Jamal but didn't seem to recognize Judd and Lionel.

Daniel, the emcee of the Meeting of the Witnesses, sat beside Yitzhak. About a dozen others sat at tables and on the floor.

"Who is our mystery guest?" Yitzhak said weakly.

Mr. Stein slowly removed the cloak from his head. Yitzhak's eyes filled with tears. He stood, then fell back against the wall. Mr. Stein rushed to him and embraced him.

"When we were told you had been sent home," Yitzhak said, "we feared they had killed you."

Others in the group surrounded Mr. Stein and hugged him. Some praised God in Hebrew. Others smiled and clapped. After a few minutes of conversation, Yitzhak lifted a hand.

"We have been given the task to go into the world and reap a great soul harvest," Yitzhak said. "My brother, Mitchell Stein, has asked for a time of intense study. We have prepared a place for that, as well as rest for those who have been through a difficult ordeal.

"God has delivered us from the hands of our enemies for a purpose. And we will fulfill our destiny as God's spokesmen to a lost and confused world. May he grant us the strength and the wisdom and the courage to do it."

Mr. Stein turned to Judd and Lionel with tears in his eyes. He cupped his hands around their necks and pulled them close to him.

"I feel so torn. I don't want to let you down but—"

"We understand," Lionel said. "We want you to go."

"I cannot say when we will be together again," Mr. Stein said.

Jamal stepped forward. "These are our young brothers in the faith. We will make sure they are safe."

Mr. Stein called for quiet in the room and explained what he, Judd, and Lionel had been through. "I would like to ask someone to pray for my young friends."

Yitzhak motioned the others forward. All the people in the room stretched out their hands toward Judd and Lionel, and those standing closest to them laid hands on them directly.

"Our Father," Yitzhak began, "we thank you for those who trust in you, no matter what their age. We remember the words of the apostle Paul who said, 'Don't let anyone think less of you because you are young. Be an example to all believers in what you teach, in the way you live, in your love, your faith, and your purity.' These friends have lived that verse, and we praise you for their lives."

Those touching Lionel and Judd said "Amen," "Yes, Lord," and other words Judd couldn't understand.

Yitzhak continued. "We give them to you now and ask that you would give them spiritual wisdom and understanding so that they may grow in their knowledge of you. I pray their hearts will be flooded with light so that they can understand the wonderful future you have promised to those you have called. Help them to realize what a rich and glorious inheritance you have given your people."

Judd realized Yitzhak was praying the same prayer for Lionel and him that Paul prayed in Ephesians.

Yitzhak continued. "O God, help our friends begin to understand the incredible greatness of your power. May they experience this power that raised Christ from the dead and seated him in the place of honor at your right hand in heaven. We know that Jesus is now far above any ruler or authority or power or leader or anything else in this world or in the world to come. May he be praised by all of our lives, and the lives of these two young men, until we see him coming in the clouds at the Glorious Appearing.

"We give you Judd and Lionel, O Father, and we give you our lives. Every breath we have is yours. In Jesus' name. Amen."

Lionel awoke before the others the next morning and opened Tsion's Web page. Tsion included some personal notes in his teaching for the day. He wrote about the heartbreak of losing family members and friends.

The death of Ken Ritz has gotten to him, Lionel thought.

Tsion ended his teaching with a reminder that *we are but a year and a half from what the Scriptures call the Great Tribulation. It has been hard, worse than hard, so far. We have survived the worst two years in the history of our planet, and this next year and a half will be worse. But the*

222

last three and a half years of this period will make the rest seem like a garden party.

Tsion always concluded with a word of encouragement, no matter how difficult the teaching had been. He quoted Luke 21: *"There will be signs in the sun, in the moon, and in the stars; and on the earth distress of nations, with perplexity, the sea and the waves roaring; men's hearts failing them for fear and the expectation of those things which are coming on the earth, for the powers of the heavens will be shaken. Then they will see the Son of Man coming in a cloud with power and great glory. Now when these things begin to happen, look up and lift up your heads, because your redemption draws near."*

Lionel flipped on the television and kept the sound low. Nicolae Carpathia was still upset about the actions of Eli and Moishe. The reporter cut to Leon Fortunato at a news conference.

"His Excellency has decreed the preachers enemies of the world system and has authorized Peter the Second, supreme pontiff of Enigma Babylon One World Faith, to dispose of the criminals as he sees fit."

The response from Peter Mathews seemed almost comical to Lionel. Mathews was furious. "Oh, the problem is mine now, is it? Has His Excellency finally given authority to the person who deserves it? When the two lie dead and the rains fall again in Israel, clear, pure, refreshing water will cascade once more, and the world will know who has the true power."

Lionel thought of Vicki and his friends at the

schoolhouse. It was midnight in the Midwest, and he guessed everyone was asleep as he saw the sun rise. He opened the door to the roof and walked quietly upstairs. He wondered what Mr. Stein was learning and what would happen to him and Judd.

There were no clouds in the sky. The sun was so brilliant that Lionel had to squint. He was high enough to see the gates of the Old City. The new temple gleamed brilliantly in the bright light.

Lionel closed his eyes and felt the warmth. Suddenly, he felt a chill. He opened his eyes to what looked like twilight. It was as if someone had let down the blinds on heaven. The sun was still visible in the sky, but it had faded. The temperature immediately fell.

Lionel rushed back to his computer and pulled up Tsion's message from the Meeting of the Witnesses. He found the section he was looking for and flipped his Bible open to Revelation 8:12. "Then the fourth angel blew his trumpet, and one-third of the sun was struck, and one-third of the moon, and one-third of the stars, and they became dark. And one-third of the day was dark and one-third of the night also."

Lionel shook Judd awake. "The next judgment's here!"

Judd rushed to the roof and pulled his blanket tightly around him. Jamal and his wife joined them.

"This is going to affect everything," Judd said, "not just how much light we get and how low the temperature will go. Plants are going to die. There'll be food shortages. Water lines will freeze."

"Communication lines will be affected," Jamal said. "Much of the new GC technology is solar powered."

"And transportation," Jamal's wife said gravely. "Travel will be impossible in a few days."

Jamal motioned them back inside. "It is time to answer your questions." He closed the door and sealed off the roof with heavy tape so the cold air could not get through.

Back in the living area, Jamal opened a box. "Tsion told us to prepare, and we have." Inside the box was nonperishable food. The next box contained warm clothes and blankets. "I also purchased these." Jamal unpacked several freestanding fireplaces. "I would never allow them in the building under normal circumstances, but these are not normal circumstances."

"These won't do us any good if we don't have fuel," Judd said.

"Have you seen the new Dumpsters at the back of the building?" Jamal said.

Lionel nodded. "They're huge."

"Each is locked and filled with firewood. I estimate one Dumpster could keep us warm twenty-four hours a day for up to two weeks."

"How many Dumpsters?" Judd said.

"Ten," Jamal said. "That could last us as long as five months. However, we may need to shelter others, and that means we will have to use more wood to heat the rooms."

Jamal showed them another source of heat he had invented. It used a simple exercise bicycle and a weird contraption hooked to it. "I have five of these. It will not only give us heat, but a good workout as well."

The phone rang. Nada handed the phone to Lionel. It was Samuel. The boy shivered at the phone booth. Lionel tried to calm him, but Samuel was frightened.

"This is exactly what the Bible said would happen," Lionel said. "God's trying to get people's attention again."

"My father left early this morning, before the sky darkened," Samuel said. "I want to tell him about my faith, but I'm scared. What if he kicks me out?"

"You can come here if you have to," Lionel said, "but try to wait until you think your father's ready to listen."

Judd asked for the phone, and Lionel gave it to him. "This may be your chance to tell your dad the truth. You can say Tsion predicted all this. If your father seems open, show him the passage in the Bible."

Lionel walked to the nearest window. There was a flurry of activity as Jamal and his family and the others staying with them opened boxes and prepared for the cold days ahead. Lionel looked out at the city of Jerusalem. He wondered if his friends back home had prepared. Surely people would die from this, especially those who were used to warm temperatures.

Lionel prayed for his friends and got to work.

23

WHEN Vicki awoke the next morning, she pulled the covers up under her chin. The air was chilly. She was used to the sunshine waking her between six-thirty and seven. Sometimes she pulled the covers over her head to sleep a little longer.

She picked her watch up from the floor and turned it several times before she could see. It was after seven o'clock.

Strange, Vicki thought, swinging her feet from under the covers and hitting the floor. She quickly jumped back into bed. The floor was icy.

No one was up yet, so Vicki went to the computer room to read Tsion's Web site. The Internet seemed unusually slow.

Vicki blew warm air into her hands and noticed she could see her breath. When a window popped on her screen with a news flash about the worldwide cold spell, Vicki finally realized what had happened.

She called the others together. Slowly people made their way into the room. Mark walked onto the balcony on the second floor to see the lack of sunlight, but he couldn't stand to stay outside long.

Vicki logged on to the local news. The report said a cold front had moved into Illinois in the middle of the night. Meteorologists and other weather experts tried to make sense of the situation, but all seemed stumped.

Janie shuffled into the room with a blanket draped around her. "Who turned down the heat? I'm freezing!"

"It's the judgment we told you about," Vicki said.

Janie looked at Vicki like she had two heads. "What are you talking about?"

Vicki picked up a Bible and read the passage that described the striking of the sun, moon, and stars.

"This means we need to get in gear," Mark said. He and Conrad ran to start the generator.

Vicki, Darrion, and Shelly inspected the house and decided the upstairs would be too difficult to heat. "Too much cold air coming through those old windows," Vicki said. "We'll need to move everybody to the ground floor."

"I don't want to be cooped up down here," Janie protested.

Vicki remained firm. When it was time for lunch, the kids huddled near the computer to watch the official reaction from the Global Community.

A spokesperson for the Global Community Aeronautics and Space Administration read a prepared statement in front of reporters. The man tried to look calm and confident.

"Regarding the incident that occurred 0700 hours New Babylon time today, the GCASA is pleased to assure the public that the darkening of the skies is the result of an explainable natural phenomenon and should not be a cause of alarm. Top scientific researchers have concluded that this is a condition that should correct itself in somewhere between forty-eight and ninety-six hours."

Reporters' hands went up and several shouted questions. The man tried to calm them, then continued. "I won't be taking questions at this time. As you were told, this is a prepared statement."

"I can tell you why he's not taking questions," Mark said. "He doesn't have any answers."

The scientist continued. "This event should not affect temperatures greatly, except in the short run."

Mark snickered. "Yeah, in the short run while all of us freeze to death."

"There may be some impact on smaller solar-powered equipment such as cell phones, computers, and calculators for a few days, but there should be no measurable impact on the power reserves."

The scientist gave one theory. He said the phenomenon's probable cause was an explosion of a massive star—a supernova. "The explosion resulted in the formation of a magnetar—a supermagnetized star—that can spin at a high rate of speed, causing elements in its core to rise and become extremely magnetic."

"See," Janie said, "this is not some kind of judgment from God. They have a perfect explanation."

"It's nonsense," Conrad said. "I read about this in school. If a magnetar would have happened as close as he says, the earth would be hurtling out into space right now."

"You think you know more than this guy?" Janie said.

Mark asked them to be quiet as the scientist continued.

"The GCASA will maintain constant watch on the situation and report significant changes. We expect things to be normal before the end of next week."

Judd wanted to watch the Global Community's coverage of the disaster, but there was too much to do. Getting heat to the rooms and opening boxes took time.

Jamal was frantic with calls from the lower apartments. Power from the Global Community was running at 50 percent strength, and the main heating unit was already struggling to pump warm air throughout the building.

"We have to make a decision," Jamal said. "There are about five hundred people living here. If the judgment continues for more than a week, some of those may die."

"We can't fit five hundred people up here," Judd said.

"But we could help some," Jamal said.

"Wait," Lionel said. "Maybe we could set up a couple of your heaters in a big room downstairs. Isn't there some kind of meeting room near the lobby?"

Jamal nodded. "Excellent idea. We could spare three

of the wood-burning fireplaces and place them about the room. We would need to find ventilation, but it might work."

"And if we find other believers, we can invite them up," Judd said.

Judd and the others were exhausted by evening. They had set up a heating center in the large meeting room downstairs. The room allowed four hundred occupants, but Jamal had knocked out a wall to an adjoining room so that everyone in the building could stay warm.

Judd ate soup and watched the evening newscast. He could tell the Global Community was scrambling, and he loved it. A newscaster recapped the story and announced that a special panel would comment about the situation the following day. The panel members included famed botanist, Chaim Rosenzweig.

"That's the guy Buck, Tsion, and Chloe stayed with," Lionel said. "He's not a believer, is he?"

Jamal shook his head. "I don't think so."

"You think he'll follow the GC party line?" Judd said.

"Rosenzweig is asked to comment about everything in Israel," Jamal said. "When the disappearances occurred, he agreed with one theory the GC gave. He'll probably agree with them again."

Vicki walked outside to look at the setting sun. The gray sky hung like a blanket over the countryside. Vicki thought it looked like snow, but she knew this was nothing that could be explained by weather patterns. This was God at work.

Vicki shivered in the cold and said a prayer. She thanked God for providing them with a place to stay and enough food to keep them going. She prayed especially for Melinda, Janie, and Charlie—that their eyes would be opened to the truth. Then her thoughts turned toward Judd. She hadn't heard from him in days. She had hoped he would be on his way home, but that would be impossible now. Wherever Judd, Lionel, and Mr. Stein were, they would be stuck there until this judgment was over.

Conrad came outside and shoved his hands into his pockets. "The news is almost on. Thought you'd want to see what the GC has been advertising all day."

Vicki nodded. As they moved toward the house, Conrad stopped her. "I really respect what you've done. You've taken a lot on your shoulders. I'll do everything I can to help."

"That means a lot," Vicki said.

Janie shivered when Vicki walked in. "Close the door!"

Vicki ignored her and went to the meeting room. It was the warmest room in the house, and it felt ice-cold. Mark had made a fire in the fireplace, and most of the kids were bundled in blankets.

The program began with introductions of the various guests. Some were scientists or representatives of the Global Community, while others were authors or even entertainers.

"I don't get it," Shelly said when they introduced one guest. "She's not an astronomer—she's a singer!"

"Every time the GC wants people to buy what they're saying," Mark said, "they make it a popularity contest. As if that's what makes something true."

The host introduced Chaim Rosenzweig. The news anchor listed his many achievements, including his winning the Nobel Prize and being personal friends with His Excellency, Nicolae Carpathia.

"I wonder how many people are watching this," Darrion said.

"It's the only game in town," Conrad said. "The GC has this on every channel and all over the Net."

Melinda, Charlie, and Janie sat close to the computer screen. Vicki wondered about people who didn't know the truth. With the disappearances, the earthquake, the meteor, and poisoned water, they had to be terrified. This program was their best hope for real answers. Vicki cringed when she saw the guests.

Each participant praised the Global Community for their work and promised this was a minor, temporary condition. A woman from Global Community Power and Light said, "As alarming as the darkness is, we agree it will have a very small impact on our quality of life. The problem should correct itself in a matter of days."

When Chaim spoke, Vicki sensed something different. He made the host squirm with his first response. When he had everyone's attention he said, "I am not a religious man. A Jew by birth, of course, and proud of it. But to me it's a nationality, not a faith."

Dr. Rosenzweig talked of his former student Tsion

Ben-Judah. Vicki's heart sank when Chaim referred to Tsion's belief in Jesus as "madness." When the host tried to interrupt him, Dr. Rosenzweig said, "I have earned the right to another minute or so.

"Ben-Judah was ridiculed for his belief that scriptural prophecy would actually happen. He said an earthquake would come. It came. He said hail and rain and fire would scorch the plants. They did. He said things would fall from the sky, poisoning water, killing people, sinking ships. They fell.

"He said the sun and the moon and the stars would be stricken and that the world would be one-third darker. Well, I am finished. I don't know what to make of it except that I feel a bigger fool every day. And let me just add, I want to know what Dr. Tsion Ben-Judah says is coming next! Don't you?"

Dr. Rosenzweig quickly gave the address of Tsion's Web site. The camera panned back to the host, who was speechless.

"Go ahead now," Chaim said. "Pull the plug on me."

"I don't believe it," Conrad said. "He just gave Tsion the best publicity he's ever had!"

Vicki watched Melinda, Janie, and Charlie carefully. While the other kids cheered, they stared at the screen.

Judd couldn't believe Dr. Rosenzweig had mentioned Tsion's Web site. Though the man wasn't a believer, he had caught the Global Community off guard. Judd wondered if Chaim would suffer for his statements, or if the host of the program would be punished for not cutting Chaim off.

Judd quickly logged on and watched the number of people accessing the site swell. Lionel said, "This is the biggest Web site in the world as it is. Now he's going to get ten times the hits."

Over the next few days, people around the world tried to adjust to the cold. Many believed the GC reports that it would last about a week. But the longer the cold continued, the more things shut down. News reports from remote areas became scarce because of the energy crisis. People who had lived near the equator all their lives died from the sudden blast of arctic air. In Israel, snow fell. The only ones who didn't seem to notice the cold were Eli and Moishe. They stood in their bare feet and preached, unaffected by the temperature change.

Jamal kept a pot of boiling water going at all times. The steam helped heat the apartment. Jamal's wife had hot cups of tea and coffee to keep people warm. Because of the power shortage, they had to cut down on their computer usage.

"Will any believers die from this?" Lionel asked one day.

Jamal shrugged. "I wish I could ask Tsion all of my questions."

With the cramped quarters, Judd found himself spending more and more time with Nada. She was easy to talk with and interesting. Judd shared some of the things he had learned from Bruce and told her the stories of the Young Tribulation Force.

"Do you think I could be a member of your group?" Nada said.

Judd smiled. "I think the only requirements are that you're ready to go anywhere and do anything that God asks you to do."

Later that day, Lionel asked to talk with Judd in private. They moved to the corner of a room.

"Nada wants to know if she can be a member of the Young Trib Force," Judd said.

Lionel looked away. "That's what I want to talk to you about. Do you think it's a good idea to get close to someone like this?"

"Close?" Judd said. "Just because two people talk doesn't mean—"

"It just seems like there's more going on than that," Lionel said.

"You're crazy," Judd said. "We're just friends."

"If I'm wrong, I'll admit it," Lionel said, "but why don't you ask her?"

"I don't want to talk about it," Judd said.

The phone rang. It was Samuel. He sounded tired and scared.

"Where are you?" Judd asked.

"I finally talked with my father," Samuel said. "I followed your advice. I mentioned the possibility that Dr. Ben-Judah could be right and that we should read his Web site."

"What did your father say?" Judd said.

"He got very angry and accused me of being a traitor. I think he suspects I helped in your escape."

Judd quickly told Samuel's story to Jamal and the others.

"Tell him he can come here," Jamal said.

Judd relayed the message through the increasing static on the phone. "If your dad throws you out or you don't think you can live there anymore, we have a place for you."

Samuel thanked Judd. "I want to give it one more try. I will call you tomorrow and let you know what happened."

24

WHEN Samuel didn't call the next day, Judd got worried. "We need to check on him."

Lionel didn't like the idea. "What if it's a trap?"

"We can't abandon him," Judd said.

"But if we go, they might be waiting for us," Lionel said.

"I'll go," Nada said. "They won't expect a girl."

"No way your dad will go for it," Judd said.

"We don't have to tell him."

Lionel shook his head. "Sounds too risky."

Nada looked at Judd. "You said a member of the Young Trib Force needs to be ready to do anything and go anywhere God wants. I'm ready."

Jamal walked into the room, and Judd took Nada aside. "Lionel thinks there's something going on between you and me. I told him we were just friends."

Nada looked away, then turned to Judd and smiled.

"Your friend has quite an imagination. It has been a long time since I have had someone my own age to talk with. If I gave the wrong impression, I'm sorry."

"Now, about you going to see Samuel—"

Nada waved him off. "It's settled. I'm going."

Before the change in the weather, Vicki had hoped to make the school a training ground for the Young Trib Force. But when the sun, moon, and stars went dark, Vicki just wanted to keep all the believers and Melinda, Charlie, and Janie warm and alive. When she postponed classes again, the kids understood, but were unhappy. They knew they couldn't learn much with the frigid temperatures. But Janie had clapped when she heard the news. "I didn't want to learn that stuff anyway," she said.

The kids watched news reports from different parts of the world. The Midwest looked like Alaska in the dead of winter. The first casualties in Chicago were at the zoos. Both the Lincoln Park Zoo and Brookfield Zoo reported all animals dead except penguins and polar bears. But things got worse. Chicago, New York, and Los Angeles estimated that hundreds of homeless people had frozen to death in the first week. Before the disappearances, many of the shelters had been staffed by Christians. Those people were gone now.

Popular resorts along warm beaches closed. Ice formed along the shoreline. As the icy weather took its toll, the Global Community was forced to change its predictions about how long the cold spell would last.

Forecasts of a few days turned into a few weeks, and
Global Community spokespersons turned the blame
on Rabbi Ben-Judah and his followers. Peter the Second
called the preaching of Eli and Moishe "black magic."
Within a few weeks the estimates of deaths related to the
weird weather was in the hundreds of thousands.

Nicolae Carpathia finally appeared before the world
in a bare television studio in New Babylon. The kids
watched, huddled together, as Carpathia clapped his
mittens and praised the loyalty and courage of each
citizen.

"I come to you at this hour to announce my plan to
personally visit the two preachers at the Wailing Wall,"
Carpathia said. "They must be forced to admit they are
behind this assault on our new way of life."

"I can't believe he's actually going to face them,"
Shelly said.

"At least he admits they have power," Mark said.

Carpathia said he would bargain with Eli and Moishe
in hopes of ending this latest affliction. "I shall make
this pilgrimage tomorrow, and it will be carried live. Take
heart, my beloved ones. I believe the end of this nightmare is in sight."

Judd knew Jamal would be enraged if he heard of Nada's
plan to visit Samuel. He fought with Lionel about what
to do. If he drove Nada like she had asked him, Jamal
would be upset. If he told Jamal of the plan, Nada would
never forgive him. Finally, his commitment to Nada won

out. They made plans to secretly take Jamal's car the next afternoon as the world watched Nicolae Carpathia face Eli and Moishe.

Judd hadn't ventured out of the apartment building since the judgment had begun. He was shocked at what he saw. The wind swept along in a howling blizzard. No one was on the street.

Jamal's car was kept in the bowels of the garage in an area sheltered from the cold. It took Judd a half hour to get it started. "If this thing stops on us, we're in serious trouble."

Even with three layers of clothes on, Judd was so cold he could hardly make it back inside to get Nada and return to the car. Snow blew through the garage and piled up in the corner. Breathing was difficult in the extreme cold. Judd felt his nostrils freezing, and he had to shield his eyes from the icy wind. "We can still turn back," Judd said as he got in the car. "Your dad will never know."

Nada got in and wrapped her arms around her knees. "Just drive."

Vicki and the others were up early to watch the coverage of Nicolae Carpathia on the Net. Conrad, who had been obsessed with opening the safe, reported that running the generator twenty-four hours a day had used up more gasoline than they had planned. "I think we should turn it off during the day and keep it going at night."

Vicki ran the idea past Mark.

"We can burn wood during the day and use the generator to heat the schoolhouse at night," Mark said. "I'm for it."

Conrad switched the computer to battery power. The Global Community announcers explained that Nicolae Carpathia was in Israel, ready to bargain with the two witnesses. A message popped up on the computer that the battery was going dead.

"Already?" Mark said.

"I don't want to miss any of this," Conrad said. "I'll start the generator again."

The kids watched Carpathia approach the fence where the witnesses sat. The announcers fell silent.

"I bring you cordial greetings from the Global Community," Carpathia said, speaking to Eli and Moishe. "I assume, because of your powers, that you knew I was coming."

As Moishe began to answer, an e-mail message popped up on the screen.

"Great timing," Janie said sarcastically.

Darrion moved closer. "Looks like it's from that GC guy, Carl."

"Get out of the way; I want to see this," Janie said.

Suddenly the computer went blank. The kids groaned in unison.

"Battery's dead," Mark said.

"Did you see the message?" Vicki said.

Mark shook his head. "I'll go see what's keeping Conrad—"

Conrad stood in the doorway, his face ashen. "The

generator won't work now. Gas line must have immediately frozen when I turned it off a few minutes ago."

"We're dead," Janie said.

———————————

Lionel promised Judd and Nada he would cover for them. When Jamal asked about them, Lionel pretended he didn't hear and turned up the volume on the television. Nicolae Carpathia went back and forth with the witnesses, who seemed not to want to let the potentate get the upper hand.

"I am seeking your help as men who claim to speak for God," Carpathia said. "If this is of God, then I plead with you to help me come to some arrangement, an agreement, a compromise, if you will."

"Your quarrel is not with us."

"Well, all right, I understand that, but if you have access to him—"

"Your quarrel is not w—"

"I appreciate that point! I am asking—"

Moishe's voice blared through the speakers. "You would dare wag your tongue at the chosen ones of almighty God?"

"I apologize. I—"

"You who boasted that we would die before the due time?"

"Granted, I concede that I—"

"You who denies the one true God, the God of Abraham, Isaac, and Jacob?"

Carpathia sputtered something about tolerance.

Moishe countered with, "There is one God and one medi-ator between God and man, the man Christ Jesus."

A few minutes later the witnesses repeated, "Your quarrel is not with us," and turned away from Carpathia.

Nicolae looked confused. "So, that is it, then? Before the eyes of the world, you refuse to talk? All I get is that my quarrel is not with you? With whom, then, is it? All right, fine!"

"What do you think he'll do now?" Lionel said.

"Watch," Jamal said.

Carpathia moved close to the main camera and spoke precisely, his face clearly freezing in the cold. Lionel thought he looked desperate.

"Upon further review," Carpathia said, "the death of the Global Community guard at the Meeting of the Witnesses was not the responsibility of any of the witnesses. The man killed by GC troops at the airport was not a terrorist. As of this moment, no one who agrees with Dr. Ben-Judah and his teachings is consid-ered a fugitive or an enemy of the Global Community. All citizens are equally free to travel and live their lives in a spirit of liberty.

"I do not know with whom I am or should be talking, but I stand willing to do whatever it takes to end this plague of darkness."

The camera followed Carpathia as he turned on his heel, sarcastically saluted the two witnesses, and reboard-ed the motor coach. Before the news anchors could speak, the witnesses said together, "Woe, woe, woe unto all who fail to look up and lift up your heads!"

Judd drove by Samuel's house. He kept moving another block and turned into an alley. "Before you go, tell me what you're going to do."

"I'm going to see if he's okay. If he's not, I'll bring him here."

"Just like that?"

"Just like that."

Nada opened the door to get out, and a blast of cold air hit Judd in the face. It took his breath away. Nada quickly closed the door again, took a deep breath, and then finally got out. Judd watched her run from the car, her hand over her face. She was either the bravest girl he knew or the most foolish.

Nada made it to the house and went straight to the front door. Judd couldn't imagine what she would say or do. If Mr. Goldberg was there . . .

The door opened. Judd stretched to see who it was. Suddenly, a hand grabbed Nada's arm and pulled her inside.

Vicki knew they were in trouble. Until now the cold had made life difficult. Some of the food had frozen. It was difficult sleeping when you could see your breath. But now their source of power was gone and, with it, their best source of heat.

Vicki sent the kids into emergency mode. While Conrad and Mark worked desperately at the generator, Vicki and the others brought in more firewood and stacked it in the meeting room. The kids moved their mattresses and sleeping bags into the room. Janie complained and blamed Conrad for their problems, but Vicki told her to keep quiet.

Shelly returned from the storage area, her teeth chattering. She held up three bottles of water, all frozen solid.

"Put them by the fire," Vicki said. "We'll ration the water until we can thaw some more."

Conrad and Mark came back. Conrad volunteered to keep the fire going all night.

"I don't know if I trust him," Janie said. "You see what he did to the generator!"

"I've had enough out of you," Mark yelled. "If you think you can survive without us—"

Vicki held up a hand. "Settle down. Let's just see if we can make it through tonight."

Vicki and a few others held hands and prayed before they went to sleep that night. "God, you were able to stop the lions from eating Daniel," Mark prayed. "You saved Noah from the water that flooded the world. Now we're asking for another miracle. Help us figure out a way to keep warm during this judgment."

When they finished praying, Melinda scooted her sleeping bag next to Vicki.

"Are we going to die?" Melinda whispered.

25

JUDD'S first instinct was to jump from the car and run to the Goldberg house, but Nada had been pulled inside so quickly that he had no chance to rescue her. He ran his hand through his hair. The gas gauge read almost empty.

Judd left the car running and raced toward Samuel's house. Icy wind whipped at his face. He had lived in Chicago all his life, but Judd had never felt such biting cold. He peeked in the window, but the drapes were closed.

Judd circled the house. He found the secret entrance he and Lionel had used to escape through a few weeks earlier, but it was nailed shut. He kept moving, rubbing his arms to stay warm. At the back of the house Judd climbed onto the wooden porch and stood on a railing to reach the bare kitchen window. He took a minute to rub a small spot in the ice so he could look inside.

Shadows in the living room, beyond the kitchen.

Someone yelled. If Mr. Goldberg had pulled Nada inside, they were in deep trouble.

Judd was surprised to find the window unlocked. Carefully he pushed it open.

"You are with them, aren't you, young lady?" a man yelled. Judd recognized the voice. It was Mr. Goldberg.

"I was worried about your son," Nada said. "Now that I know he is all right, I will go."

"Sit down!" the man screamed. "You're not going anywhere."

Judd pulled himself inside, careful not to make noise.

He closed the window quietly and walked toward the living room. Mr. Goldberg shoved Nada into a chair. "How do you know my son?"

Nada looked away.

The man raised a hand. Samuel shouted, "Stop!" making his father turn. "Don't hurt her," Samuel said, stepping between them. "I was supposed to call her house to say I was all right. You wouldn't let me outside."

"What are you saying? Why would you have to go outside—"

"I've been trying to tell you for days," Samuel interrupted. "I helped Judd and the other boy escape. They showed me the truth about God."

Mr. Goldberg stepped back. "Traitor," he muttered.

"I couldn't call them from here or you'd trace it," Samuel said. "What they've said about Jesus is true. He is the Messiah. I've wanted to tell you so badly—"

"Enough," his father said.

"I have the mark of the believer now—"

"Be quiet!" Mr. Goldberg slammed his fist into a lamp and knocked it to the floor. "You're the same as Ben-Judah."

"Listen to me," Samuel pleaded. "Rabbi Ben-Judah is right. This weather phenomenon was predicted in the Bible thousands of years ago. At least let me explain it."

"The only thing I want from you is the location of the hiding place of those two."

Samuel shook his head. "I cannot betray my friends."

Mr. Goldberg turned to Nada. "Unless . . ." He leaned close.

"Father, no!"

"Perhaps *you* know where they are."

Nada glanced past the man into the shadows. Judd put a finger to his lips.

Mr. Goldberg picked up a telephone. "We'll see how quiet you will stay when we have you at headquarters."

Lionel Washington worried about Judd and Nada. Nada's father, Jamal, had watched Nicolae Carpathia's news conference intently. Now he paced the floor, asking questions. Each time Jamal asked about Nada and Judd, Lionel changed the subject.

"Do you think Carpathia means what he said about people who agree with Dr. Ben-Judah?" Lionel said.

"Carpathia will do whatever it takes to stop these plagues," Jamal said, "just like Pharaoh in the Old Testament."

"But if this is true, we can go home," Lionel said. "And Judd and Nada—"

"What?" Jamal said.

Lionel pressed his lips together and rolled his eyes.

Jamal gritted his teeth. "Where are they?"

Lionel shook his head, angry with himself. "That kid . . . Samuel . . . he was going to talk with his dad about God. He didn't call us. Judd thought something might have happened. He and Nada—"

"How foolish! I told Judd to stay away from my daughter."

Lionel nodded. "Judd tried to make her stay, but she wouldn't listen."

Jamal grabbed his coat and gloves from the closet and explained to his wife what had happened. She put a hand over her mouth.

"Carpathia says we're free to travel and that no one's a fugitive," Lionel said, "so we don't have anything to worry about."

Jamal glared at him. "If I get my daughter back, you and your friend may leave."

Jamal slammed the door. Lionel grabbed a coat and followed, calling after him, "They took your car!"

"I have another."

"Let me go with you."

"You've caused enough trouble!"

Lionel raced down the stairs behind Jamal. When they made it to the garage, both were out of breath. Lionel helped remove a tarp from the car. The plastic was so cold it snapped.

Jamal tried to start the car but the battery was dead. He dug around in the garage and installed another battery. The car sputtered and coughed, then finally came to life.

"I have to come with you," Lionel said. "You have no idea where Samuel lives."

"Your daring does not impress me. It is my job to keep my daughter safe."

Lionel lowered his voice. "I don't mean any disrespect, sir, but your daughter has a mind of her own. I know what happened to Kasim, and I'm sorry—"

"What does my son have to do with this?"

Lionel shook his head. "Maybe nothing. But maybe you're so scared of losing your other child—"

"I trust God with my family every day," Jamal said. "We risk our lives to protect his servants. We must not take needless chances."

"But just because a person is young," Lionel said, "doesn't mean God can't use him or that his ideas are too dangerous. God wants to use everybody who believes in him."

"Just tell me where this Samuel lives," Jamal said.

"Only if you let me go with you."

Jamal shook his head.

"Come on," Lionel said. "We both want them back. I can help. I'll show you exactly where they went."

Jamal frowned. "No matter what happens, you will leave my home when this is over."

Vicki and the other kids at the old schoolhouse were freezing. She believed that those with the mark of the believer would not die from this act of God. The others, who didn't have the mark—Janie, Melinda, and Charlie— looked as cold as she was and stayed as close to the fire as they could.

Melinda's lips were blue and she trembled. She asked again, "Are we going to die?"

"I hope not," Vicki said, "but I don't know."

"For somebody who says they know the future, you're not much help."

"We don't know everything that's going to happen," Vicki said, "just what God wants us to know." Vicki put an arm around Melinda. "You don't have to be scared. You can know what's going to happen to you after you die."

"I want to know what's going to happen to me now," Melinda said, "and I want to get warm. Is that asking too much?"

Janie and Charlie scuffled near the fire. They both wanted Phoenix to sleep beside them. Mark separated them and placed Phoenix between them. "Now you see why we asked you to carry all that firewood."

Janie cursed. Mark looked over at Vicki.

"Just leave her alone," Vicki said.

The wind howled through the walls. The generator was dead, so only the fire lit the room.

"We're going to do everything we can to stay alive," Vicki said, "but if you're afraid of dying, why not give your life to God and take care of it forever?"

Melinda pulled the cover up to her chin. "If God gets me out of this, maybe I will."

"Why wait?" Vicki said.

"I'd feel like I was cheating, you know, praying just because I'm in trouble."

"God doesn't care what gets your attention," Vicki said. "All these things—the earthquake, the cold—they're to get to you."

"They've done that."

"Good. Just ask God to forgive you and help you."

Melinda put her head back. "I'm too cold. I can't think." She grew pale. Vicki asked Conrad to help her pull Melinda closer to the fire.

"Just let me sleep," Melinda groaned.

"No way," Vicki said. "Go to sleep when you're this cold and you're dead."

"Fine," Melinda said.

Vicki patted Melinda's face and propped her against the brick fireplace. Conrad gave Melinda one of his blankets.

Vicki prayed silently. *Please don't let her die.*

As Mr. Goldberg dialed the GC, Judd darted into the room and unplugged the phone.

"You!" the man said.

Judd looked at Samuel and Nada. "You okay?" They nodded. He turned to Mr. Goldberg. "Before you call anyone, listen to your son."

The man raised his eyebrows. "You want *me* to listen?"

"He had the chance to run, but he decided to come back for one more try. He deserves to be heard."

Judd was stunned when Mr. Goldberg sat and said, "Fine." This was too easy.

Samuel looked shocked, but he quickly stood and began. "At the stadium, the final night of the Meeting of the Witnesses, I told you I went to catch the Ben-Judah-ites. That wasn't true. I wanted to know more about God.

"What happened amazed me. People were going forward, falling on their faces. I wanted to go too, but I was scared. I was afraid of what you would say."

"You should have been," his father said.

"When I saw my friends afterward," Samuel said, pointing to Judd, "I knew they would be in trouble. I thought I could save them."

"They are enemies of the Global Community!"

"The more we talked and the more I thought about what the rabbi had said, the more sense it made."

"Nothing that man says makes sense," Mr. Goldberg said. "He is against our leader, the one man who has a plan for this world."

Samuel sat down and put his elbows on his knees. "Father, I know now that there is a God and that he loves me. He loves you. He died for us."

"You say this of a god who would take your mother? A god who would allow millions to disappear and millions of others to die in the earthquake and the war?"

"My friends say there are worse things to come," Samuel said, "but this is God's way of calling us."

Mr. Goldberg smirked. "You have peculiar friends. Nicolae Carpathia is my god."

Samuel fell to his knees. "I don't want to disappoint you or disobey you. But I beg you to consider that this may be the truth. On my forehead is the mark of the sealed believer."

"Son, I see nothing on your forehead."

"You cannot see it because you are not one of us."

"Oh, I get it. You have an exclusive club where only the members can detect other members. That would be brilliant if it were true. What does this mark look like?"

Samuel looked at Judd. Judd shook his head. He didn't want anyone knowing the shape of the mark, especially a member of the Global Community.

As Samuel continued, Judd noticed a light blinking on Samuel's father's belt. Why hadn't the man pulled a gun or tried to call the GC again?

Nada jumped into the conversation. "I know all about the Global Community because my brother worked for the potentate."

"I don't care," Mr. Goldberg said. "You have information about the followers of Ben-Judah, and I want that information."

"I would never tell you," she said.

Judd knew something wasn't right. The man was too calm, almost like he was trying to keep the kids talking. A door slammed outside.

Mr. Goldberg smiled. "You didn't think unplugging my phone would keep me from signaling my superiors, did you?" He pulled back his coat to reveal a button.

"When I pressed this it was only a matter of time before they got here."

"You shouldn't have come," Samuel told Judd.

Someone pounded on the front door.

26

JUDD grabbed Nada and ran for the kitchen. Mr. Goldberg jumped in front of them and Judd blasted into him, sending them both to the floor. Judd tried to get up, but Mr. Goldberg pinned him down.

The front door splintered and a cold wind blew in. "Nada?" came a scream from outside.

"Father!" Nada yelled.

Nada ran to Jamal and hugged him.

"Leave!" Samuel yelled. "The GC will be here soon."

"Come with us," Nada said to Samuel.

Judd flipped over and lay atop Mr. Goldberg, struggling to hold him down.

"Just go, Samuel," Judd yelled. "I can't hold him much longer."

"What about you?" Nada yelled.

Jamal pulled Nada outside. Samuel paused in the doorway. "Father, I'm sorry. Please consider what I said."

Mr. Goldberg struggled under Judd. "I'll find you and the rest of them!"

Samuel disappeared, and their car pulled away. Judd let go and scrambled to the kitchen. He unlocked the back door and ran through the alley for the street where he had left Jamal's car.

Will it still be running?

A siren wailed a few blocks away. Judd slipped on the ice and crashed into a row of trash cans. A car pulled away from the curb on the other side of the street. Lionel was behind the wheel.

Judd jumped up and called to him, but Lionel sped away. Judd flailed and shouted, then stopped dead in his tracks. Two GC squad cars slid to a stop, barely missing him.

A man yelled, "Get your hands up!"

Vicki fought to keep Melinda awake and alive. Phoenix whimpered as Janie and Charlie still bickered over who would sleep next to him. Finally, Charlie gave up and let Janie pull Phoenix close. Janie said, "I read a book once where this guy was freezing to death and he used his dog to stay alive. Won't tell you what the guy did, but he had to kill the dog."

Throughout the night Vicki listened to the occasional groan from the kids, the crackling fire, and the whistling wind. At sundown, the wind had seemed to pick up and send the temperature plunging way below zero. Tonight it howled, as if a storm were brewing.

Branches from a nearby tree scratched at the window-pane.

Mark scooted close and asked about Melinda.
"I can't get her any nearer to the fire without burning her clothes," Vicki said.

"How long will this last?"

Vicki studied Melinda. "I don't think we can take much more and still keep them alive. This fire's all the heat we have."

Mark asked Vicki about Judd and Lionel, then brought up Carl Meninger's mysterious e-mail. Carl had known Mark's cousin John and wanted to meet with Mark. Others questioned whether Carl was a threat to the Young Tribulation Force.

"I have to see him and find out what's up," Mark said, "but I'll make sure we don't meet nearby—"

A thunderous crack interrupted Mark. Glass and snow flew about the room as a branch rammed through the window. Snow gushed in, dousing the fire instantly with a loud hiss.

The kids were plunged into total darkness.

Lionel hated the thought of leaving Judd, but Jamal had ordered him. Lionel waited as long as he could, but when he saw the lights of the GC squad car, he hit the accelerator and sped away.

Lionel had never driven a car alone. He had backed out of Judd's driveway a few times just for grins, but this was different. A wave of relief swept over him when he finally arrived at Jamal's house. When he had the car safely sheltered, he trudged upstairs.

Jamal scolded Nada, but she didn't back down. "What would you have done if a friend said they were going to call and didn't?" she said.

"Go," Jamal said, pointing to her room, "I don't want to hear it."

"You treat me like a child," Nada said.

"You act like one—I treat you like one."

"Sir, she was just trying to protect me," Samuel said.

Jamal stared at the boy. "I am glad you have become a true believer in Jesus, your Messiah. However, that does not excuse my daughter's disobedience."

Nada came into the room again, her hands clasped in front of her. "Father, you know how much I love you. I want to obey you, and I'll admit I made a mistake."

"It could have cost your life," Jamal said.

"Yes, but it is *my* life. I have to make decisions on my own."

Lionel paced the floor. "Let's focus on Judd right now, okay? What are they going to do with him?"

Samuel shrugged. "They'll take him to headquarters and question him."

"And he will lead them directly here," Jamal said.

Lionel sighed. "Judd won't do that."

"Don't you remember what the GC did to your friend Mr. Stein?" Jamal said. "They only let him go because they thought he was dead!"

"Wait," Lionel said, "what about the potentate's order? Won't they have to let him go?"

"What order?" Nada said, poking her head back into the room. "We didn't hear anything."

Lionel explained that Nicolae Carpathia had tried to bargain with the witnesses, Eli and Moishe, at the Wailing Wall. When the two witnesses stopped talking, Carpathia had cleared the Trib Force of any wrongdoing. "He also said nobody who agrees with the teachings of Dr. Ben-Judah is considered a fugitive or an enemy of the Global Community. Believers are supposed to be able to travel and do what any other citizen can do."

"That means they'll release Judd," Nada said.

"What the potentate says in front of the cameras and what happens in a Global Community jail cell are two different things," Jamal said.

"What if we reach him?" Nada said.

Lionel looked at Samuel. "Know anyone you can trust who works with your father?"

Samuel pursed his lips. "A lieutenant who knew my mother might—"

Jamal interrupted. "It is too great a risk. You will not make the call from here."

"What are we supposed to do?" Lionel said. "We have to let Judd know—"

"Pray that God will intervene," Jamal said.

Vicki yelled, "Is anyone hurt?"

"My leg's broken!" Janie screamed. But when the kids moved the branch, Janie only had a scratch.

Conrad found an old newspaper in the next room, lit

a match, and set the paper on fire. The wind blew it out. He stepped into the hallway and lit it again. "Grab anything that will keep you warm and follow me!" Conrad yelled.

Vicki helped Melinda to her feet. Flakes of ice clung to the girl's eyebrows, and she shivered violently.

Phoenix bounded away from Janie and down the stairs toward Conrad. "It's gonna be colder down there than it is up here!" Janie whined.

Mark helped Charlie to his feet, and they stumbled down the stairs. Vicki hated to admit it but Janie was right. As they moved farther underground, the temperature fell.

"Trust me," Conrad said.

Vicki was the last through the underground entrance. She closed the door. The icy wind no longer whipped at her clothes, but she could barely stand the freezing cold.

Conrad and Mark brought wood stored in the tunnel and piled it on the earthen floor. "If we can get a fire going, the wind won't be able to blow it out."

Janie picked an icicle off the side of a wall. "We're all going to wind up human Popsicles."

"Stop it," Vicki said.

"At least there aren't snakes and bugs," Shelly said.

Vicki bundled Melinda in blankets and rubbed the girl's arms and shoulders.

"I can't feel my feet," Melinda said.

Smoke filled the room when the fire started. The kids gasped for air. Conrad opened the entrance to the tunnel. "This will work as a flue."

Smoke floated through the opening, and the kids breathed easier. "It's going to take a while to warm up," Conrad said.

In the corner, Darrion and Shelly prayed softly. Janie cornered Phoenix again and dragged him as close to the fire as he would go.

While Mark stoked the fire, Conrad joined Vicki. "This is the only place I could think of. Any other spot in the house and we'd burn the place down."

Vicki nodded. "It was good thinking."

"I'm sorry about turning off the generator—"

"You were trying to conserve energy. It's not your fault."

"I keep thinking about Eli and Moishe. I wish we could have seen what happened. Do you think they killed Carpathia?"

Vicki shook her head. "It's not his time yet. Tsion says the witnesses will die before Nicolae. I just hope God puts a stop to this judgment soon."

Melinda moaned and complained about her feet. Vicki carefully pulled the covers back and helped take off her shoes and socks. The right foot was pale but looked okay. When Vicki took off Melinda's left shoe, she gasped. Three of her toes were turning a dark blue.

"That's frostbite," Conrad whispered.

———

Judd sat in an interrogation room at the Global Community precinct. Only a few officers were at their desks when he was brought in from the cold. He rubbed his wrists where the icy handcuffs had been. *At least the station is warm,* he thought.

Judd hoped Nada and the others had gotten away without being seen. He wondered whether the GC would track them down. He kicked himself for putting Nada in that situation and resolved that no matter what the GC did to him he would never tell them about Jamal's apartment building.

Judd's thoughts turned to the kids in Illinois. What would Vicki say about this? Judd figured she had the generator going and the schoolhouse warm. He smiled.

Without thinking, Judd began to pray. It was as natural as breathing. Just speak to God. He knew the Bible said believers should pray continually. That was something his mother had quoted when he was younger. He had laughed at her. He used to think it meant you had to be in a church service your entire life. Now he knew it meant just giving your thoughts and concerns to God.

Judd asked God to give him the right words to say to the GC. As he prayed, he wondered if God had placed him in the hands of the Global Community for a reason. His friend Pete had talked about God to a GC officer. It was a stretch, but there might be someone here who needed to hear the truth.

A man entered the interrogation room, then quickly retreated, leaving the door open. A nearby television showed a report about the two witnesses and Potentate Carpathia. Judd couldn't believe what Nicolae was saying about the Trib Force and the followers of Tsion Ben-Judah.

Mr. Goldberg entered with a tall man. Judd looked

down at the small wooden table and shifted in his seat. The tall man riffled through papers, then stared at Judd. When he spoke, Judd thought he recognized the voice, but he couldn't place it.

"I am Deputy Commander Woodruff," the man said, looking at Judd's fake papers. He read the information aloud and said, "Is that correct?"

Judd stared at the man.

"Are you a follower of Ben-Judah?"

"Have the things the rabbi predicted come true?" Judd said.

Deputy Commander Woodruff folded his arms.

"Even the brilliant Chaim Rosenzweig has said we should look to the rabbi for wisdom," Judd said, "so I guess the answer is yes."

Mr. Goldberg jumped from his chair. "You'll be sorry you talked that way!"

The deputy commander calmed Mr. Goldberg and turned to Judd. "We have reason to believe you know where Ben-Judah is hiding. If that is the case, we will get the information from you."

Judd leaned close and lowered his voice. "Why would you need to know the hiding place of someone who is not wanted by the Global Community?"

Woodruff frowned. Judd repeated what he had heard Nicolae Carpathia say on the news report. "I'd say you are in direct violation of an order given by the potentate himself. And if those two witnesses at the Wailing Wall hear you're holding someone simply because I agree with the rabbi, things are going to stay cold for a long time."

The two men stepped outside the room. "I didn't hear that the potentate had lifted—," Mr. Goldberg said as they closed the door. A few minutes later a guard escorted Judd back to his cell.

27

VICKI helped Melinda through the night. Mark had learned first aid in the militia and grabbed a pot from the kitchen to melt snow. When the water was warm, he soaked Melinda's foot and rubbed the darkened toes.

"Can't make this water too hot or it'll hurt her," Mark said.

When Melinda moaned, Vicki found aspirin in a bottle and gave her a drink. When morning came, Melinda's toes were blistered but she could move them slightly.

"Normal," Mark said. "The color looks better. We have to make sure they don't freeze again."

While Melinda, Charlie, and Janie huddled by the fire downstairs, the others headed upstairs. The kids removed the tree limb and nailed boards over the windows.

"That should keep the wind out," Conrad said.

While Darrion and Shelly built another fire upstairs, Conrad and Mark inspected the generator. Vicki found the canned food, but it was frozen. She placed several opened cans of soup directly on the fire. When the soup was warm, Vicki brought it downstairs. Janie complained but wolfed it down and asked for more.

Melinda wore four pairs of socks and shivered under several blankets. "What's going to happen to us?" she said.

Vicki patted her shoulder. "We'll take care of you."

Lionel and Samuel prayed for Samuel's father and Judd. Nada and the rest of her family remained behind closed doors. Late in the morning, Lionel heard a report from the Wailing Wall. The two witnesses, Eli and Moishe, had spoken out against the Global Community again.

"Woe to the leaders who make promises but do not do what they say," Eli wailed. "The eyes of the Lord watch over those who do right; his ears are open to their cries for help. But the Lord turns his face against those who do evil; he will erase their memory from the earth."

Moishe picked up the message. "This judgment shall not pass until those who are sealed are released from their bondage."

Vicki found Mark and Conrad working on the generator. The sun was out, but the light was weak and the temperature hadn't risen much. The two blew into cupped hands to stay warm.

Mark shook his head. "This line won't thaw anytime soon."

When they were back inside, Conrad asked about Melinda's foot.

"It blistered some more and she's in a lot of pain," Vicki said, "but I guess that's good."

Mark nodded. "If we can, let's get her back up here so—"

"Already done," Vicki said. "Charlie and Janie, too."

Vicki led them to the three, who were huddled close to the fire. Janie held tightly to Phoenix. The room flickered in the firelight.

"How much wood do we have left?" Vicki whispered.

"We've gone through it faster than I thought," Mark said. "If we stick with one fire, we might be able to keep this room warm for another week or so."

Judd's cell was chilly, but he wasn't affected by the cold like some of the other prisoners. They moaned and cried for more blankets. One man hadn't moved in hours. When guards carried him out on a stretcher, Judd realized he was dead.

On Friday evening Judd noticed a flurry of activity in the jail area. Several times a guard walked near Judd's cell to check on him. Finally, Judd was led to a room where Mr. Goldberg met him.

The man fidgeted with a pink piece of paper. "We have reviewed your file—"

"You have no reason to hold me," Judd interrupted.

"The potentate said followers of Rabbi Ben-Judah are free to move around."

"The deputy commander has spoken with New Babylon about the meaning of the potentate's statement."

"The meaning?" Judd said. "Seemed pretty clear to me. I've done nothing wrong."

Mr. Goldberg leaned close. "You have taken my son away from me. You brainwashed him with your religion. You are a dangerous young man."

Judd paused. Instead of hating the man, he felt pity. "My parents and my whole family were taken in the disappearances. Before that, my mom and dad tried to get me to go to church and listen to the same things your son believes. I wish I'd listened to them. I wish *you'd* listen. You don't have to be separated from your son or from God."

A guard opened the door and motioned for the man. Mr. Goldberg left. A half hour later, Judd was returned to his cell.

Later that night, Judd noticed an older, dark-skinned man in the next cell. The grizzled man scooted his cot close to the bars and said, "American?"

Judd was cautious but moved closer. "Yeah."

"I tell you something important. In return, you give me blanket."

"What could you possibly tell me that—"

"You get out soon," the man said. "Heard it from guard. But I tell you something else. First, blanket."

Judd folded a blanket and shoved it through the bars.

The old man wrapped it tightly around him. "When you leave before, guard came. Take coat from bed."

"They took my coat?" Judd said. "What would they want with—"

"They bring it back. Did something to it."

Judd felt his coat. Nothing was different. "What would they have done?"

The man shrugged. "Heard something else. You must be important person."

"Why?"

"New Babylon say you get released. Others like you."

Judd nodded and told the old man about Rabbi Ben-Judah. The man turned and pulled the covers over him when Judd explained the message of the gospel.

"No God," the man mumbled.

Judd tried again, but the man yelled and others nearby awoke. Judd thought about what the man had told him. If the GC had planted a tracking device somewhere in his coat, he would lead them straight to Jamal and the others. Later in the night, Judd woke the old man and proposed an even exchange: the old man's coat for Judd's. "All you have to do is keep quiet about the coat for a few hours."

The man handed him an old coat about the same color as Judd's. Judd wrapped it around his shoulders and fell asleep.

The next morning keys jangled Judd awake. He could see his breath in the frosty jail. A guard opened the door and motioned Judd outside.

Judd stood up. "What's going on?"

"Bring your coat," the guard said. "You're free to go."

The guard led Judd to the front of the station, where he signed for his wallet and fake ID. Judd shoved them into a pocket.

Judd looked around for Mr. Goldberg or the deputy commander. Neither was in sight. Outside the station he quickly pulled out his ID and money and threw the wallet in a nearby trash can. If there was a transmitter in his coat, they might have planted one in his wallet as well.

Judd ran a few blocks until he came to a familiar street name. He was at least an hour's walk from Jamal's apartment building. He passed several bodies of those who had frozen to death.

Judd ducked into a crowded coffee shop and sat on a stool by the window. As he sipped a warm drink, he listened to the conversations around him. People spoke of the cold and the two crazy men here in Jerusalem. A few minutes later, as Judd suspected, GC squad cars raced past. He stood up and pushed his way to the front. Before he could get to the door, something stopped him in his tracks.

The sun.

At 10:30 A.M. Jerusalem time, the bright, yellow sun appeared. People who had been inside for weeks ran into the streets and lifted their faces toward the sky. Crowds blocked traffic, but no one seemed to mind. The earth had broken out of its icy spell.

A monitor inside the coffee shop showed a replay of the entire conversation between Nicolae and the two

witnesses. Commentators praised the work of the potentate. Judd smiled. He knew God had been looking out for
him and other believers.

Early Saturday morning, Vicki awoke and noticed something different. She stumbled to the kitchen. Brilliant
sunshine streamed through the windows. She let out a
whoop, and the other kids came running.

Mark and Conrad quickly got to work on the generator. The others helped pull food from the frozen storage
area. Melinda stayed inside with her foot still wrapped.
Color had returned to her toes, and Mark thought she
would be okay in a few days.

Vicki boiled drinking water and thawed enough food
for dinner. She wanted to resume classes on Monday and
had planned a worship service to celebrate the end of the
judgment.

Vicki noticed Janie was missing. She found her walking by the river. Vicki wanted to scold the girl or punish
her in some way but decided to let it go.

"I'm glad that's over," Janie said. "Feels like spring
again."

"It's not over," Vicki said.

"You mean it's going to get cold again?"

Vicki shook her head. "The judgments get worse and
worse. That's part of what we're learning in our classes.
See, God wants us to come to him now while there's—"

Janie patted Vicki on the shoulder and interrupted.
"Just wait. When the guys get the computer working, I'll

bet it shows Nicolae had something to do with getting things back on track."

Judd walked into the crowded streets and made his way toward Jamal's hiding place. He watched for any sign of a Global Community squad car. Once, a siren blared behind him and Judd darted into an alley. Later, he found they were headed to an accident scene.

Judd waited near Jamal's building until dusk, scanning the street for anyone suspicious. When he was sure no one was watching, he slipped into the underground garage and found the back entrance. He knocked on Jamal's door. Someone opened the peephole and closed it. A few seconds later, Lionel let Judd in.

"Man, it's good to see you," Lionel said, leading Judd to his room. Samuel greeted Judd.

Judd told them his story. Samuel quizzed him about his father.

"He seems closed to the truth, at least for now," Judd said.

"I've been praying for him ever since I received the mark of the believer," Samuel said. "I don't understand."

"It took you a while to come around," Judd said. "Maybe it's just going to take time."

Lionel took Judd aside and apologized for not waiting at Samuel's house. "I didn't have a choice. Jamal said I had to follow him closely or he wouldn't let me in the garage."

"What about Nada?"

"Basically he's keeping her locked up," Lionel said. "Samuel and I have been working with people in the building since the sun came out. We've been helping Jamal get them back into their apartments, but the guy is as cold as ice toward us."

"Doesn't he know it was Nada's idea to—"

"Doesn't matter," Lionel said. "He blames you for what happened. He said she could have been killed."

Judd shuddered. "It could have been a lot worse, but everything turned out okay."

Lionel pulled out a sealed envelope. "I don't think so. I haven't seen Nada since we got here. She slipped this note under my door last night. She said to make sure you got it when you returned."

Judd opened the envelope and scanned the note.

Judd,
Remember when you asked me if I had feelings for you? I said I didn't, but that wasn't the truth. Lionel was right. Since you came, my feelings for you have increased. I pray you see this note and that we will be able to talk soon. Don't let my father scare you. Please write me as soon as you can.
Love,
Nada

Judd handed the note to Lionel. Lionel read it and shook his head.

"Don't say it," Judd said.

"Man, I told you—"

Judd grabbed the note and stuck it in his pocket. "I don't need that right now."

The door opened and Jamal stepped in. His face was grim. "I have made a difficult decision. Your presence here is not good for my family. I will have to ask you to leave."

"Can't we talk about this?" Judd said.

Jamal held up a hand. "I have made my decision."

28

VICKI and the others were amazed by how fast the snow melted. The river rose just as quickly. Conrad sealed the outside entrance to the underground tunnel. Shelly asked if they should move to higher ground.

"It would have to rise another ten feet before we'd have to move," Mark said.

The generator finally began working late Saturday night. Mark checked their e-mail messages. There was nothing from Judd or Lionel, but he did find two messages from Carl Meninger. Mark opened the first, the one he had been reading when the computer had gone dead.

Carl wrote that he had been released from the hospital in South Carolina and was ready to visit Mark. "I'll take a military transport and get as close to Chicago as I can. Just give me the word."

Mark opened the second e-mail, which had been

written the night before. *I want to take a flight soon, but I haven't heard from you*, Carl wrote. *Are you still alive? Has something happened? Please contact me as soon as possible.* Carl included a phone number at the bottom of the e-mail.

Mark picked up the phone, but Conrad stopped him. "I still don't like this," Conrad said. "I know you want to hear about John, but this might be a GC trap."

"I told you I was going to be careful," Mark said. "I'll drive a cycle to meet him somewhere away from here. Maybe Indiana."

"I think it's a good idea," Vicki said. "If this guy Carl isn't on the level, Mark can find out and get away."

Mark dialed the number and asked for Carl. He went into the next room to talk and returned in a few minutes.

"Carl's not there," Mark said. "His roommate said he took a transport flight early this morning. He thought something had happened and wanted to find me."

"Just what we need," Conrad said, "the GC looking for our hideout."

"Did he say where he was headed?" Vicki said.

Mark shook his head. "It could take him a while and a few different planes to get close. One thing's for sure: he's not coming to Chicago."

"Why not?" Vicki said.

"There are reports of big-time radiation downtown," Mark said.

Vicki gasped. "Nuclear?"

Conrad scratched his head. "I don't remember Chicago getting hit with any nukes."

"Whether they did or didn't isn't the point," Mark said. "The GC and everybody else are staying as far away from it as they can." Mark typed a response on e-mail. "Carl's supposed to check this every day."

"What are you telling him?" Vicki said.

"As soon as he gets close, I'm on my way."

Judd, Lionel, and Samuel ate breakfast Sunday morning and waited.

Samuel talked about his father and the possibility of seeing him again. "I want you to call me Sam. It's what my friends call me."

Lionel brought Judd up to date on the warming center Jamal had set up downstairs. "A lot of those people seem interested in learning more," Lionel said, "but Jamal is cautious. He doesn't want to alert the GC."

Jamal's wife brought them food and gave Judd a pained look when he tried to talk with her.

"We don't have money," Judd said. "Where are we supposed to go?"

Jamal's wife shook her head but didn't speak.

Judd wrote a quick note to the kids in Illinois. He explained their situation, leaving out the part about Nada.

"What are we going to do when he kicks us out?" Lionel said.

"He can't kick us out," Judd said.

Sam said, "You have to understand how important family is to Jamal. You have offended him."

"But we're spiritual brothers," Judd said.

"True," Sam said, "and I'm new to this so I don't understand everything, but you have offended him. You have come between him and his daughter. That is not good."

Judd felt helpless. Since the disappearances he had been a take-charge person. When a problem came up, he solved it. Sometimes not the best way, but he acted. Now he was at the mercy of someone else. Someone who didn't trust him.

"You have to tell me," Lionel said when he got Judd alone. "Do you have feelings for Nada?"

Judd looked down. "I don't know. I mean, she's easy to talk to. I like her as a friend. She's got a heart for God—"

"And she's a knockout," Lionel added, "but that has nothing to do with it."

Judd blushed. "Jamal has been good to us. I can't go against him. Besides, I don't think this is the time to start a romance."

"Especially when there's someone waiting back in the States."

"What do you mean?" Judd said.

Lionel frowned. "You know exactly what and who I mean. Vicki."

"No way," Judd said. "We fight too much."

"You're different from her," Lionel said. "You're supposed to be."

Judd put a finger to his lips. Voices in the next room. The phone rang. Lots of activity.

"I've got a feeling we're moving," Lionel said. "And you'd better write a note to Nada."

Vicki and the others were up early Sunday morning. Mark packed food and a change of clothes and checked on the motorcycles. Only one worked since the freeze. The rest of the morning was spent preparing for the worship service. The kids didn't know many songs, but they typed up the ones they knew and put them on the computer screen.

They took turns reading verses from the Bible and telling what God was teaching them. Melinda and Charlie seemed to listen closely. Janie sighed a lot and stared out the window.

When it was Vicki's turn, she pulled up news coverage the kids hadn't seen. "I got up early to find out what happened with Nicolae and the witnesses. Carpathia made a deal and promised safety for those who believe the message of Tsion Ben-Judah."

"So it was Nicolae that made it happen," Janie said.

Vicki smiled. "He may have made a deal, but it was God who lifted the judgment from us."

Janie rolled her eyes.

Vicki pulled out a sheet of paper. "I found something interesting on Tsion's Web site this morning. It proves my point that we have a lot to learn from the Bible, but we also have to be students of what's happening around us. Tsion says the next judgment from God will be the most dramatic yet."

"How could it get more dramatic than a worldwide earthquake?" Darrion said.

"I'll read you what Tsion says," Vicki said. *"Because of*

the proven truth of Luke 21, I urge all, believers and unbelievers alike, to train your eyes on the skies. I believe this is the message from the two witnesses."

"I don't get it," Shelly said.

Vicki pulled up the computer video of the Meeting of the Witnesses. Tsion Ben-Judah cleared his throat and began. "This passage warns that once the earth has been darkened by a third, three terrible woes will follow. These are particularly ominous, so much so that they will be announced from heaven in advance."

Vicki moved the video forward and said, "We've just been through that judgment. Now Eli and Moishe come up from behind him and read the Scripture Tsion had picked out."

Vicki's voice caught when she saw the two prophets standing directly behind Tsion. It was like watching something from a biblical movie, only this was real.

Moishe recited the text without looking at a Bible. "'And I beheld, and heard an angel flying through the midst of heaven, saying with a loud voice, Woe, woe, woe, to the inhabiters of the earth by reason of the other voices of the trumpet of the three angels, which are yet to sound!'"

Vicki paused the clip.

"What does all that mean?" Melinda said.

"It means you don't want to wait another minute to make your decision about God," Shelly said. "This next thing that's coming is going to be awful."

"You're just trying to scare us," Janie said.

Melinda looked hard at Janie. "I don't think so. They've been right about everything so far."

Judd gave Sam the note and asked him to slip it under Nada's door when no one was looking. Sam returned, shaking his head. Jamal walked in behind him.

"Come with me," Jamal said.

"Do you want us to get our stuff together?" Lionel said.

Jamal turned. "Just follow me."

"Wait," Judd said. "Before we go I'd like to speak with your daughter."

Jamal stared at Judd.

"I know how you feel," Judd said, "but this might be my last chance to talk with her."

Jamal opened the door to Nada's room and called her. Nada walked out, her head down. "Two minutes," he said sternly.

Judd looked at Sam and Lionel. The two walked into the hallway.

"I got your note," Judd said.

"It was foolish of me," Nada said. "I should never—"

"It was sweet," Judd said. "You're so easy to talk to. It was like instant friendship between us."

"But you don't feel the same for me?" Nada said, finally looking at Judd. Nada had deep brown eyes and brown hair that touched her shoulders.

"I don't know how I feel, especially if your dad is making us go away," Judd said.

"I'll go with you," Nada said.

"We only have a minute," Judd said. "I just wanted to let you know I care about you. I'm not sure if this

goes deeper than friendship or not, or if this is the
time to—"

"You don't have to say anything more," Nada interrupted.

"Please," Judd said, "I want you as part of the Young
Trib Force no matter what happens."

"How can you hope to fight the Global Community
when you won't even stand up to my father?"

Judd rubbed his forehead. "Right now the best thing
for me to do is honor your father's wishes. Then, at some
point, I hope—"

"Go," Nada said. "Just go."

Nada turned and retreated to her room, crying.

Jamal took him by the arm and led him into the hall.
"You will have no further contact with her," he said.

Judd didn't argue. He followed the others to the small
car and got in the backseat. They stopped at a house that
looked familiar. When the front door opened, Judd realized it was the home of Yitzhak, the man who had first
helped them when they had arrived in Jerusalem. Yitzhak
warmly greeted them, hugged Sam tightly, and ushered
them into the dimly lit living room.

A bearded man sat in the shadows. His face seemed
to glow.

"It is good to see you," the man said.

"Mr. Stein?" Lionel said, moving closer.

"Yes, it is me," Mr. Stein said, and he hugged Judd
and Lionel. Judd introduced Sam and told Mr. Stein what
had happened with Sam's father.

Mr. Stein put a hand on Sam's shoulder. "We will be

your family now. Perhaps your father will come around.
We will leave that to God."

"Would you speak with him, sir?" Sam said.

"When the chance comes, I will speak with him."

Mr. Stein asked them to sit. "My time away was
incredible. Yitzhak and I were up until all hours of the
night studying, praying. I would wake up after only two
or three hours of sleep and be ready to go again."

Yitzhak laughed. "I wanted to give him sleeping pills."

"Were you affected by the cold?" Lionel said.

Mr. Stein smiled. "It was like living in a refrigerator,
but God kept our hearts warm. He has confirmed to me
that I am one of his witnesses. I believe I have been given
a special mission."

Judd looked at Yitzhak. Had Mr. Stein gone over the
edge? "What kind of mission?"

"In our cabin was a huge map of the world," Mr. Stein
said. "I was drawn to it. I kept looking at the different
countries, wondering what God was saying to me.

"I believe God has selected me to travel to a group
of people I have never heard of and have never seen."

"What?" Judd said.

"I prayed in front of that map every day. Sometimes
for hours. Last night I had a dream. I was floating toward
the ground. A huge desert stretched before me. And then
I saw a river and people, hundreds of them, thousands
who had no contact with the outside world.

"They wore strange clothing and talked in a language
I have never heard. I asked, 'Who are these people?'
I sensed I was being called to tell them the gospel."

"What country is it?" Lionel said.

Mr. Stein smiled. "I don't know. I can only surmise it is somewhere in Africa. I am leaving tomorrow."

"What?" Judd said. "How are you going to go if you don't know what country they're in? How will you talk without an interpreter? A trip like that could take weeks, even months."

Mr. Stein stroked his beard. "I gave my word to God that I would make myself available. If this is what he wants me to do, I know he will make the way clear to me."

"The GC took all your cash!" Judd said. "How will you—"

"I have some," Yitzhak said. "It should be enough to at least get you there."

"Wait," Judd said. "You need to plan this better."

"I do not know how much longer before the next judgment," Mr. Stein said. "I must go as soon as possible."

Jamal looked at Mr. Stein. "There is one other thing, correct?"

"Oh yes," Mr. Stein said. "In the vision I was not alone. There was someone beside me the whole time."

"Who?" Lionel said.

Mr. Stein turned. "It was you, Judd. I believe God wants you to come with me."

29

JUDD blinked. It was one thing for Mr. Stein to go off the deep end, but another to drag him along. "You want me to go?" Judd said.

Mr. Stein turned to Jamal. "I understand from Yitzhak that my friends have caused trouble in your home."

Jamal looked at the floor. "My daughter won't speak to me. My wife is upset. I am in a difficult position."

"If you will care for Lionel and Samuel while we are gone, I promise to take full responsibility when I return."

"And when would that be?" Jamal said.

Mr. Stein sighed. "I do not even know where I am going, much less when I will return. I suppose we could find another—"

"No," Jamal said, "leave them with me. Before we came here I heard about an important job. I think they can help." He put out his hand. "We will pray for your safety and that God will be glorified through this."

"Thank you," Mr. Stein said. He turned to Judd. "Are you willing to go?"

Judd closed his eyes and breathed a prayer. "If this is really what God wants you to do, and I'm supposed to be part of it, I'll go."

Judd slept at Yitzhak's home and awakened early the next day. Though Nicolae Carpathia had promised that believers in Christ could move about freely, they didn't want to take any chances. Mr. Stein had his photo taken, and a new fake passport was made for him.

Monday afternoon they pooled the money they needed and traveled to the airport. Yitzhak drove Mr. Stein and Judd and hugged them both.

"May you have great success!" Yitzhak shouted over the roar of a jet engine.

Judd and Mr. Stein waved and walked through the GC security.

Monday morning in Illinois, Vicki set up the room for the first day of classes since the judgment. Melinda hobbled into the room and put her foot on a chair. "Figured I'd get here early to get a good seat," Melinda said.

Conrad came into the room, shaking his head.

"What's up?" Vicki said.

"It's that safe I found in the bell tower," Conrad said. "I poured water in the lock and left it outside in the cold. Thought the freeze might bust it. Nothing. I've drilled a hole in the lock, tried to saw it off. It simply won't open."

"Forget the lock and work on the box," Melinda said.

"It's solid steel," Conrad said. "This thing was made more than a hundred years ago, and it was made to last."

Vicki counted heads as the others came into the room. "Where's Janie?"

"I saw her after breakfast," Shelly said. "Said she was going for a walk to meditate."

"Okay," Vicki said, "we'd better get started."

Vicki pulled together material from Tsion Ben-Judah's Web site. She also included much of the daytime teaching the kids had recorded from the Meeting of the Witnesses.

When lunchtime came, the kids took a break. Mark checked for a message from Carl but found none. While the others ate, he went outside. A few minutes later he returned out of breath and took Vicki aside. "Janie's not back, and I've looked all around the house and by the river."

"This is her choice," Vicki said. "I can't make her study with us. Besides, the class went better without her. Charlie and Melinda are actually paying attention."

"That's not the point," Mark said. "What if she wanders off and the GC find her?"

"We can't baby-sit her—"

"But she could lead them back here," Mark said. "You know she'd trade her freedom for a chance to watch some music videos."

Vicki stared out the window. She had known it would be a risk allowing Janie into the schoolhouse. She had hoped the girl would be a believer by now.

"I feel like this is my responsibility," Mark said. "I was the one who brought her here."

"You and Conrad look for her," Vicki said. "We'll do chores the rest of the afternoon."

"Maybe she's just on some rock, chanting to Nicolae," Mark said, "but I'd feel better if we found her."

Lionel was cautious around Jamal the next day. Finally he decided to talk with the man. When the two were alone, Lionel said, "I know you don't like what happened with Judd and Nada, but I have to know if that's going to affect us."

"I have no hard feelings for you personally," Jamal said. "If you become a father someday, perhaps you will understand."

After the conversation it seemed like a weight was lifted from the house. Nada came out of her room and talked. Jamal's wife appeared less upset, and the conversations seemed lighter.

Sam asked how to talk about God with others. Lionel showed him transcripts from Tsion's messages. Before long, Sam asked to set up a meeting with his father.

"Let's take it slowly right now," Lionel said.

"But Tsion says the next judgment could come at any time."

"I know," Lionel said, "but let's give your father time to cool off."

Monday afternoon, after Jamal had dropped off Judd's clothes at Yitzhak's house, Jamal took Lionel, Sam, and Nada to an empty warehouse on the outskirts of Jerusalem. "This is the important job I spoke about last night," he said. He put a finger to his lips and knocked on the door four times. There was a faint sound of a machine running inside. It stopped, but no one came to the door. Jamal led them inside. The metal door clanged shut behind them.

The room was nearly empty and eerily quiet. Jamal grabbed one end of a desk that sat in the middle of the room. Lionel and Sam took the other end, and they slid it toward the wall.

Jamal bent down and lifted what looked like a paperweight on the floor. Lionel gasped when a trapdoor opened. There was modern printing equipment, and a dozen workers were packing small boxes in the basement. The workers were of different nationalities, but all had the mark of the true believer.

Jamal hugged one of the men leading the operation. They talked in a different language. Lionel scanned the boxes. "Property of the Global Community" was printed on the side. Lionel looked in an open box and saw pamphlets. The stack was printed in weird characters, like Chinese. The next set of pamphlets was printed in Spanish. Another in French. Lionel had taken a semester of French and recognized words from the Bible.

"It's all stuff about God," Sam said, picking up a stack printed in Hebrew.

Jamal introduced the kids. "The material in this room will be sent around the world."

"How?" Lionel said.

"With the help of the Global Community," Jamal said.

"What?" Sam said. "They would never—"

"They don't know we're sending it," the leader explained. "These boxes all go to the airport. Some people on the inside sneak it onto the Condor 216."

Lionel's mouth opened wide. "You mean Carpathia's plane?"

"Christian literature is flooding the globe, and the potentate has no idea it's his own plane spreading it!" Jamal said.

Judd was amazed at the busy airport. The freezing temperatures had grounded most flights. Now, hundreds of people were trying to get out of Israel. Judd looked at the monitors for flights to the U.S. Many big cities like Chicago weren't listed.

"Which airline?" Judd asked Mr. Stein.

Mr. Stein looked at the row of ticket agents. "We need to find someone who can be used by God."

Judd shook his head. "We don't know where we're going or if we have enough money to get there. People back home would call me crazy if I did this."

"Yitzhak explained it this way," Mr. Stein said. "These are incredible days when we must have incredible faith in an incredible God. Since the Rapture, God is showing his miraculous ability in new ways. Don't underestimate the power and the love of the Almighty. He cares for the people we're going to."

"I believe that. I just wish we knew more."

"Faith means taking one step at a time," Mr. Stein

said. "If we knew the whole plan, we might trust in ourselves or become scared."

Mr. Stein had come a long way in a short time. It seemed only a few weeks ago that he had been so against his daughter, Chaya, and her belief in Jesus.

They chose a counter with only a few people in line. When it was their turn, the ticket agent smiled and asked if they needed to check baggage.

"We simply need two tickets," Mr. Stein said.

The agent entered their information. "Destination?"

"We're not sure."

"Excuse me?"

Mr. Stein smiled. "This is rather difficult to explain. But I think there's a desert nearby."

The agent stared. "You're kidding." She looked at Judd. "He's kidding, right?"

Judd shook his head. "He's serious."

"I know what the people look like, what they wear, and that—"

"Sir, we're very busy. Why don't you figure out where you need to go and then come back—"

"Africa," Mr. Stein said.

"Africa," the agent said. "That's a continent. I need a city."

Mr. Stein scratched his beard. "Is there someone who could help, a pilot or a manager?"

People lined up behind Judd. Some shoved suitcases forward with their feet and sighed. Someone said, "This guy is loony."

The ticket agent took a deep breath. "You said there

was a desert nearby? The biggest desert in Africa is the Sahara, so we're probably talking about northern Africa."

"Very good," Mr. Stein said. "Now we're getting somewhere."

"The Sahara is three million square miles, sir. We're not even close."

Judd spotted a man in uniform talking with a baggage handler. He had the mark of the believer on his forehead. "Perhaps that man could help us," Judd said.

The agent shook her head. "That's my boss; he's much too busy—"

"What's his name?" Mr. Stein said.

"Mr. Isaacs is in charge of all the daily—"

"Mr. Isaacs!" Mr. Stein yelled. "Please, come help us!"

There was more grumbling behind Judd as Mr. Isaacs slowly walked forward. He was stocky, in his late forties, and had a round face. He smiled when he saw that Judd and Mr. Stein were believers.

"Is there a problem, Vivian?" Mr. Isaacs said.

The agent spoke through clenched teeth. "These gentlemen want a ticket but don't know where they're going."

"Let me take them down here," Mr. Isaacs said, motioning Mr. Stein and Judd to an empty spot. The man hit a few computer keys, then shook hands with Judd and Mr. Stein. "How can I help?"

Mr. Stein explained his dream and their need to leave as soon as possible.

Mr. Isaacs studied the monitor. "We're definitely talking northern Africa. My guess is west of the Sahara." He pulled up an on-screen map and turned the monitor so

Judd and Mr. Stein could see. The man pointed to lines on the screen.

"This area is known as the 10/40 window. Many people who have not responded to the gospel live between ten and forty degrees latitude. Missionaries had broken through to the area before the Rapture, but there are still people who haven't heard."

"That is why God is sending me," Mr. Stein said.

"And others like you," Mr. Isaacs said. "We've had about a dozen witnesses looking for flights to remote areas in the last few days, but no one to this specific area. It's incredible what God is doing."

Mr. Stein described the people in his dream.

Mr. Isaacs nodded as he listened and pulled up a smaller map. "I've heard of nomads in this area taking their flocks wherever they can find food and water."

"How could they have survived the recent cold?" Mr. Stein said.

"Good question," Mr. Isaacs said. He punched in some data and pointed to a small dot in a country called Mali. "We can fly you into the capital, Bamako, but from there you'll have to find a way into the countryside. Maybe a chartered flight or a Land Rover could get you to those people."

Mr. Stein pulled out a wad of cash. The cost of the ticket was more than they had. "How much for two tickets?"

Mr. Isaacs smiled. "But you have come on the very day we're offering a discount. I'll make up the rest of the money."

"We couldn't let you—"

Mr. Isaacs leaned over the counter. "It is a privilege to be involved in some small way in God's work. Don't take this away from me."

Mr. Stein beamed and looked at Judd. "I told you our God would provide."

Judd shook his head. He couldn't believe it.

Mr. Stein took the tickets. His eyes filled with tears. "How can we ever thank you?"

"Thank God," Mr. Isaacs said. "He is the one who brought you to me, and he is the one who will lead you to the people who need to hear your message."

"Amen," Mr. Stein said.

30

CONRAD and Mark searched the woods for Janie. When Phoenix lost her trail, they headed toward town on the motorcycle.

Conrad knew it was dangerous anytime the kids got near other people. If the authorities knew the kids lived alone in the country, the GC social services would be after them. The fact that most of the kids believed the message of Tsion Ben-Judah and that they housed a wanted Morale Monitor and an escaped prisoner made Conrad feel queasy.

Mark stopped as they neared the town. Something in the road caught Conrad's eye. "That's a person!"

Mark hid the cycle in some brush. "They must have been trying to find firewood or food during the freeze."

Conrad shook his head. The sight and smell of the body in the road was awful. He counted five people and several animals alongside the road as they walked into town.

Conrad gave Janie's description to a mechanic at a gas station. The man shook his head but said he'd watch for her.

Conrad turned a corner onto the main street and saw Janie a block away, talking with a woman. Mark pulled him back quickly. A GC squad car passed on another street.

"We have to get to her before they do," Mark said.

Judd's plane left Israel Monday evening. He sat by a window and didn't notice any other believers on the flight. Mr. Stein sat in the middle and talked with an African man. When he brought up the subject of God, the man said he wasn't interested.

The plane landed after midnight in Bamako, Mali. Judd and Mr. Stein passed through the GC checkpoint and wandered into the terminal. Many people had used the airport for shelter during the cold. Clothes and personal belongings sat in piles in hallways.

"What now?" Judd said, feeling a little helpless.

Mr. Stein turned, put a hand on Judd's shoulder, and closed his eyes. "Father, you have led us this far and we thank you. Now we ask you to direct us to the people you want us to reach. We pray in Jesus' name and for his glory. Amen."

Judd looked around. People were staring at them. They moved to the baggage carousel.

"We will wait here," Mr. Stein said.

Judd stretched out on the floor. He was tired and hungry. *I wonder where we'll be this time tomorrow?*

Conrad raced to Janie and pulled her into a nearby alley. Mark kept watch for the GC. The woman with Janie stood near the street, crying. She was holding something under a blanket.

"What's the big idea?" Janie said.

"I can't believe you'd be this stupid!" Mark said.

"I had to get out for a little while," Janie said. "I needed a smoke like you wouldn't believe."

"You didn't see the GC?" Conrad said.

"They're here?" Janie said.

"A squad car just passed a block away before we got here," Conrad said. "Come back to the school."

"I can't leave her," Janie said, pointing toward the woman. The woman was pale and had long, stringy hair. Her ragged clothes hung on her, and the quilt she carried was filled with holes.

"Lenore," Janie said, "these are two of my friends I was telling you about."

"What?" Mark said. "You told her—"

"She needs a place to stay," Janie said.

"Are you nuts?" Mark said.

"I told her how nice you guys were," Janie said. "Other than the religious stuff, it's okay. Plus there's plenty of food."

"I don't believe this," Mark said.

The woman, sobbing still, put a hand on Mark's arm. "Please, let me come with you. We have nothing. My husband went to find food last week. . . ." Her voice trailed, and she put a hand to her face and wept.

"She found his body this morning," Janie whispered.

"What do you mean, *we?*" Mark said. "Is there somebody else with you?"

Conrad put a hand on Mark's arm and pointed to the edge of the quilt. Sticking out was a tiny, still hand.

"That's her baby," Janie said.

Conrad gasped. "Is it . . . is it dead?"

Lenore pulled the quilt back, showing the baby's face. It was a boy, his tiny hand holding tight to a button on his mother's shirt. Conrad moved closer and noticed the child's chest rising and falling.

Conrad sighed. "I thought he was dead."

"This is Tolan," Lenore said weakly. "He's all I have left."

"I'll help her," Mark said. "There must be some kind of shelter around here. You and Conrad get to the motorcycle."

Janie shook her head. "I'm not leaving her. I'm supposed to do unto others and all that, right? I mean, what if I don't help this lady and her baby dies? You think God would let me into heaven with that on my conscience?"

"It doesn't work that way," Conrad said. "God doesn't let you in because of the good things you do—"

"I don't care what you say," Janie said. "I'm not leaving her."

A car approached. Mark pulled the group behind a huge Dumpster. A GC squad car drove by slowly.

When it was gone, Lenore turned to them and whispered, "I won't be a bother. I promise to work for any food we eat. The place this girl told me about sounds wonderful. Please."

Mark pulled Conrad aside. "I don't think we have a choice."

"If we take her, we've opened ourselves up again."

"We have to chance it," Mark said. "If the GC pick Lenore up, she might say something about us. Or she could try and follow us. We can't leave her and the baby alone."

Conrad nodded. "Maybe Z can take her to a shelter on his next run through here."

Conrad went ahead of the group, watching for any sign of the GC squad car. When it was safe he motioned to the others. When they found the motorcycle, Lenore and the baby rode with Mark while Janie and Conrad walked.

"Our spiritual guide back at the prison said we're all God's children," Janie said. "Anything we do to another child of God will be repaid in the next life. If we don't do good, we come back as an ant or a snail."

Conrad scratched his head. "God did make all of us, but we aren't all his children."

"You don't think I'm God's child?" Janie said.

"God created you and loved you enough to die for you, but until you receive—"

"I can't believe you don't think I'm a child of God,"

Janie said. "And that woman and her baby aren't either? No wonder they call you people narrow-minded."

"What you believe is that we're all a part of God and that God rewards and punishes people simply by what they do."

"Yeah, so?"

"God's not like that. He wants to be our friend, but we sinned, and that separates us from God."

Janie interrupted Conrad several times before he gave up. The girl simply wouldn't listen to the truth.

Judd awoke early Tuesday morning with a pain in his neck. He was sore after sleeping against the wall all night.

Mr. Stein sat beside him. "I brought you a donut and some coffee. You like cream and sugar?"

Judd nodded and rubbed his eyes. The donut was stale and the coffee watery, but they still tasted good. He stretched and leaned back against the cold wall. The airport was quiet. A few baggage workers and flight crews walked the halls. Passengers waited for flights in the terminal. A businessman lugged a suitcase up a flight of stairs.

"So what's up?" Judd said.

Mr. Stein smiled. "The sun, for one. And we are both well. We can be thankful for that." Mr. Stein leaned against the wall and cradled his cup of coffee. "If you could have known me before, Judd, you would see what a miracle this is. I am the least likely candidate to be a messenger of God, and yet, here I am."

"But what are we supposed to do?" Judd said.

Mr. Stein closed his eyes. "The psalmist says, 'Wait patiently for the Lord. Be brave and courageous. Yes, wait patiently for the Lord.'

"I think that is the most difficult task we have as followers. Believe. Wait. Let God work in his own time. It must have been very difficult for my daughter to know the truth and still have to wait for me to understand it and believe it."

Judd thought of Chaya and how much she had prayed for her father. "I wish your daughter were here now."

Mr. Stein nodded. "She would be thrilled to see how God has changed my life. Just that I have memorized Scripture would make her laugh with glee."

Mr. Stein said he had read Scripture throughout the night and kept coming back to another passage in the Psalms: "'You will keep on guiding me with your counsel, leading me to a glorious destiny.' And at the end of the psalm he says, 'I will tell everyone about the wonderful things you do.' That is what I want to do more than anything, Judd. Tell people of the wonderful things God can do."

Judd sipped the coffee. He noticed a man in uniform near the baggage carousel watching them. "We have company."

Mr. Stein stood. When the man came closer, Judd saw that he was a pilot and had the mark of the believer.

Mr. Stein shook hands. "Good day to you, my brother."

"Welcome to Mali," the man said. "I am Immen. Did you fly from Jerusalem?"

"Yes," Mr. Stein said. "How did you know?"

"Come with me," Immen said.

"Why?" Judd said.

"God has a job for you," Immen said, "and he has sent me to take you to it."

Vicki was cranky the rest of the day. She barked at Charlie for messing up the food pantry. Mark and Conrad weren't back when it got dark, and she wondered if something was wrong. If they hadn't found Janie in the surrounding woods, they may have gone toward town. That meant possible contact with the GC.

She found an e-mail from Judd and shared it with the rest of the group during dinner. He was off with Mr. Stein to some unknown country. Judd wrote that he didn't know when he and Lionel would be back in the States and asked the kids to pray for Sam, a new friend, and for a "situation" he didn't go into.

"What do you think the other thing is?" Shelly said later as she and Vicki did the dishes.

"Knowing Judd, it's probably something dangerous," Vicki said.

Shelly smiled and looked down at the water.

"What?" Vicki said.

"You and Judd," Shelly said. "I can tell how you feel about him."

Vicki rolled her eyes. "Stop."

Shelly giggled, then put a hand on Vicki's shoulder. "Do you realize how long it's been since any of us has laughed?"

"Just don't make fun of me to get your kicks," Vicki said. "I don't have a thing for Judd."

"Sure," Shelly said.

Outside, a motorcycle revved. Vicki dropped the dishcloth and rushed out. She stared as Mark and an unfamiliar lady stepped off. When the motor died, she heard a baby cry.

Vicki didn't ask questions. Instead, she told Shelly to fix up a room downstairs. Darrion made dinner for their guest. Vicki told Charlie to come up with a crib.

"It's okay," the woman said, "he can sleep with me."

"I'll try anyway," Charlie said.

"Please," the woman said, "don't go to any trouble. I'm just glad to have a place to stay tonight."

"Do you have family?" Vicki said.

The woman began to explain but couldn't continue. She clutched the baby and sobbed.

"It's okay," Vicki said. "We'll get you something to eat and you can rest."

Mark explained what had happened in town. "We're ahead of Janie and Conrad by a few minutes."

Vicki nodded. "We have to figure out what to do with Janie."

31

JUDD and Mr. Stein followed the pilot through a security door and down a flight of stairs. As they walked onto the runway Judd said, "Where are you taking us?"

Immen stopped. "Are you not the two God has called?"

"We are," Mr. Stein said.

"Good, follow me."

The plane was small. Judd and Mr. Stein had very little room. When they were buckled, the pilot quickly went through the preflight procedure and was cleared by the tower.

The plane shook on takeoff, and Judd held on until his knuckles turned white. As they gained altitude, Immen put the plane on autopilot.

"I fly with one of the smaller airlines," Immen said. "I use this to travel home when the roads are impassable."

"How did you know we would be at the airport?" Mr. Stein said.

Immen smiled. "First, you must tell me why it is so urgent that you travel into such a dangerous area."

Mr. Stein shrugged. "We don't know where we're going, my brother. Or what we'll do when we get there. But God has called us." Mr. Stein told Immen about his dream and what he had seen.

Immen shook his head. "God is amazing. I had a dream as well last night. It was during a long flight. My first officer said I was talking in my sleep, but since he's not a believer, I didn't dare tell him what I saw."

"What was the dream?" Judd said.

"I was walking through a remote area, and I came over a sand dune and saw hundreds and thousands of people. I have seen them before from the airplane. They are nomads; they move about the country with their flocks and herds.

"In the dream, these people tried to speak with me. They looked frightened and excited. I was frustrated because I couldn't talk with them or understand them."

"What happened then?" Mr. Stein said.

"I was at the airport. I saw an older man with a beard and a younger man. 'Find them,' a voice said to me. I awoke from my dream sweating. It seemed so real."

"We are glad you followed instructions," Mr. Stein said.

The pilot followed a river through the parched land. Judd wondered how the freezing temperatures had affected the desert. A few hours later they landed on a private airstrip, where a friend of Immen's waited. The man greeted Judd and Mr. Stein. He spoke in an

African language to Immen, then opened the doors to his home.

"We'll rest here a few hours until sunset," Immen said.

Judd fell into bed and was asleep immediately. When he awoke, Immen's friend had prepared a meal. When they were finished, the man led them outside to his Land Rover.

"Take," the man said.

Mr. Stein hugged the man, and they were off. As they made their way across the rough roads and places where there were no roads, Immen explained. "Many people died from the effects of the cold. My friend told me where he thinks the tribe is staying."

"Do you know their dialect?" Judd said.

"A few words," Immen said. "No one knows their language completely. They have kept to themselves. A few years ago I heard that some of them left the tribe. A few even became Christians. But most remain isolated."

"How did you become a believer?" Judd said.

Immen smiled. "By listening to and reading Tsion Ben-Judah."

Immen drove the Land Rover into the night. Sometime after midnight, they bounced along a dry creek bed, then rose straight up over a sand dune. Immen stopped and pointed. "Down there."

Judd gasped. In the moonlight he saw hundreds of campfires. Tents filled the valley, and thousands of dark-skinned people lay sleeping. Goats and camels were tied up at the edge of the camp.

Someone blew a horn, and people shouted and rushed out of their tents. They ran to the center of the village, then headed toward the vehicle. Some carried long, pointed sticks and waved them over their heads.

Judd panicked. "Are we in trouble?"

Immen gunned the engine and raced toward the people. "Not if this is where God wants you to be."

Vicki finally got the woman and baby settled in a room. The baby slept peacefully on a crudely constructed crib Charlie had made from pieces of wood and a few blankets.

As Vicki went for another blanket, Conrad returned with Janie. "I didn't do anything wrong," Janie said when she walked into the kitchen.

Vicki pulled her into the pantry and told her to keep quiet. Vicki shook from anger but tried to control herself. "I can't believe you'd do this to us!"

"This isn't about you," Janie said. "I needed to get away—what's so bad about that?"

Vicki shook her head. "You don't get it, do you?"

"I know the GC could have picked me up, but I wouldn't rat you guys out."

"You have no idea what they can do to you."

Janie stared at Vicki. "Yes I do, but I don't expect you to care about it." She opened the pantry door and slammed it behind her. Vicki sighed and walked into the kitchen.

"I tried to talk with her on the way back. She wouldn't listen," Conrad said.

"I shouldn't have yelled at her like that, but it's so frustrating!"

Vicki took the woman another blanket and a pillow. "My name is Lenore Barker," the woman said quietly. She looked at the sleeping child. "This is Tolan."

Vicki introduced herself and asked if the woman needed anything else.

"No, and I told those two boys that I'm willing to work for any food that I eat."

Vicki smiled. "You'll be safe here tonight."

"Just tonight?" Lenore said. "My husband is gone now and . . ." Lenore put a hand to her mouth and wept.

Vicki patted her shoulder and waited.

"We ran out of food," Lenore said. "We'd burned everything in the house we could to keep warm. Finally, Tim had to go out and try to find some food, or we were going to starve.

"This morning I found him lying in the street a few blocks from our house." Lenore bowed her head and whispered, "He had a loaf of bread and some meat he had found somewhere. He died trying to save our lives."

Vicki shook her head. "I'm so sorry."

"That girl, Janie. She saved my life. I don't know what I would have done if she hadn't come along."

"Somebody would have taken you in," Vicki said.

Lenore shook her head. "When I saw my husband in the street, I thought about killing myself and my baby. Janie talked me out of it. She said she knew some people who really cared and could help."

"Janie said that?"

"Yeah. She said you were a little weird about reading the Bible but that she was sure you'd give me a place to stay."

Vicki looked at the floor. "She was right. You can stay here as long as you'd like."

Judd watched people swarm around the Land Rover. They shouted and chanted, some with spears held high. They wore loose clothing and many had a cloth around their faces. Their tents were made of camel skin.

"What do we do?" Judd said.

"We will speak to them," Mr. Stein said.

Immen grabbed his arm. "I'm telling you, I only know a few words."

Mr. Stein nodded. "Can you make out anything they're saying?"

Immen listened. "It's something about God. He brings something . . . I'm sorry. I can't make it out."

"He has brought us this far," Mr. Stein said. "He will show us."

The people stood back as the three got out; then the crowd rushed them and took them to their tents. Judd almost fell and feared being trampled, but they made it safely to the middle of the camp and into the tent of what Judd thought was the leader of the group.

Mr. Stein, Immen, and Judd were forced to sit before a small table. The leader stared at them, then whipped a cloth away, revealing several plates of food. Flies were all

over the meat. Judd was handed something warm
to drink. He took a sip and nearly gagged.

Immen sat forward and spoke to the leader. The
leader replied and Immen asked a question. The leader
answered for almost a minute.

"I told him you come in peace and in the name
of God," Immen said, "and he said something about a
movement of their people. For some reason they've been
brought together."

The meal lasted until daybreak. Finally Immen turned
to Mr. Stein and said, "They are waiting for some kind of
message from the Great Spirit who caused the freeze."

Mr. Stein whispered, "Have them come outside and
gather round the Land Rover."

Mr. Stein led Judd through the sea of people. Some
were teenagers. They followed him, touching his clothes
and chanting something.

When they reached the car, Mr. Stein put a hand on
Judd's shoulder. "Please pray as you have never prayed
before."

"Immen can't translate," Judd said.

"God will have to provide some other way then."

A few minutes later the leader of the people approached
the vehicle. He blew into an animal horn. The people
crowded close. Judd figured there must be at least five
thousand people.

The leader raised his voice and shouted something.
Mr. Stein looked at Immen. "He has introduced you as
someone who knows God," Immen said. "I will do my
best to translate."

Standing on top of the Land Rover, Mr. Stein raised his voice. "Hear the word of the Lord, the maker of the universe, the creator of every living thing."

Before Immen could speak, the people fell to the ground. Even the leader of the group was on his knees.

"Why are you speaking in my language?" Immen said.

"I'm speaking English," Mr. Stein said.

As the people whimpered on the ground, Judd understood. "We're all hearing in our own language. It's just like the witnesses, Eli and Moishe. Tell them something else."

Mr. Stein seemed overwhelmed at the thought that these people were hearing their language supernaturally. He composed himself and said, "Please, stand."

Immediately the entire group stood as one. Judd shook his head. Mr. Stein had been right again. God had worked a miracle to get them here and another after they arrived.

"There is one God and Creator," Mr. Stein continued, "and he has sent me to tell you he loves you."

As Mr. Stein talked, people looked at each other in amazement. Mr. Stein explained that Jesus, the Son of God, had died as a sacrifice for the bad things people had done. If anyone would come to Jesus and ask forgiveness, God would come into that person's life.

Mr. Stein held up his Bible. The people inched forward, trying to get a look at it. Mr. Stein quoted several verses from Romans that showed that everyone had sinned and that the payment for sin was death and separation from God forever. The people gasped.

"But," Mr. Stein said, "the gift of God is eternal life through Jesus. You will live forever with God if you ask him to forgive you and become your leader."

Many wept when they heard what a terrible death Jesus had died. The leader of the people stepped forward, tears streaming down his cheeks. Mr. Stein led the people in a prayer. Judd couldn't understand anything anyone said except Mr. Stein.

When Mr. Stein finished, the leader of the group climbed onto the Land Rover and hugged him. The people clucked their tongues and cheered. The leader called for quiet and asked a question.

Mr. Stein looked at Immen. "I think," Immen said after a moment, "he said something about their enemy."

"What enemy?" Mr. Stein said.

"There have been many tribal wars throughout the years," Immen said. "People have been killed over a few missing animals. I believe he wants you to give the message to them."

Mr. Stein smiled. "It is proof that they understood my words. We will go wherever God leads us."

32

VICKI called an emergency meeting Wednesday morning. The schoolhouse now housed four unbelievers and an infant.

"This is getting crazy," Mark said. "I thought this place was for training."

"We've asked God to show us what to do, and it seems like he keeps bringing people without the mark," Vicki said. "Maybe that's the kind of training we need."

"More outsiders, more trouble," Mark said.

Shelly sighed. "What about this Carl guy you're supposed to see? You going to bring him back if he's not one of us?"

Mark looked out the window. The sun was coming up and cast an orange glow around the room. "Carl is different. I have to know what happened to John."

The kids were quiet. Darrion leafed through her Bible and cleared her throat. "I've been reading the book of

James. One of the verses says, 'Pure and lasting religion in the sight of God our Father means that we must care for orphans and widows in their troubles, and refuse to let the world corrupt us.' I think all four of our guests qualify."

Vicki nodded and the others agreed. They would care for anyone God brought their way.

While Mark searched the Web, Vicki went to Janie's room. She knew she hadn't treated the girl well the night before. Even if Janie had put them in danger by going off alone, she had cared for Lenore and her baby. Vicki rehearsed what she wanted to say, took a deep breath, and knocked on Janie's door. When there was no answer, she peeked in and found Janie's bed empty.

Not again, Vicki thought.

She searched the house and was about to tell the others when she heard a noise in Lenore's room. The door was slightly open, and Vicki saw Janie holding little Tolan. She was trying to get him to laugh. Lenore lay on the bed behind them, half asleep.

Vicki got Janie's attention. Janie put Tolan beside his mother and walked into the hall.

"You going to yell at me for being in there? I was just trying to help."

"I'm sorry about last night," Vicki said. They walked to Janie's room. "I won't make any excuses. I was wrong to yell at you."

Janie sat on her bed. "And I was wrong to go off like that without talking to you guys."

Vicki sat beside her. "I've been thinking about some-

320

thing you said last night. I couldn't get to sleep wondering what you meant."

"What?" Janie said.

"I said that you have no idea what the GC can do to you if they want information. You said you did. What did you mean?"

Janie put a hand on her elbow and pulled her arm tightly to her chest. "I don't want to talk about it."

Vicki leaned closer. "Maybe it would help."

Tears came to Janie's eyes. "The first place they sent me was awful. I was thrown in with criminals. I thought the detention center was bad, but this was ten times worse.

"I got mixed up with the wrong people. They were bringing drugs into the place. The GC nabbed me and wanted to know who was selling. I wouldn't tell. I knew what would happen as soon as I got back."

Janie pulled up her shirt and turned so Vicki could see. "They stuck this electric thing in my back to get me to talk. The mark's still there."

Vicki shook her head.

"So I know what the GC can do, and I'll say it again. I wouldn't rat on you guys."

Someone shouted in the study room. Vicki excused herself and found Mark typing an answer to an e-mail.

"Carl's going to be dropped off near Kankakee day after tomorrow," Mark said. "I'm going to meet him there."

Conrad looked over Mark's shoulder. "It might be a trap. You know the GC are going to be all over the place."

"We've been through this before," Mark said. "I'm going to hear him out."

Mark searched for the best route to Kankakee, due south of Chicago. Conrad pulled up the latest news, and the others gathered around.

The top story highlighted a shiny object in the sky. At first, stargazers considered it a shooting star. It had first been seen during nighttime hours in Asia. But this star didn't streak across the sky or circle the earth.

A scientist from a leading university said, "Due to the speed of light and the distance from the earth of even the nearest stars, events such as this actually occurred years before and are just being seen now."

But the man had to retract that statement a few hours later. Both amateur and professional astronomers agreed this was no ordinary star and certainly not an event that had happened years before. Though the experts couldn't identify it, they agreed it was falling directly toward Earth. It seemed to emit its own light, as well as reflect light from stars and the sun, depending on the time of day.

The head of the Global Community Aeronautics and Space Administration, GCASA, said it posed very little threat. "It has every chance of burning up as it hits our atmosphere. But even if it remains intact, it will probably land harmlessly in water. If it doesn't vaporize, it will no doubt break apart once it hits the earth."

Vicki watched the coverage with interest. She flipped open her Bible, then asked if she could use the computer. She scrolled through the text of Tsion Ben-Judah's message, looking for a clue.

"What do you make of this?" Conrad said.

Vicki whirled around. "Get downstairs. We don't have much time."

Early Wednesday morning Judd and Mr. Stein arrived at the camp of the enemy tribe. They had driven to a river and floated in a small boat with the leader and a few others who came with them.

After docking, they hiked to the camp. Several times they heard weird birdcalls. "Those are the scouts sending signals," Immen said. "They will be waiting for us."

"Are you sure about this?" Judd said to Mr. Stein.

"God has not called us to be careful. He has called us to give the message."

A group from the enemy tribe met Judd and the others at the edge of the camp. Judd noticed freshly dug graves nearby and wondered if these people had died from the freeze.

"I know even less of this language," Immen said.

A fierce-looking man from the tribe yelled at them. The others nodded and spoke in agreement. Judd closed his eyes, sure that they would soon be surrounded and killed. But the next voice Judd heard was Mr. Stein's.

"We come on behalf of the Prince of Peace," Mr. Stein said.

Judd could tell the men were amazed that someone was speaking their own language. A crowd from the village gathered. Before long, hundreds were listening

to the gospel message. When he finished, Mr. Stein
invited the tribe to pray with him.

People knelt and lifted their eyes toward heaven.
Many wept. The villagers repeated Mr. Stein's words,
though Judd heard what sounded to him like gibberish.
When he was finished, Mr. Stein invited the leader of the
first tribe to greet the enemy tribe leader. He pointed
out the mark of the true believer on their foreheads, and
they were both amazed. Two men who had been sworn
enemies only minutes before hugged and smiled. Then
they hugged Mr. Stein.

"You are to take this message of love and forgiveness
to all who need to hear it," Mr. Stein said.

Lionel kept feeding Sam information and Scripture.
Like other new believers he had known, Sam was like a
sponge. He couldn't get enough teaching about Jesus and
the Bible. Though Sam talked about his father often,
Lionel was able to keep him from going to see the man.

"I think you'll be able to see him again," Lionel said,
"but it's too early right now."

Nada met secretly with Lionel. They talked about the
falling object from space and what it might mean. Their
conversation finally turned to Judd.

"I am worried that he won't speak with me," Nada
said, "that he'll be too concerned about my father."

"Judd respects your dad, and he's grateful for what
he's done for us," Lionel said. "But I won't let him leave
here without having a talk with you."

"I want more than a talk," Nada said. "I want to go to your country. I feel so trapped here. I want to be a part of the Young Tribulation Force."

Lionel smiled. "You don't have to go back to the States to be part of our group. As a matter of fact, you might wind up being more help to us staying here. If it weren't for you, we probably wouldn't have gotten Sam out of his dad's house."

Nada's father knocked on the door. She put a finger to her lips and stood behind it. The door opened, and Jamal handed the phone to Lionel. "Please speak quickly," Jamal said, "I am waiting for an important call."

Lionel took the phone. It was Judd.

"You won't believe what's happened," Judd said. He explained the adventure he and Mr. Stein had been through.

"Where are you now?" Lionel said.

"We're spending a couple more days here so Mr. Stein can train the new evangelists," Judd said. "The guy who flew us here is taking us back to Bamako on Sunday. We're hoping to get a flight into Israel from there. Can you meet us at the airport?"

"I'll be there," Lionel said.

"Good. I want us to fly to the States from there. We have to get back to the others."

"Sounds great," Lionel said, "but what about money?"

"God is working," Judd said. "If he wants us to get home, we'll get there."

When Lionel hung up, he went to the computer.

"What are you doing?" Nada said.

"Maybe there's some way the others can help us get back," Lionel said.

Vicki helped Mark load his backpack onto the motorcycle. He said it would take him a day to get to Kankakee, and he wanted to get there early to scope things out before he met with Carl. "Sorry I can't help with downstairs," he said.

"We'll manage," Vicki said. "We've got the lower room almost sealed off."

"Are you sure about what you're doing down there?" Mark said.

"No," Vicki said, "but if I'm right, all this work will pay off."

Mark said good-bye to everyone and rode off. Shelly called the others inside. She had just gotten Lionel's e-mail.

Conrad slammed some tools down and said, "That's it. I'm going to get that safe open if it's the last thing I do."

Vicki met with Lenore briefly to make sure she had what she needed. "What are you doing downstairs?" Lenore said.

"We're preparing," Vicki said. "I don't want to scare you, but I think this judgment will be even worse than the others."

Lenore frowned. "Janie said you people were kind of strange when it came to religion."

"I'd like to explain what we believe if you'll let me," Vicki said.

Tolan stirred in his crib and started crying. "I need to feed him right now. Maybe later."

Vicki went back to the study room, where the kids watched the latest on the falling object. It had landed without doing any damage. The head of GCASA was back at a news conference to explain.

"The point of impact is in a remote area near the border of Syria and Iraq," the man said. "We have not been able to locate the object in our aerial studies. It appears to have slipped past the earth's surface into a deep crevice."

A reporter shot up a hand. "Sir, can't you get teams in there to find it and study it?"

"It's impossible to get a vehicle in that area or even get a team in there on foot. Our main concern is what might have been done to the earth's crust. We haven't been able to detect a problem at this point, but we want to make sure."

Suddenly Vicki and the others felt a tremor. The schoolhouse shook slightly, and then all was calm. "Did you feel that?" Lenore said as she ran in with her baby. "It's not another earthquake, is it?"

The head of GCASA was handed a piece of paper from an aide. "I've just received this report and won't be able to answer any questions. It says there's been an eruption near the place where the object fell. We have data from different countries coming in that say their sensors went off the scale a few moments ago. Our pilots monitoring the area were blown off course and forced to escape the area."

The GCASA leader quickly exited the news conference with reporters screaming questions. A few minutes later, pictures from a news flight showed the beginning of a mushroom cloud a thousand times bigger than anything seen in history.

"We are now told," a news anchor reported, "that this object has somehow triggered volcano-like activity deep beneath the surface of the earth's crust."

Judd and Mr. Stein were in the Land Rover when the thick, black cloud rolled across the desert. There was no wind to speak of, but the cloud moved rapidly, blotting out the sun. The thick cloud almost seemed solid as it rolled over the landscape. As it traveled quickly above them, Judd could tell this wasn't a smoky cloud that thinned as it moved. It was dense and as black as the base of a gasoline fire. From the radio Judd learned that scientists feared the source of the smoke was a huge fire that would eventually rise and shoot flames miles into the air.

"We must hurry if we hope to get back to Israel by Sunday," Mr. Stein said.

33

MARK arrived in Kankakee, Illinois, Wednesday night. It had been a grueling ride. He found a cheap hotel by the interstate and fell asleep.

The next morning, he drove to the airport but saw no Global Community officers. An older man at the information desk told him the Global Community had a temporary post set up outside the terminal. The man had no idea when Carl's flight might arrive.

Mark kept his distance from the GC. Though Nicolae Carpathia said everyone could travel as they pleased, Mark knew he had to be careful. He saw one officer walk outside to smoke near a chain-link fence. Mark approached him and said hello.

The man ignored him. His nameplate said "Kolak."

"I'm wondering about the transport flight that's supposed to be here today," Mark said.

"Nobody's supposed to know about those flights," the officer said.

"I don't know what's on them," Mark said quickly. "I've got a friend coming in from South Carolina who said he'd be here today. I told him I'd pick him up."

Kolak blew smoke in Mark's face and laughed. "Heard there was a flight from down south that got cancelled because of the cloud. Might be here Saturday."

"Saturday!?" Mark said.

"Could be Sunday," Kolak said. "What's your friend's name?"

Mark didn't want to give the man too much information, but he also didn't want the guy to get suspicious.

"Carl Meninger," Mark said.

Kolak threw his cigarette to the ground and smashed it with his foot. "You mean one of the guys on the sub?"

"I don't know," Mark said. "What sub?"

"Communications guy on the *Peacekeeper 1*, right?"

"I guess so," Mark said.

"How do you know him?"

"I had a cousin on that ship," Mark said. "Carl wanted to talk to me."

"Come with me," Kolak said. He pointed to the gate in the fence.

Mark hesitated.

"Well, come on. I want to make sure you and your buddy get hooked up."

Mark followed the man inside the fence to a small building. Inside were three GC officers standing by television monitors.

Nicolae Carpathia smiled at the camera. "I bid all workers of the Global Community greetings. Your hard work and efforts to bring peace and harmony to people around the globe do not go unnoticed."

Carpathia held a piece of paper in his hand. "As you know, a few days ago I gave approval for all those who follow religions other than Enigma Babylon One World Faith to travel about freely. I also cleared them of any wrongdoing in Israel.

"At the request of people I trust, I am today issuing an order that gives Peter the Second, Supreme Pontiff of Enigma Babylon One World Faith, the authority to handle this situation. Since it is a religious issue that separates the followers of Dr. Ben-Judah from the One World Faith, I am giving him full power to handle this in whatever way he chooses.

"After Pontiff Mathews looks the matter over, I assume he will make a statement to the media. Until then, be alert for any terrorist acts these followers may attempt. Thank you for your service."

The men clapped. One said, "I hope they get those jerks and put them in jail."

The head officer turned and looked at Mark. "How long's he been here?"

Kolak stepped forward. "This kid says he's here to meet with Meninger, one of the survivors from the *Peace-keeper 1*."

The officer nodded. "All right. Give us your number and we'll let you know when he's supposed to get here."

Mark nodded and wrote the number of the hotel on a scrap of paper. As he walked out, he wondered if he had just done something that would come back to haunt him.

Vicki took some food to Lenore. Tolan had a runny nose and a cough, and the woman seemed upset. Vicki looked for some infant medicine but couldn't find any.

She heard a commotion in the study room. When she arrived, everyone was crowded around Conrad. "I did it!" Conrad said when he saw Vicki. "I got it open, and you're not going to believe what's in here."

Conrad lugged the safe to the computer table. "I took Melinda's advice and worked on the body instead of the lock. There was a little rust in one corner of the bottom. I got a drill bit through—"

"Who cares how you got it open," Janie said. "Just show us what's inside."

Conrad flipped the safe upside down and put his hand through the small opening. He pulled out a gold coin. "It's full of them. Has to be worth thousands, maybe hundreds of thousands!"

"We have to call Z," Vicki said. "If he gives us the okay, we could sell some of them and get the money to Judd and Lionel."

"Why do we have to call anybody?" Janie said.

"This is Z's property," Conrad said. "We don't do anything until we've cleared it with him."

Vicki dialed the number and explained to Z what had happened.

"That's good work," Z said. "We been lookin' for that box since I was a kid. Never looked in the bell tower."

"We'd like to sell a few of the coins and get the money to Judd and Lionel to get back to the States," Vicki said.

"Might take a while to get a buyer," Z said. "Tell you what I'll do. I'll wire the money to Israel. You find out where to send it and all the details. I'll come pick up the coins on my next run."

"Do you have any infant medicine?" Vicki said. She explained about Lenore and how it seemed God was bringing them more and more nonbelievers to live with them.

Z laughed. "Sounds like he's throwing a few monkey wrenches into your plans."

Vicki sighed. "If this is what God wants us to do, we'll do it."

"I may have some aspirin for the baby," Z said, "but it might take a few days. Call me if things get worse."

Judd awoke in the middle of the night, troubled. The temperatures during the day had risen above a hundred degrees. During the night he tossed and turned inside the Land Rover, trying to figure out what to do. Mr. Stein had said he felt God wanted him to stay and train more people.

In the morning, Judd walked with Mr. Stein. Yet another encampment of people stood before them. Hundreds milled about with what was left of their flocks and herds.

"I can't leave," Mr. Stein said. "I believe God has called me to this."

"I wouldn't ask you to leave," Judd said, "but I think I should get back to Lionel and Sam."

"I understand," Mr. Stein said, looking at the people. "Isn't this amazing? God has prepared their hearts for his message. It is almost as if I don't need to say anything. They already hunger for God's forgiveness."

Judd looked up at the cloud that didn't end. God was up to something. He was also working in Judd's life. Judd had grown spiritually as he watched Mr. Stein speak to the new believers. He had seen God work in a way Judd would never dream of, and it had changed him.

But Judd also felt a longing to share his experiences with someone. Even with his friends around, he felt lonely. He wanted to share this experience with someone close.

Judd thought of Nada. She was certainly interested in him. But his thoughts turned to Vicki. *Could anything ever work out between us?* he thought.

Mr. Stein handed Judd the rest of his money. "I will see if Immen can get you to the airport in Bamako. You should be able to get a flight to Israel if the planes haven't been grounded."

"What about you?" Judd said.

Mr. Stein smiled. "God is looking out for both of us. He will show us where to go and what to do."

Lionel was excited to hear the news from Vicki that their plane fare could be wired to Israel. Lionel figured it would be safer if the money was wired in Sam's name, so he gave Vicki the information.

"Z says the money should be there Saturday afternoon," Vicki said.

"Is everybody all right back there?" Lionel asked.

"We had a pretty big scare through the freeze, but everybody's pulling together now. Well, almost everybody."

"I think I know who you mean," Lionel said.

"Have you heard from Judd?"

Lionel briefly gave Vicki Judd's report. "I hope we can get back home before the next judgment hits."

———

Mark waited in his hotel room. Friday came and went with no sign of Carl's plane. Mark watched the TV coverage of the cloud that had enveloped the earth. It looked as dark as night outside, and he wondered how any plane could get through the inky blackness.

———

Lionel told Nada about the money they were expecting. She closed her eyes and frowned. "Are all three of you leaving?" she said.

"We hope to take Sam with us if he wants to go," Lionel said.

As the two talked, Jamal walked in. "Father, I'm going with Lionel to retrieve a wire."

Jamal looked at Lionel. "She goes nowhere with you."

Lionel held up both hands. "I didn't ask her, sir."

Jamal ordered Nada to her room and turned to Lionel. "This is the final warning. If you talk to my daughter again, I will ask you to leave."

"Understood," Lionel said. "Can we borrow your car to pick up—"

Jamal shook his head. "It's too dangerous now. I can't let you out with my vehicle."

Lionel and Sam left through the back entrance and found a bus that ran close to the bank. Before they reached it, Lionel and Sam split up. Lionel sat in an outdoor café across the street and watched.

As the plane touched down in Bamako, Judd thanked Immen and offered to pay him.

"Do not insult me," Immen said. "Besides, I believe you will need all of that cash to get back to Israel."

Immen gave Judd the name of another believer he could call on in case he had trouble. Inside the airport Judd discovered that many flights had been cancelled because of the dark cloud. The only airline that offered flights to Israel wouldn't get him there until Monday. Plus, the airfare was more than Mr. Stein had given him.

Judd tried to bargain with the ticket agent, but he wouldn't budge from the listed price.

Great, Judd thought, *what do I do now?*

At the outdoor café, Lionel asked for a glass of water. The waiter scowled and said something in another language. Lionel pointed to a soft drink, and the waiter frowned and took his menu.

Sam entered the bank. Lionel could see him through a row of windows in front. The boy stopped and said something to a security guard, then got in line. *So far so good,* Lionel thought.

As Sam moved forward, Lionel noticed two men in a car scanning the bank with binoculars. As Sam reached the teller the men quickly exited the car and headed for the front door. They didn't wear GC uniforms, but Lionel knew they were probably working with Sam's father.

Lionel stood. He wanted to get Sam's attention, but he couldn't. If Lionel didn't act now, Sam and the money would be gone. He glanced up the street for any other suspicious cars. Nothing.

Lionel crossed the street. Someone behind him shouted. It was the waiter holding a soda. Lionel shrugged and kept moving.

Sam signed something at the teller window and waited for his money. Lionel moved past the two men at the door and reached the security guard. He asked where the men's rest room was, and the man pointed to a hallway.

"There's a couple of suspicious guys out front," Lionel said. "Looks like they're about to jump somebody. Thought you oughta know."

The guard thanked Lionel and spoke into a walkie-talkie.

That ought to keep them busy a few minutes, Lionel thought.

Sam stuffed a wad of cash into a pocket and turned. Lionel called out and motioned for him. Sam looked around nervously, then followed. When they were inside the bathroom, Lionel said, "Give me the money. There are two guys outside waiting for you."

"My dad," Sam said, handing over the money.

Lionel looked for a window but found none. "The security guard may keep them busy for a couple of minutes. Is there a back way out of this place?"

Sam nodded. "An alarm will sound."

"Good," Lionel said. "Stay right here."

34

AS LIONEL exited the bathroom door, he saw the two men still outside in a wild conversation with the security guard.

Lionel crept down the carpeted hallway and hit the door, sounding the alarm. He rushed back to the men's room and shoved Sam out of sight.

Keys jangled outside. People ran past. "Okay," Lionel said, "follow me."

Lionel and Sam calmly walked into the lobby. As Lionel suspected, the two men had rushed out the back door. The security guard wasn't in sight.

Lionel and Sam didn't run until they left the bank and turned the corner. They stayed out of sight until they reached the bus stop.

Judd phoned Immen's friend and explained the situation. The man asked which airline he had chosen and told

Judd to wait fifteen minutes, then return to the ticket window. Judd got back in line and a half hour later was talking with the same ticket agent who had turned him down earlier. Judd gave his information and said, "I've made arrangements with a friend."

The ticket agent scowled and tapped his keyboard. The man raised his eyebrows. "It looks like someone has made up the rest of the price of the ticket."

Judd handed the cash to the man and signed a form. "When will that flight leave?"

"They're talking about Sunday evening. Perhaps Monday morning."

Judd shook his head.

"It's the weather phenomenon," the agent said. "If you'd like a refund, I can—"

"No," Judd said, "I'll take it."

Judd took the ticket and went to his gate. He called Lionel, but there was no answer. He found a restaurant that had e-mail access and typed a message to Lionel, then sent one to Vicki and the others back in Illinois.

Mark wished he had brought Judd's laptop with him. Late Sunday evening he watched the GC coverage of the cloud. He clicked to other channels and found psychics and fortune-tellers. Viewers wanted to know the future, and they were willing to take answers, even if the answers were wrong.

Flipping through more channels, Mark landed on a movie and thought of his cousin John. They used to love watching action flicks together. This one had some bad language, but he overlooked it because he was so interested in the plot. But things on the screen got worse. He reached for the remote and turned off the television.

Mark shook his head. Before he had become a believer in Christ he had watched things he knew were wrong. The images had stayed with him, even after becoming a believer. Now he felt ashamed that he had been drawn in. He unplugged the television and opened his Bible.

The phone rang. It was the guard, Kolak. "Boss wanted me to tell you that transport plane is supposed to get here between 8:00 and 9:00 tomorrow morning."

"Do you know if Carl is on the flight?" Mark said.

"Don't know anything other than that the flight's due in the morning. I'd be here if I were you."

Judd ate an overpriced meal at an airport restaurant. He had saved a few dollars to get him to Israel, but his money supply was down to almost nothing. His flight number was called over the loudspeaker. An airline representative said the flight had again been delayed. They hoped to get off the ground at some point Monday morning.

Judd groaned and settled into a chair in the waiting room. He propped his feet up and watched the television monitors. The continued effects of the worldwide cloud were the top story. Scientists speculated that the falling object had created a volcanic disturbance underground.

"We should see this cloud cover dissolve within the next few days," one scientist said.

The news switched to a statement from Peter the Second. The man was wearing his full clerical outfit. "The Global Community may have an agreement with these religious terrorists, the followers of Rabbi Ben-Judah, but the time has come to enforce the law. Enigma Babylon One World Faith is the accepted religion for the whole world. I have read the rules listed in the Global Community charter, and I believe it is now within my power to punish offenders.

"So that all may be clear, I consider the intolerant, one-way-only beliefs as a threat to true religion. Therefore, Enigma Babylon must go on the offensive.

"To be an atheist or an agnostic is one thing. Even they are welcome. But it is illegal to practice a form of religion that opposes our mission. Followers of Dr. Tsion Ben-Judah will suffer."

Judd felt a chill run down his spine. *So much for being able to live your life in freedom*, Judd thought.

"As a first step to rid the world of intolerance, it shall be deemed criminal, as of midnight Tuesday, for anyone to visit the Web site of the so-called Tribulation Force. The teachings of this cult's guru are poison to people of true faith and love, and we will not tolerate his deadly teachings."

Several people in the airport clapped and cheered. Judd looked around for someone with the mark of the believer but saw no one.

"Technology is in place that can monitor the Internet

activity of every citizen," Mathews continued, "and those who visit this site after the deadline shall be subject to fine and imprisonment."

Mark awoke early Monday morning, checked out of the hotel, and drove to the airport. He parked his motorcycle a good distance away from the GC post. He had seen and heard very few planes land at the airport and wondered whether the flight might again be cancelled.

Kolak came to the fence and gave Mark a thumbs-up sign. "Ten more minutes!" he yelled.

A few minutes later the jet engine screamed overhead. The plane descended through the dense cloud with a roar. Through the noise, Mark heard a voice. He turned, thinking someone was behind him. There was no one there.

Monday afternoon in Israel, Lionel and Sam said good-bye to Jamal and his family. Nada came out of her room and hugged Lionel. She began to speak, then looked at her father and stepped back. Her mother put an arm around her and pulled her close.

"I can't thank you enough for taking us in," Lionel said. "I don't know what we would have done."

Jamal nodded. "If I had come to your country, I'm sure you would have done the same for me."

Jamal drove Lionel and Sam to the airport and dropped them at the terminal. "May God protect you, my friends," Jamal said before he drove off.

Lionel checked the monitors inside and found the right gate. His heart sank when he heard an announcement that said all outgoing flights had just been cancelled. Lionel rushed to Judd's gate and talked with the attendant.

"That flight is already in the air," the attendant said. "It should be here within the hour."

"Why is everything being cancelled?" Lionel said.

"Radar shows that the cloud mass is increasing," the attendant said. "There's a good chance of severe weather ahead."

Lionel sat with Sam in the waiting area. The boy was quiet.

"Want to talk about it?" Lionel said.

Sam looked out the huge windows. "It's my dad. I want to talk with him."

Lionel nodded. "You know if you reach out to him what's going to happen. Those guys at the bank showed you that."

Sam stared out the window.

Announcements were made over the loudspeaker about cancelled flights. People hurried back and forth. Some shouted at attendants.

Lionel closed his eyes and put his head back. He heard a voice that sounded like it was right next to him. He opened his eyes and stared at Sam.

"Did you hear that?" Lionel said.

"Yes," Sam said, "it was perfect Hebrew."

"Hebrew?" Lionel said. "I heard it in English."

Others around them had heard the voice as well.

Some women ran screaming into the rest room. A businessman carrying a briefcase fell to the floor and scampered under some seats. A woman at the gate got on the loudspeaker. "Please stay calm!" she shouted.

"What was it?" Sam said.

"The angel," Lionel said. "It's sounding the next judgment."

Judd sat on the crowded airplane. The seats were small and the plane seemed ancient. He thought of the trip with Mr. Stein and what he had learned. Once again he ached to share the experience with someone close to him. Then he fell asleep.

He awoke suddenly, thinking another passenger had said something. The man next to him shrieked, unbuckled, and jumped into the aisle. A woman in front of Judd did the same, and the two ran into each other.

"What's happening?" a woman yelled behind Judd.

The plane descended into the thick cloud and was enveloped in darkness. Those who weren't screaming or crying whimpered in fear.

Judd thought of Mr. Stein and the kids back in Illinois. If he could hear the voice of the angel in an airplane, could everyone on the ground hear it too? Judd sat forward and looked around. He was the only one with the mark of the believer. He was the only one who knew what was about to happen.

Vicki asked the group to come together in the study room early Monday morning. Melinda was walking with only a slight limp now, her foot almost back to normal. Conrad couldn't wait for Z to come so he could show him the gold coins. Thankfully, Tolan's temperature was normal. Janie complained about the meeting but showed up anyway.

Vicki turned on a light and ran through the changes that had been made downstairs. "We've made it as airtight as possible. I don't think it can be any more secure."

"Why'd you guys do all that work?" Janie said. "Doesn't make sense."

Vicki put her hands on her hips. "We did it for you. And for the others here who don't believe what we're telling you is true."

Janie rolled her eyes.

Vicki began the teaching for the day. Tsion Ben-Judah's latest teaching concerned the next judgment. She called up notes on the computer.

"I've told you what Dr. Ben-Judah thinks about the cloud that's covering the earth. Tsion says the things that come from it will not be part of the animal kingdom at all, but actual demons that—"

Vicki stopped when she heard the noise. It sounded from the heavens, reverberated outside, but they could all hear it clearly in the room.

"Woe, woe, woe to the inhabitants of the earth, because of the remaining blasts of the trumpet of the three angels who are about to sound!"

Phoenix barked at the voice of the angel. Charlie's eyes widened. He grabbed the dog in fear.

"What was that?" Melinda said.

Janie shook her head. "You think we'll fall for anything. That came from the computer."

Conrad stared at Janie. "No, it didn't."

"She had it on a timer or something," Janie said. "You guys can't scare us into believing."

"We wouldn't do that," Conrad said.

Vicki held up a hand. "These judgments are going to get worse and worse. The only way to survive is to ask God to forgive you."

Before anyone else could speak, Janie said, "If you're so smart, tell me what's going to happen." She snickered and looked around the room. "Is it going to be a God-sized tornado? Is that cloud going to spew out a bunch of little green men? Sounds like I'm not the only person here who's smoked some weed."

Darrion got in Janie's face. "These are going to be the scariest things you've ever seen in your life. I wouldn't make fun of them if I were you."

"We may not have much time," Vicki said. She and Shelly helped Lenore carry the baby and his crib downstairs. Melinda and Charlie weren't far behind.

Janie stayed in the room. "I'll ride this one out with the religious weirdos!"

35

AS JUDD'S plane descended into the cloud, the captain
of the flight spoke on the intercom, first in French, then
in English. "Do not be alarmed by the voice you just
heard. We believe there was some kind of interference
with the plane's sound system."

Judd shook his head. *These people will never believe,*
he thought.

The announcement by the pilot seemed to calm
people. Those who had gone into the aisle made their
way back to their seats. Some laughed nervously, as if
they hadn't really been frightened.

The pilot came back on the intercom. "We're descend-
ing into the cloud. Don't be alarmed by the darkness as
we prepare for landing."

Judd sat in the middle seat and craned his neck to
see out the window. "You want to move over here?" the
man beside him said. "There's nothing out there but
pitch-black."

A flash of lightning lit the cloud. In that split second, Judd looked past the man and saw something swirling, almost like a tornado, inside the cloud. "If you don't mind, I would like to switch seats."

"Suit yourself," the man said.

Judd moved over and peered out the window. A flight attendant instructed everyone to put down their window shades. Judd dutifully followed orders, then lifted it slightly and bent to see outside.

Another flash of lightning revealed an incredible sight. In the swirling blackness, small pieces of the cloud were breaking off. The pieces scattered and flew through the air. At first, Judd thought it was an actual tornado. He had heard how fierce winds could lift pieces of wood and stone into the air thousands of feet. But these bits of debris seemed to have a mind of their own. They flew in all directions.

"Close that now!" the attendant yelled from the aisle.

"Sorry," Judd said. He put the shade all the way down and sat back.

The man in the middle seat snickered. "She really told you." He patted Judd on the shoulder. "Don't worry. We'll be out of the cloud in a few minutes and you can look all you want."

"Flight attendants, prepare for landing," the pilot said over the intercom.

Suddenly, the plane was splattered with small objects. It sounded like hail. The plane dipped and veered to the left, as if trying to avoid something. The pilot came back on the intercom. This time he sounded out of control.

"Please do *not* look out the window! We're experiencing some kind of weather phenomenon." Judd heard someone scream in the cockpit. The captain turned off the intercom.

People around Judd began to whimper again. The man in the aisle seat nervously fidgeted with an in-flight magazine. He turned to the man in the middle. "I've been through hail in a plane smaller than this one. This shouldn't be a problem."

From three rows behind Judd came a piercing scream. Then another. Someone had ignored the captain's order and had looked out.

Judd slammed open his window shade.

Mark watched the GC plane land and taxi to the end of the runway. Kolak and two other officers drove a jeep to pick up the pilots. Mark saw a younger officer with a backpack get out. He was tall with dark hair and eyes. The man jumped out of the jeep before it stopped and trotted toward the fence. "Are you Mark?"

Mark nodded. "Carl?"

They shook hands. "Man, that was scary up there," Carl said, taking off his hat. There was no mark on his forehead. "We heard a voice in the plane."

Mark's heart sunk. He couldn't take Carl back to the schoolhouse. And with the judgment coming, Mark knew he had only a little time to convince him of the truth.

"The pilots said it might be somebody jamming the

GC radio signals," Carl said. He grabbed a jacket from his backpack, and Mark spotted a Bible inside.

"I wish your cousin were here," Carl said. "Bet he could explain all this."

"Yeah," Mark said, picking up the Bible. John's name was written on the front.

"He gave me that before he died. I want to explain what happened. I have some questions, too."

"We have to talk," Mark said.

"Yeah, but I want to get away from here first."

"We may not have much time," Mark said.

"What do you mean?"

"Carl, I heard the voice down here."

"You had a radio?"

"It didn't come over the radio." Mark stepped closer. "It was an angel announcing—"

"No way," Carl said. "You're trying to scare me."

"The angel sounded a warning to everybody on earth. You'd better listen to it."

"You don't even know what the voice said."

"'Woe, woe, woe, to the inhabitants of the earth . . . ,'" Mark said.

Carl squinted. "How did you know that?"

"God is about to bring a judgment on the people who haven't given their lives to him. Did John talk to you about this?"

"Sort of," Carl said. "He wanted me to pray with him, but I didn't feel right about it."

"What more do you need to know?" Mark said. "All you have to realize is that—"

Carl shook his head and interrupted. "Let's get away from here so I can think clearly. Take me to you guys' hideout and I'll tell you all about it."

Mark blinked. How did Carl know they had a hideout? He pushed the thought from his mind and led Carl to his motorcycle. "Hope you don't mind riding on the back."

Carl smiled. "I haven't ridden one of these in a couple of years. It'll be great."

As they pulled out, the wind picked up. Dust and sand flew at them from the runway. Mark headed toward the interstate and noticed the cloud changing as they drove. The underside turned from a dark blue to a yellowish brown.

"Something's happening," Carl yelled over the noise of the motorcycle engine.

Mark turned his head to answer, but the sight over Carl's shoulder sent a chill through him. The cloud was falling to the earth. Mark couldn't speak. He knew what was about to happen, and he had no way of stopping it.

Lionel took Sam to the corner of the airport waiting area and watched as people scurried about. The minutes just after the angel spoke were chaotic. People screamed and ran for cover, but they didn't know what they were running from. Finally things calmed. People checked on incoming flights. Others who had just discovered that all outbound flights had been cancelled complained and stomped off.

Lionel stood by the window and watched for Judd's plane. As it descended from the cloud, it veered to the right, then angled downward toward the runway.

"Look," Sam said, "the cloud is changing."

Sam was right. The bottom of the cloud swirled, like a beehive suspended in midair. Instead of dark blue, the cloud had taken on a yellowish color. As the plane fell from the sky, the cloud seemed to follow it.

"What's that noise?" Sam said.

It began as a low humming sound and became louder. Lionel looked up. The cloud was breaking apart. Little pieces fell to earth.

The noise was deafening, like a helicopter, only higher pitched and metallic.

"Sounds like a gigantic lawn mower," Sam said, covering his ears. Others in the airport did the same as the clanging continued. Lionel's body shook from the beating and rattling outside the window. His heart raced.

On the other side of the terminal came a tapping on the windows. People shrieked and scattered, pointing and crying. Lionel glanced out the window and saw creatures fly out of the cloud. They flew fast and swarmed like bees.

A mix of brown, black, and yellow, the locusts were hideous. They looked like tiny horses about six inches long with scorpion-like tails. Lionel was close enough to the window to look into their eyes. They were on the attack. The creatures seemed to look past Lionel and Sam to the others in the terminal. The earthquake and meteors had been devastating to live through. But these beings were the most horrible things he had ever seen.

Lionel noticed a door that led to the gate. Someone had left it open. He sprinted across the waiting area and slammed it shut. Then came the anguished scream of a worker just outside the door. The man was covered with the creatures and was trying to get inside.

Judd had read Tsion Ben-Judah's description of the demon locusts, but it had not prepared him for his first sight of them. *Ugly* was too nice a word. Just a glimpse at one turned Judd's stomach. The man next to him fainted. People all around Judd screamed for help. Judd pulled down the window shade.

Tsion had taught that these creatures wouldn't harm plants like normal locusts did. Instead, they would attack those who did not have the seal of God on their foreheads. If that was true, Judd was the only one on the plane who wasn't a target.

Another frightening observation of Rabbi Ben-Judah was that the people who were stung would be in so much pain that they would want to die, but God would not allow them to. Tsion said these beasts were not part of the animal kingdom at all. Instead, they were actual demons taking the form of living organisms. Even though the plane was traveling at a high speed, the demon locusts swarmed over it.

Screaming continued throughout the cabin as an explosion rocked the plane. The pilot came back on the intercom, panic in his voice. "We've just lost our right engine! We have to make an emergency landing. Everyone assume the crash position."

Some of those things must have gotten sucked inside, Judd thought. He opened the window shade again. A huge ball of fire engulfed one engine. White liquid poured into the hole, putting out the fire, but they were falling fast. An emergency crew drove wildly toward the runway. Judd shook his head. *They'll get stung before they can ever help us.*

Somehow the pilot managed to get the plane safely on the ground. People clapped nervously, but as soon as they rolled to a stop, the shrieking and wailing began again. The metallic sound of the locusts roared outside.

The creatures surrounded the plane and hovered, beating their wings and driving their heads into the windows. The sound of scratching at the roof of the plane made passengers cower in their seats.

Judd opened the shade and put his face close to the window. One of the beasts rammed its head into the glass and was stunned. It shook and looked directly at Judd. Judd was sickened by what he saw. The face of the locust looked like a man's. The eyes were hollow and piercing. The mouth dripped saliva from teeth that were long and pointed, like a lion's. Another disgusting feature was the demon's long, flowing hair. It spilled out from under what looked like a gold crown.

The creature flew forward and hovered at the top of the window so it could look past Judd to the other passengers. When it caught a glimpse of the others, the locust bared its teeth and struggled desperately to get inside.

Judd shuddered. No way they could open the door without those things getting inside. Everyone on the plane was trapped.

Mark gunned the motorcycle, but he couldn't outrun the beasts from the sky. They fell from the dark cloud above and scattered. Mark figured he had only seconds to find shelter for Carl.

Mark spotted a car under a bridge and screeched to a stop. "Quick, get inside!"

Carl jumped from the cycle and lifted the door handle. "It's locked!"

"Try the other side!" Mark yelled.

The noise from the approaching creatures grew to a roar. Cars passing above on the bridge crashed into each other at the sight of the oncoming horde. Mark looked up and saw the beasts already on the bridge.

"The back door's open!" Carl yelled.

"Get in and make sure the windows are all up!" Mark shouted.

Carl closed the door just as the locusts descended, skittering on the windshield and banging their heads into the windows. Carl scooted to the other side and reached for the doorknob.

"No!" Mark yelled. "I'm okay. Just stay where you are!"

Mark knew from his study that he wouldn't be stung by the locusts, but his heart raced when he saw them swarm around the car. Their wings clattered, and they hissed at the sight of their victim. Mark wondered if Carl could be stung more than once.

Someone screamed from above, and Mark ran to the edge of the bridge. A man had gotten out of his car, and several of the demon locusts had swarmed around him. "They're biting me!" the man yelled, climbing onto the bridge railing.

Mark yelled at him but it was too late. The man stepped off and plunged to the pavement. Mark knew the fall had to be fatal. He ran to the man's side and was surprised to find a pulse. A huge welt appeared on the man's arm where a locust had stung him. Mark leaned over the man's face and said, "Sir, can you hear me?"

To Mark's surprise, the man rolled over and groaned. "I wanted to kill myself. It hurts so much. I want to die!"

Mark turned back to the abandoned car and felt a chill. Someone or something was chanting. He walked closer to the car and listened as more locusts swarmed near Carl.

"Apollyon!" the beasts shouted. "Apollyon, Apollyon, Apollyon!"

Vicki closed the door to the secret room downstairs and made sure the second door was secure as well. She was glad she could offer shelter to those who wanted safety. She hoped all their work on the rooms would pay off.

Upstairs, Janie was still making fun of the kids. She believed the voice of the angel was a hoax.

"You'd better get downstairs while you can," Conrad said.

A low rumble shook the windows of the schoolhouse.

"It's too late," Vicki said, coming up the stairs. "They'll be here any minute."

"Who'll be here?" Janie said.

Vicki shook her head. "We tried to warn you, Janie. You wouldn't listen."

Janie went to the window and looked out. "Something's happening. What's that sound?"

"Your worst nightmare," Conrad said.

Something banged into the windows in the front room. Roaring, buzzing, and clanging filled the house.

"Okay, okay," Janie said, "take me downstairs."

"We can't put the others at risk," Vicki said.

"Just open the door and let me go down!" Janie screamed.

The demon locusts angrily converged on the schoolhouse. Though Conrad and Darrion had checked all the windows, somehow a few locusts managed to get inside.

"The kitchen pantry!" Vicki yelled.

Janie ran for the back of the house, but a locust roared down the stairs and attacked. Janie flailed at the creature and knocked it to the wooden floor, but another flew after her. Conrad picked up a piece of firewood and knocked the beast against a wall. It lay there, stunned.

Janie rushed into the pantry and grabbed the door. Just as she closed it, another locust darted inside.

Janie's screams pierced Vicki's heart.

36

VICKI opened the pantry door and jumped back as the locust skittered out, flapping wildly and screeching, "Apollyon! Apollyon!"

"I didn't know those things could talk," Conrad said. The locust flew past him and Conrad turned his head. "Disgusting."

Janie was still screaming, slapping at her legs and hair. "Get it off me! Get it off!"

"It's gone," Vicki said.

Janie quivered and twitched from her locust bite. The demonic venom was shooting through her veins. Vicki saw only one bite, on Janie's face, and it was beginning to swell. "Am I—am I going to die?" Janie managed.

"No," Vicki said. *But you'll wish you could,* Vicki thought.

Vicki and Conrad helped Janie into an upstairs room and tried to make her as comfortable as possible. When they returned downstairs, a dozen locusts were gathered around the door to the basement, biting, clawing, and scratching to get inside. One flew menacingly at Vicki and landed on her back. The thing hissed, as if trying to keep Vicki from helping the people downstairs.

Conrad knocked the locust off. "Plug any holes you can find. I'll see if I can get rid of these guys."

Conrad picked up a piece of firewood and swung at a hovering locust. He hit it solidly, and the creature crashed into the wall behind Vicki and fell to the floor.

Vicki bent over to inspect it. She was sickened by the sight but at the same time intrigued. "Conrad, come look at this."

The blow from the firewood had stunned the locust. Its segmented belly rose and fell as it breathed. Its body was shaped like a tiny horse armed for war. The thing had wings like a flying grasshopper.

"Fascinating," Conrad said as he inched closer. "It's a mix between a horse and a man."

"Look at those teeth," Vicki said.

The locust opened its eyes and screamed, "Apollyon!" It flew toward Vicki, but Conrad had a bead on it. He swung the wood and knocked the locust against the wall with a terrible blow. Vicki thought the beast would surely have cracked in two, but it lay in one piece, its wings clicking.

Conrad picked it up. "No wonder we can't kill the thing—its back feels stronger than the safe. And it's got little spines."

"Put it down," Vicki said.

"Grab that bucket by the fireplace," Conrad said. "We'll trap it."

Vicki brought the heavy bucket and put it upside down. Conrad held the locust close to her. "This is the stinger here. You can almost see through it. And that has to be the venom." A liquid substance sloshed as Conrad moved. "What do you think it's saying?"

"Tsion told us that the king over these things is the chief demon in the pit. He rules over all the demons of hell. In Greek the name is Apollyon. It's something different in Hebrew."

"If these really are demons," Conrad said, "they've got to want to kill us."

"But they can't," Vicki said. "Just shows you God can use even his enemy for his own purposes."

The creature opened its eyes. Vicki screamed. Conrad threw it on the floor and quickly put the bucket over it. The locust beat its wings against the bucket but couldn't get out. Inside, the tiny voice screamed again and again, "Apollyon! Apollyon!"

Mark ran back to the car and found Carl in the backseat, stuffing tissues and trash into a crack in one of the back windows. The locusts had found the spot and were trying to crawl through.

Mark found an empty beer bottle nearby and swatted the locusts away. The metal backs of the monsters pinged as Mark swung the glass.

"What are these things?" Carl yelled frantically.

"Demons," Mark said.

"Why aren't they bothering you?"

"They know I have the seal of God on my forehead," Mark said. "They can't hurt me."

Carl looked puzzled. "That stuff John told me about God . . . it's really true?"

Mark leaned close to the window. "It's your only hope against these things and against being separated from God forever."

"I came up here to tell you John's story," Carl yelled. "What he did haunts me. I read some of the stuff about God, but I felt so worthless. I could never do what John did. I don't deserve—"

"None of us deserves what God gives us," Mark said. "But he wants to forgive us and make us part of his family."

"I want that," Carl said.

Another swarm of locusts descended on the car. Their beating wings were deafening. Some landed on Mark, hissing. He was surprised by how much they weighed. He shook them off and tried to clear the window. It was as if the demons didn't want Mark to talk with Carl about God.

"What do I need to do?" Carl shouted.

"Pray with me," Mark said. "God, I'm sorry for the bad things I've done. I believe Jesus died for me and took my punishment. Change me right now and make me your child. And help me to live for you. In Jesus' name, amen."

The locusts hissed as Carl said, "Amen."

Judd sat still as the plane taxied to the terminal. The locusts covered the plane, hissing and chanting something. It sounded like "A bad one! A bad one!" Finally Judd recognized the word from having read Tsion Ben-Judah's Web site. It was *Abbadon*, the Hebrew word for the chief demon of the bottomless pit. "Abbadon, Abbadon," the locusts hissed, calling out to their demonic leader.

People around Judd were terrified, holding hands over their ears and crying. Judd knew if they did manage to get to the terminal, it was unlikely anyone would be able to help them connect the ramp. Already he could see baggage handlers and maintenance workers writhing in pain on the runway.

As they approached the terminal, Judd stood and squeezed into the aisle. He searched for anyone with the mark of the believer.

When he reached first class, a flight attendant yelled at him to sit down. He shook his head.

"Get back in your seat, sir, or I'll have to call the captain!" the flight attendant said.

"I want to volunteer," Judd said. "Those things out there are stinging people, but I can help."

The flight attendant pulled Judd into the galley and closed the curtain. She whispered, "I won't have you upsetting the passengers."

"I'm telling the truth," Judd said. "If those things get inside the plane, they'll sting everybody."

"Everybody but you?" the attendant said skeptically.

"I'm not a target. I can't explain right now why—"

"Then get to your seat. We're responsible for your safety and if you can't explain—"

"Okay," Judd said. "Since I believe in Jesus, those locusts won't bother me. They're only after people who . . . who don't believe in God."

"You're one of those people," the woman said. "I believe in God, but I don't follow that crazy rabbi."

The plane stopped. Judd put a hand out to steady himself. "You've got to believe me."

Passengers whimpered and cried. They were too frightened to retrieve their things from the overhead bins.

"Wait here," the attendant said.

A few moments later she returned with a member of the flight crew. "Linda said you've volunteered to go outside and help with the ramp," the pilot said. "All of our personnel are down."

Judd nodded. "If you can get me out of here without letting any of those things in, I can help. But if even one of them gets inside the cabin, it'll sting all the passengers."

Lionel felt sorry for the worker trapped outside the door, but he knew he couldn't risk opening it and letting the locusts inside. Besides, Lionel knew that once the man was stung, there was nothing anyone could do.

Lionel ran to a security worker. "You've got to seal off the terminal!"

The man seemed dazed. He nodded, then lifted his radio. "Seal off all the entrances to the terminal!"

Lionel found Sam, and they watched Judd's plane taxi toward the terminal. The smoky cloud that had hung over them for days was gone, but the spread of the demon locusts was as thick as the cloud had been. The locusts flew into the window, piling on top of each other to get a look inside.

A worker on the tarmac screamed and beat his head against the concrete. Lionel shook his head.

"He's going to kill himself," Sam said.

Lionel stared through the thousands of demons looking straight at them. "'In those days people will seek death but will not find it,'" he said, quoting the verse from memory. "'They will long to die, but death will flee away!'"

Mark peered through the car window, knocking away the locusts that kept coming. The car was covered with the beasts now, and he couldn't see Carl.

Mark raced to the other side and opened the door.

"Are you crazy?" Carl said.

Mark smiled. "Get out."

Carl's eyes darted from Mark's face to the locusts buzzing around his head. Carl slid out of the car. "They're not stinging me."

"They won't," Mark said, pointing to his forehead. "See this?"

"It's a cross," Carl said. "I didn't notice that when I first met you."

"You have one just like it. Come on," Mark said,

"I want to get you back to meet the others. And I want to hear John's story."

Vicki checked on Janie later in the day. The girl thrashed and moaned. She shivered as if it were the middle of winter.

Conrad brought some cool cloths and stood by Vicki. "We gave her every chance."

Vicki nodded. Finally, Janie relaxed enough to speak. "Why didn't you tell me?"

"We tried," Vicki said. "You wouldn't listen."

"Why would God do such a thing to me?" Janie said. "I can't stand the pain."

"Give your life to God now, Janie," Vicki said.

"Will it make it stop hurting?" Janie said.

"I don't think so, but—"

"Then what good is your God anyway?" Janie yelled. "Get out! Both of you, get out!"

Conrad followed Vicki downstairs. They had closed every opening in the house and still the locusts were finding their way inside.

Vicki had prepared enough food and water downstairs to keep people alive for a few weeks. At some point they would need to get more supplies, assuming the locusts continued their attack. Vicki couldn't wait to log onto the Web and see what more Tsion Ben-Judah had to say.

Someone screamed. Darrion and Shelly were calling for help.

"Can you clear these bugs off the stairway door?" Vicki said.

"I'll do my best," Conrad said. He grabbed the piece of firewood and started whacking. There were at least a hundred locusts chewing, biting, and scratching to get inside. A few minutes later the locusts lay in a heap, stunned.

Vicki grabbed a flashlight from the kitchen and opened the stairwell door. She ducked inside and slammed it behind her, inspecting the basement as she walked downstairs. Locusts scratched on the walls, but none were inside.

She raced to the secret entrance to the room below. She lifted the trapdoor and gasped. Charlie, Melinda, and Lenore cowered in one corner of the room. Shelly and Darrion stood by the tunnel door, their feet planted firmly in the dirt.

"They're digging through the mud underneath the door," Darrion shouted. "We can't hold them much longer!"

Vicki raced back to the room above and grabbed a loose board. Shelly screamed again. "One of them's getting through!"

"Come up here!" Vicki shouted, motioning for Charlie, Melinda, and Lenore to follow her.

The three scrambled up the stairs into the room. Shelly and Darrion struggled to keep the locusts from working through the mud. One of the demons clawed its way through and showed its ugly head. Shelly was terrified. She jumped back from the doorway just as Vicki brought the board and slapped it on the ground.

But it was too late. One of the demons flew into the room, its teeth bared, looking for a victim.

Lenore screamed from above, "My baby! Don't let it hurt my baby!"

Vicki glanced down into the corner at the makeshift crib Charlie had made. Tolan was awake and thrashing under the covers.

The locust glanced at Vicki, Shelly, and Darrion, then darted for the corner. It hovered over the crib, its teeth dripping with venom.

"No!" Vicki shouted.

ABOUT THE AUTHORS

Jerry B. Jenkins (www.jerryjenkins.com) is the writer of the Left Behind series. He owns the Jerry B. Jenkins Christian Writers Guild, an organization dedicated to mentoring aspiring authors. Former vice president for publishing for the Moody Bible Institute of Chicago, he also served many years as editor of *Moody* magazine and is now Moody's writer-at-large.

His writing has appeared in publications as varied as *Reader's Digest, Parade, Guideposts*, in-flight magazines, and dozens of other periodicals. Jenkins's biographies include books with Billy Graham, Hank Aaron, Bill Gaither, Luis Palau, Walter Payton, Orel Hershiser, and Nolan Ryan, among many others. His books appear regularly on the *New York Times, USA Today, Wall Street Journal*, and *Publishers Weekly* best-seller lists.

Jerry is also the writer of the nationally syndicated sports story comic strip *Gil Thorp*, distributed to newspapers across the United States by Tribune Media Services.

Jerry and his wife, Dianna, live in Colorado and have three grown sons.

Dr. Tim LaHaye (www.timlahaye.com), who conceived the idea of fictionalizing an account of the Rapture and the Tribulation, is a noted author, minister, and nationally recognized speaker on Bible prophecy. He is the founder of both Tim LaHaye Ministries and The PreTrib Research Center. He also recently cofounded the Tim LaHaye School of Prophecy at Liberty University. Presently Dr. LaHaye speaks at many of the major Bible prophecy conferences in the U.S. and Canada, where his current prophecy books are very popular.

Dr. LaHaye holds a doctor of ministry degree from Western Theological Seminary and a doctor of literature degree from Liberty University. For twenty-five years he pastored one of the nation's outstanding churches in San Diego, which grew to three locations. It was during that time that he founded two accredited Christian high schools, a Christian school system of ten schools, and Christian Heritage College.

Dr. LaHaye has written over forty books that have been published in more than thirty languages. He has written books on a wide variety of subjects, such as family life, temperaments, and Bible prophecy. His current fiction works, the Left Behind series, written with Jerry B. Jenkins, continue to appear on the best-seller lists of the Christian Booksellers Association, *Publishers Weekly*, *Wall Street Journal*, *USA Today*, and the *New York Times*.

He is the father of four grown children and grandfather of nine. Snow skiing, waterskiing, motorcycling, golfing, vacationing with family, and jogging are among his leisure activities.

areUthirsty.com

well . . . are you?